LIA ANDERSON
DOG PARK MYSTERIES

MAXIMUM SECURITY

LIA ANDERSON MYSTERIES
by C. A. Newsome

A SHOT IN THE BARK
DROOL BABY
MAXIMUM SECURITY
SNEAK THIEF
MUDDY MOUTH
FUR BOYS

MAXIMUM SECURITY

LIA ANDERSON DOG PARK MYSTERIES 3

C. A. NEWSOME

TWO PUP PRESS

MAXIMUM SECURITY

Two Pup Press
1836 Bruce Avenue
Cincinnati, Ohio 45223

Newsome, C. A.
Maximum security: a dog park mystery/ C. A. Newsome
Pages cm
ISBN 9780996374231 (paperback)—ISBN 9780996374286 (ebook)
1. Murderers—Fiction. 2. Family Violence—Fiction 3. Cincinnati (Ohio)—Fiction. I. Title.

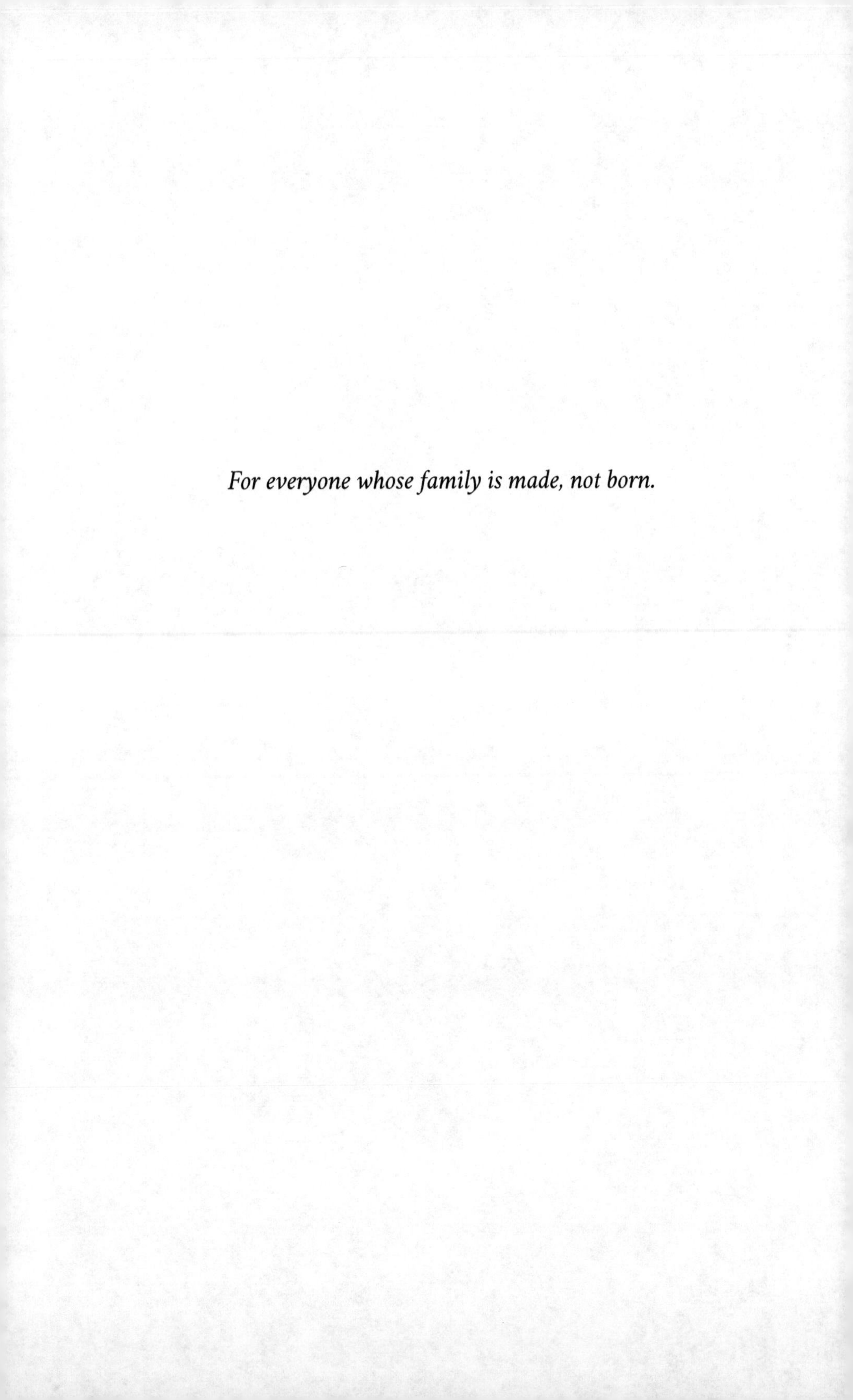

For everyone whose family is made, not born.

PROLOGUE

THIRTY YEARS AGO, IN NORMAN, OKLAHOMA

Madonna blared from maxed-out speakers as Kitty stumbled from the house, away from the juvenile puke fest going on inside. She was furious at herself for letting Tom bring her when she knew it wasn't her kind of party. Blinded by the night and unsure of her direction, she checked her momentum and blinked, adjusting to the darkness.

She spotted Joe across the road, leaning against his Chevy pickup under a burned-out street light. He had one foot propped behind him on the rusted fender and his arms folded across his chest.

His real name was George, but only his teachers called him that. Everyone called him Injun Joe, or just Joe. She wondered if the tough crowd he hung with knew he'd named himself after a Mark Twain villain. Probably not.

He was a little shorter than she was, with skin that

browned as soon as the sun came out and straight black hair almost down to his shoulder blades. He wore jeans and work boots in spite of the summer swelter. His shirt was unbuttoned and a narrow strip of chest showed in a concession to the heat. He remained motionless while smoke curled from his cigarette, playing hide and seek with one high cheekbone.

Joe watched her with those dark eyes, his chin lifted, provoking her with a hint of a sneer. He gave her a faint nod. Acknowledgment? Or just affirming his own judgement of her personal drama?

Oh, Yeah? Kitty abruptly changed course and headed for the old truck. *Think you know me?*

"Give me one of those," she demanded, gesturing to his cigarette.

"You don't smoke, Buttercup." He lazily placed the filter between his lips and drew. The end lit up, illuminating his face, red pinpoints in his eyes giving him a predatory look.

"Don't call me that. And how would you know?"

"I know a lot of things about you. Buttercup."

She ignored the provocation. "Like what?" She challenged.

"Like you're too smart for that asshole you date, for one."

"And?"

"What are you doing here, Buttercup? Aren't you afraid your grade point average is going to drop?"

"I'm not some nerd. Give me one of those," she repeated.

"Aren't you, now?" He kept his eyes on hers as he

pulled the pack of Marlboros from his shirt pocket and shook one out.

Kitty took the cigarette and held it up, waiting. "What are you doing out here, anyway? This isn't exactly your scene."

"Just enjoying the show." He lit a match, cupping it in the still air as he held the flame for her. His hand brushed hers. An electric sensation pulsed through her as their fingers touched. Had he felt it? She stepped back and puffed, nurturing the ember.

Kitty looked away and dragged on her cigarette. She knew better than to take it into her lungs. She blew out carefully to avoid coughing.

She looked sideways at him. "You don't talk much, do you?"

He shrugged. "You going to inhale that thing?"

"Are you always this rude?"

"Usually. Remind me not to share a joint with you. I hate waste."

"Do you want it back?" Kitty held her cigarette out to him. He took it from her, gently tamped it out on the side of his truck, put it back in the pack.

She crossed her arms. "I just wanted something to do with my hands."

"I can think of plenty you could do with your hands, Buttercup."

"Why do you call me that?"

He grinned. "Because it bugs you."

"Gee, thanks, *George*."

"Now that's just mean."

Kitty huffed. Light and noise erupted from the house as the front door opened, drawing her attention. Tom was silhouetted in the party din. He stormed into the yard, bearing down on them.

"Get me out of here."

"Trouble in paradise, Buttercup?"

"Can we just go?"

"Where to?" The driver's-side door squealed as he opened it for her.

She climbed in and scooted past the steering wheel. "Anywhere."

"Not home?"

"No way."

She looked through the rear window as they pulled out. Tom was in the middle of the street, hands fisted on hips, enraged. She leaned back against the bench seat, smug.

She'd spent the last month as Tom's girl. Being Tom's girl mostly meant being the adoring witness to his awesomeness. It was boring. She could be one of a dozen females, and any one of the others could slide neatly into her place without Tom ever noticing or caring.

At least she hadn't "done it" with him. He'd pushed, he'd kept pushing. Whatever she was supposed to feel when the most popular guy in school wanted you, she hadn't felt it. So she kept saying no. She took a moment to be relieved.

Joe had been her only option for a quick escape from the party. She now took a moment to wonder if she'd jumped from the frying pan into the fire. At least he was fully aware of her. She couldn't explain how she knew this. She felt amazingly ... *something*. Amazingly ... *alive*. The New Age types talked about about "being present in the present moment." She'd never known what that meant before now.

She lowered her lashes and observed Joe from the corner of her eye as he tucked another cigarette between his lips, the same one she'd started, and coaxed it back to life from the old one. They rode in silence punctuated by the whining and grinding of the truck's gears. He headed out of town, then turned off on a section line road.

"Where are we going?"

"We're going anywhere, Buttercup. You ever been there?"

"I guess not."

Should she be worried? She'd heard about boys who drove girls out in the country and refused to drive them back home unless they put out. The stories were vague. It always happened to "this girl," or "my friend told me about a friend of hers." Never any names, of the girl, of the guy.

If it came to that, she'd be able to spot the town lights over the tree line. A long walk might be just what she needed to cool down. She discovered part of her was still spoiling for a fight.

The boy beside her was silent as he drove, right hand on the wheel, left elbow resting on the door frame. He'd barely touched her, just the once, when he lit her borrowed cigarette. He gave no hint to his intentions, no clue what was going to happen next. She felt prickly all over, as each moment, each mile took her further into the unknown. She didn't know if she liked the feeling, but she wasn't bored.

The motor droned as she hung her arm out the window and felt the air rushing through her fingers. She wondered what he was thinking.

The fields gave way to woods that crowded the road, rising over them and blocking out the sky. Joe turned onto a lane that was barely more than a pair of tire tracks in the high grass. He jammed his cigarette into the ashtray and put both hands on the wheel. The truck humped and bucked over ruts and fallen branches. Trees closed in around them, shutting out everything except the bouncing headlights. Then the track disappeared.

"End of the line, Buttercup. Everybody out." He grabbed a blanket from behind the seat and hopped down.

"What is this place?"

"You'll see. Come on."

She got out of the truck, stumbled on a tussock of grass. "I can't see anything. You must have eyes like a cat."

"Scared?" He was a gray smudge against the trees.

"You wish," she lied.

He ghosted over to her.

"Here." He took her hand in his own firm, dry one, leading her down an invisible path. Gradually her eyes adapted to the void and she began to see a faint movement in the air ahead.

A clearing opened up around them, full of flitting, flickering points of light dancing in the night air. Thousands of fireflies filled the space. They blinked in the grass, they hung from the branches, they flashed in the surrounding air. The minute beacons spiraled from the ground up into the tree tops, merging with the stars in an endless kaleidoscope.

"Oh!" She grabbed Joe's arm. She could feel him grinning beside her.

He spread the blanket on the ground, pulling her down next to him as he sat. She bolted up, startled. His arm came around her, warm and strong. She stiffened, caught in her own indecision like a small forest creature trapped in headlights. She should protest. Why wasn't she protesting?

"Relax," he whispered into her ear. She turned to look at him. His face was deep shadows and silver in the starlight. "You don't have to do anything you don't want to. I just like to come here when I'm mad at the world. You seemed plenty mad to me."

"How did you find this place?"

He shrugged. "Just driving around. Sometimes I like to camp out. This is one of my spots."

"This is amazing."

"I like it. All those bugs are supposed to be mating. The ones sitting still and blinking are the females. The males are the ones flying around. Only some of them are a different species, and they mimic the females to draw the other males near so they can eat them."

"That's terrible."

"It's life. Firefly light is the most efficient in the world. It's called cold light because all of the energy becomes light. In a light bulb, almost all of the energy creates heat and only ten percent becomes light."

She turned to him. "How do you know all this?"

He shrugged again. "I like knowing stuff."

"You've got everyone fooled."

"I like finding out about things. It's school I can't stand. Some species have eggs that glow when they're poked."

"You're putting me on."

"Nope." He grinned like a small boy with a secret.

She looked up, taking in the luminous display above her. She felt light, as if she might float up among the tiny insects winking their love songs. "It's like I'm inside an atom."

"Nerd."

"That's just mean."

"But you're real cute for a nerd, Buttercup."

"Gee, you say the nicest things, *George*."

"Still mad?"

She blinked, aware her disagreeable mood had evaporated. "No, why?"

"Because." He tugged on a lock of her hair, pulling her closer to him, then leaned in to bridge the gap between them and closed his lips over hers. Kitty's world tilted. She fell through stars, kept falling as fireflies lit her up from inside. She felt like a pop-bottle rocket with a lit fuse.

She wrapped her arms around his neck to save herself, anchoring to the warm reality of his tongue in her mouth. He lowered to the blanket, taking her with him. Burying his face in her neck, nibbling his way up to her ear and sucking on the lobe, hot breath sending frissons of pleasure through her. She made little mewling noises that had him smiling against her skin.

Kitty lowered her arms and placed her palms against the hot skin of his chest, tentatively exploring. Joe leaned over her, his hair a curtain around his face, shutting out everything except his gleaming eyes. As his hand slid up under her top and the heat arrowed down inside her, she realized he was right. She wasn't going to do a thing that she didn't want to do.

Kitty never told anyone about that Friday night. She

spent the rest of the weekend cherishing the sweet, secret ache between her legs. She lied to her friends and said Joe had just given her a ride home. They thought it was bad enough that she'd gotten into his truck. She was not about to admit she'd given him her virginity.

Tom called her a whore for leaving the party with Joe. She called him a drunk pig and broke up with him. After she slapped him.

She played imaginary scenarios in her head where she presented Joe to her friends as her new boyfriend. These went badly, so she stopped.

She waited for Joe to call.

The following Monday, she looked for him at school. She found herself walking by the smoking area when her classes were on the other side of the building. She stole looks at the parking lot, searching for his truck. On Tuesday, her mood sank.

She finally saw him as she arrived for school on Wednesday. He was leaning against the building with one foot propped on the wall, talking to his buddies. Her heart lifted as she drew near and she sent him a tentative smile. He gave her an inscrutable look and turned his back on her. She walked on by, her face burning, mortified.

She didn't let herself cry until she got home and was able to shut herself up in her room, refusing to come out until the following morning. She worried about pregnancy for two weeks until her cramps came. And she hated Joe with all the animosity shame could muster.

1

WEDNESDAY, OCTOBER 9

Lia Anderson unclipped her furry trio in the dog park corral and hung their leashes on the fence. She pulled a coiled training lead off her shoulder and attached it to Max's collar.

"Ha! Try getting away now, Girlfriend."

The Beagle-Boxer mix turned her nut-brown eyes toward Lia and gave her a hurt look.

"That won't work on me, so forget it." She leaned over the horde milling in front of the gate and lifted the latch. Honey nosed the gate open and all three dogs bolted. Twenty feet away, Max stumbled, halting at the end of the lead. She did a one-eighty and glared at Lia.

"Sorry, Max, you're on lockdown."

"Poor Max," a willowy redhead said, joining Lia.

"Bailey, don't you start. She's been driving me crazy. She stays on the lead until I find the hole in the fence." Lia looked out over the park, morning sun piercing the surrounding trees and shooting long shadows across the grass.

"How are you going to do that?" Bailey asked.

"Max is going to show me. Keep me company while I walk the perimeter."

The pair strolled along the back slope of the four-acre enclosure, parallel the fence separating the dog park from the rest of Mount Airy Forest. Honey, a Golden Retriever, stayed by Lia's side while holding a convo with Bailey's Bloodhound, Kita. Lia's silver Miniature Schnauzer, Chewy, sniffed at Max, jumping up on her and provoking a game of chase. The game was short, over when Max hit the end of the lead. Chewy quickly discovered Max's limits and stayed just beyond. He barked and cavorted while Max pretended she didn't care.

"Little Brat, you should be ashamed of yourself," Lia called, laughing.

"Can't blame him for using every advantage he's got. All the other dogs are bigger than he is." Bailey punctuated this assessment with a long, graceful hand that flitted like a bird when she talked.

"I suppose so, but it's mean. Even if Max does deserve to be kept tied up."

Halfway along the fence line, Max stopped and looked oh-so-casually over her shoulder, grinned and bolted for the barrier. She succeeded in wiggling her forequarters under the wire before Lia pulled the lead up short and stopped her progress.

"Ha! Found it." Lia reeled the lead in as she approached the fence, keeping tension on it so Max couldn't complete her escape. Bailey lifted the bottom edge of the field fencing while Lia knelt and pulled straight back on the lead. Max rumbled in disgust and slowly backed up. Back in custody, she gave Lia an affronted look, then lay down and sighed audibly as she settled her head on her paws.

"She's so expressive," Bailey commented.

"What she's expressing now can't be repeated in polite company."

"I see you found her way out," Jim said as he walked up. The retired engineer was a slight, grizzled man with a large nose and a beard that defied all attempts at grooming. Kind blue eyes floated in the rumpled bed of his face. He always carried a walking stick that he'd made from a honeysuckle branch.

Stumping along with his stick and accompanied by his Border Collie, Fleece, he could have been Saint Francis. Today he was also accompanied by a small Norfolk Terrier mix named Chester who resembled an ambulatory dust mop. Chester waddled up to Lia, sat up on his hind legs and licked her nose.

Lia gave Chester a scratch and stood up. "Her latest one, anyway. This was hidden by the grass." Keeping Max on a tight rein, Lia moved closer to the fence and peered over. "Look how the ground drops away on the other side. How are we going to fix that?"

"Looks like Max found another way out. You got some wire?" Jose asked, joining the group.

"I gave it to you to fix the last hole she found," Lia said. "Then she got out yesterday and came back with the carcass from someone's turkey dinner. Jim had to steal it away from her before she started a riot. Who eats turkey in October?"

Jose considered the gap. "We could pin it down somehow, maybe pile some wood in front of it so she can't get at it."

"I've got camping gear in the car," Lia said. "How about tent stakes?"

"We can give it a shot. We'll look after Max while you get them. Got something to hammer them in with? If you don't, I think I've got something in the van," Jose said.

"I've got a rubber mallet," Lia offered.

"That'll do 'er."

Lia handed Max's lead to Jim, then made a quick trip to her car trunk. She returned with a tote bag containing a variety of tent stakes and her mallet. She clipped Max's lead to the fence using a carabiner. Max lay down and settled her head on her paws with an offended huff. Honey and Chewy sniffed at the prisoner. She refused to look at them.

"Poor Max," Jim said. "She should be free. Look at how sad she is. You won't try to get out again, will you, Max?"

Max lifted her head at her name, then gave Lia a dirty look.

"Ha. That's what you said the last time."

"We found the hole. She can't get out while we're all standing here."

"Wanna bet?"

"She can't get out, can she, Jose?"

"Leave me outta this," Jose said. "I don't want to have nothin' to do with it."

"You really want me to let her go, Jim?" Lia asked.

"I do."

"It's on you, then. She gets out, you find her."

"Agreed." Jim leaned over and unclipped the lead from Max's collar. Max stood up, stretched, then looked around, suspicious of her sudden freedom. She took a cautious step, then another, then trotted off without looking back.

"See how happy she is?" Jim said.

"Uh huh. I'm just waiting to see how happy you are when she's gone again."

"Children," Bailey interrupted, "no squabbling."

"Yes, Mom," Lia and Jim said in unison. They turned to watch Jose as he sized up the mismatched array of tent stakes.

"Lose many of these, Lia?" Jose asked.

Lia shrugged. "Is there anything you can use?"

"No problemo. Jim, you're the engineer, what do you think is the best way to stake this?"

"I say we pull the bottom of the fence inward, then go straight down."

"I'm with ya."

The pair put their heads together, deciding to cover their bases with two styles of stakes: shorter, U-shaped, wire stakes and longer, plastic stakes that looked like railroad spikes with a hook on the top. Bailey and Lia watched as they selected five stakes and positioned them.

Honey nudged Lia's hand. Chewy barked, bouncing against her shin. "What's up with you guys? Why aren't you playing?" She looked around. "Where's Max?" She scanned the park, spotting a tan and white blur racing for the far corner.

"Oh, no, not again!" Lia moaned as she watched Max sprint down the hill toward the fence.

"It's a four-foot fence. She can't make the jump," Jim insisted.

"I wouldn't put it past her," Jose said.

The four of them watched as Max built up speed on the grass. She leapt across the last bit of slope, boosted herself on the horizontal corner brace and went over the top. Her tail high, she disappeared into the woods.

"Smart dog," Jose said. "We keep plugging the fence and she keeps finding new ways out. You could hire her out as a security consultant."

"What am I going to do?" Lia moaned. "I've got a meeting at Renee's in a couple hours."

"She always comes back," Tom said. "You just need to wait."

"I just need to wait? What happened to you being responsible?"

"I just promised she wouldn't get back out of the hole. I didn't say anything about her jumping the fence."

"Well, that's a weasely way to get out of it. I thought you were an engineer, not a lawyer."

Repair finished, Jose stood up and handed the tote to Lia.

"Thanks a lot," she grumbled.

"Any time."

They turned away from the fence and headed for a picnic table.

"Maybe she'll bring you a present this time," Bailey said.

"Like I needed that turkey carcass she stole yesterday," Lia groused.

Lia climbed on top of the picnic table. Leaning her elbows on her knees, she dropped her head in her hands. She blew out noisily, sending a stray wisp of hair flying. Honey walked up and nosed her arm. Chewy propped his front paws on the bench and head-butted her leg. She ruffled the fur on Chewy's head absently.

"You guys don't run away. Why does your foster-sister have to be so bad?"

Honey whuffed sympathetically, as if to say such a thing was incomprehensible to her.

"And why aren't you getting along with her?" She asked the dogs. "Maybe if you were nicer, she wouldn't run away. The one time I agree to foster a dog, and I wind up with a kleptomaniac Houdini. 'I'll take that one,' I said. 'She has such sweet eyes.'" Lia snorted. "Looks like we're stuck here until your delinquent sister comes back."

Honey and Chewy looked at each other.

"Too bad it's not winter," Jose said. "If there was snow we could track her."

"Gee, yeah, too bad it's not freezing outside," Lia groused. She got up off the table and the quartet headed to the front of the park, trailed by their pack of dogs.

"Don't you worry," Jose said. "She'll be back. She knows where her kibble comes from." In his forties and balding, he looked like someone who had played ball in high school, or spent time in the military. Jose claimed Italian ancestry, despite his name. "I gotta get to work, but I'm sure Jim will stay with ya. C'mon, Sophie," he called to his Mastiff. "We gotta go."

"I've got an appointment at the optometrist," Jim mumbled, following Jose. "Gotta go. Fleece! Chester! Home!"

"Way to abandon a sinking ship," Lia called after the retreating figures.

"I'll stay."

"Thanks, Bailey. You're a true friend." She turned back toward the entry corral. "Not like some people I could name," she yelled. Jim shrugged his shoulders and kept going.

"How long do you think she'll be gone?" Bailey asked.

"Hour, hour and a half, at most. I hope. Guess I'd better call Renee."

LIA ANDERSON WAS A PRETTY WOMAN, thirty-ish, with slanted green eyes and high cheekbones. Her firm chin was accented by a slight dent that her boyfriend, Peter, liked to tap with his forefinger.

She sat on a picnic table with Bailey and repaired her I-haven't-had-coffee-yet knot of streaky chestnut hair, anchoring it more firmly with a butterfly clip. Her slim figure was arrayed in oversized, paint-spattered, studio clothes that doubled as dog park gear. Lia called this her bag-lady look.

She and Bailey had already walked a mile to pass the time, crossing the park ten times. The dogs realized they weren't going anywhere during the fourth lap and sat down in the middle of the park to watch.

After their walk, they threw balls for the dogs until the dogs stopped chasing them. They questioned everyone who entered the park. No one had seen Max.

A silver pickup sporting a camper shell and a kayak rack pulled into the parking lot, honking. Terry Dunn parked next to the fence and jumped out, leaving his dogs in the truck. He was a portly, ruddy-complected man bearing a strong resemblance to Teddy Roosevelt.

"Hey, Lia," he yelled. "Max is headed this way. I saw her along the side of the road on Westwood-Northern."

Lia hopped off her perch. "Thank God." She ran for the corral, grabbed Max's leash off the fence and draped it around her neck as she headed down the service road. She hit the parking lot, joining Terry in time to see Max enter the lot from the street. Max maintained a jaunty trot despite a heavy load.

"What is that?" Lia asked Terry.

Terry squinted behind his wire rims. "Don't know. I thought it was a branch, but it doesn't look right. Maybe a bone? It's awfully big. I'd say it's a moose bone, but you don't see moose this far south. Can't keep them in zoos, either–"

"You think she found a deer skeleton?"

"Could be. I imagine there are a few field-dressed carcasses lying around. Which does nothing to reduce the resident coyote population. Coyotes are scavengers just as much as they are predators. They aren't picky."

Terry continued his foray into the habits of the local wildlife as she watched Max approach. Max stopped at Lia's prehistoric Volvo and looked toward her expectantly while struggling to balance her newest find, an eighteen-inch-long bone with knobbed ends. Bits of gore clung to the joints.

"Of all the nerve! She's had her little field trip, and now I'm supposed to chauffeur her home. Terry, will you circle behind her? I don't want her running off if she gets another wild hair."

Lia approached the car cautiously, then opened the rear door. Max gave Lia a dubious look as she dragged her treasure into the back seat. Lia shut the door, trapping

Max inside. "Thanks, Terry. Now all I have to do is get that bone away from her. You want to volunteer?"

Terry peered into the car, through windows smeared with nose prints. "You really ought to clean these off."

"Yeah, Yeah. So how do I get that bone from her? I have no problem with her having a deer bone, but I don't want her fighting with Honey and Chewy. I think she could be food-aggressive."

"You've got a bigger problem."

"What do you mean?"

"That's not a deer bone. It's too thick."

"I really don't care what kind of bone it is. I just need to get it away from her without her escaping again."

"That's a femur. A human femur."

Lia gaped at Terry. "Are you sure?"

"It's unmistakable. Can't tell if it's from the left leg or the right. It's a bit on the smallish side …. Could be female."

Lia shut her eyes and slumped against the car with a pained expression. "Oh, God, I think I'm going to vomit." She kept her eyes shut and concentrated on calming the heaving in her stomach. She tasted bile along with coffee and hazelnut creamer.

Terry went back to his truck and retrieved a bottle of water. He handed it to Lia. She carefully sipped on the water and wiped her mouth.

"Thanks. I guess I'd better call Peter. He's going to say, 'I told you so.'"

Max settled down on the seat and began gnawing on her prize.

Terry raised his eyebrows. "Our resident detective had Max pegged as a body snatcher?"

"He just thought she would be more trouble than she's worth." Lia noticed Max chewing her gruesome toy. "Dammit, we can't let her eat that. You have anything tasty in your truck?"

"Dog biscuits. I doubt she'll see that as a desirable trade."

"We've got to give her something good to get her away from that. This is creepy enough without getting into a tug of war over human remains." She reached into a cargo pocket, pulled out her wallet and extracted a five. "Can you run up to UDF and grab a pack of hot dogs?"

As Terry made his way to his truck, Bailey walked down to the fence, accompanied by her furry charges. "Is there a problem? How long do you need me to hang here with the dogs?"

"Geezelpete, Bailey, you're not going to believe this. Terry says Max got hold of a human thigh bone."

"You're kidding!" Bailey craned her head, attempting to see. "And you haven't taken it away from her?"

"You want to do it?" Lia challenged. "I haven't had her long enough to feel comfortable reaching into her mouth to take away food. Terry's getting a bribe."

"She's eating it?"

"Um," Lia said, looking into the car. "Right now, she's licking it. I've got to call Peter. Can you hang on until we get it away from her?"

"Yeah, as long as I don't have to watch." Bailey headed back up the hill, then stopped when she realized all three dogs were still at the fence, avidly aware that a drama was unfolding. "Seriously?" She shook her head. "Sorry, Lia, looks like you've got an audience. I'll keep an eye on them, but I'm doing it from the top of the hill."

Lia sighed, rolled her eyes, and pulled out her phone. Peter answered on the third ring. When she was finished with her explanation, all she heard was dead silence. "Um, Peter? You there?"

"Yep."

"What should I do?"

She heard a gusting noise that could only be Peter sighing. She imagined him rubbing his temples.

"I'll call it in and be right down."

PETER DOURSON WAS A TALL MAN, over six feet, and lanky in a way that looked excellent in blue jeans. His dark hair was usually worn in a modified Paul McCartney cut that curled over his collar and gave his captain fits. The resemblance to the former Beatle was reinforced by puppy-dog eyes that drooped slightly at the outside corners. His good looks were understated, being pleasant more than handsome. Lia appreciated this. She'd learned to distrust overly attractive men.

When he arrived, he found Lia using Terry's pocket knife to open a pack of hot dogs while Max eyed her from the back seat of the car, one paw firmly possessing a bone that was clearly human in origin. He'd bagged too many deer to mistake Max's prize for the animal remains he'd been expecting. His pulse accelerated as adrenaline trickled into his system, sharpening his senses.

"Hail, my good man," Terry said. "Are you joining our siege?"

"Looks like. Hey, Babe," he said.

"Babe," Lia gritted out, "is a pig."

"From the looks of it, the pig is in the back seat. How many of those have you fed her already?"

"None, so far. We're working up a battle plan. Can you pull your Blazer over here, just far enough away so I can open the door?"

"Sure." Peter went back to his SUV and drove it over, parking four feet away from Lia's Volvo. He hopped out. "What next, Boss?"

"Stand on the other side of the car, by the back door. When I lure her out, you can reach in through the window and grab the bone." Peter pulled a pair of neoprene gloves out of his pocket, putting them on as he took his position.

Lia turned to Terry. "Terry, you stand by the front passenger door, so you're behind the rear door when I open it. Your job is to keep her from escaping that way."

Once Terry and Peter were in place, Lia opened the back door to her sedan. Max lifted her head, making a low, rumbling sound of displeasure. Lia held up the package of hot dogs and removed one, laying it on the seat just out of Max's reach. She stepped back several feet, leaving the door open. Max cautiously inched her nose forward on the seat, then gobbled the hot dog down and returned to guarding her bone.

Next, Lia placed a hotdog on the edge of the seat. She remained standing just outside the car. Max eyed the wiener hungrily but didn't move. Lia held out the pack of hotdogs and removed them one at a time and laid them in a pile on the pavement. Max watched every move she made with a level of concentration sufficient for neuro-surgery. Saliva began to drip from her jaws. Lia shifted over by the car's rear fender, out of Max's line of sight.

"Now what?" Terry stage-whispered.

"We wait," Lia whispered back.

By this time, Bailey had spread the news of Max's find across the park. The inside of the fence was lined with people and dogs, all waiting for a circus. The dogs were drooling as they watched the pile of wieners. The hushed crowd reminded Peter of a lurking mob of zombies.

Thirty seconds ticked by. Then a minute. Max's nose appeared, then her head. She inhaled the single hot dog on the seat then looked around, calculating. Released by some unknown mechanism, she jumped for the pile of processed meat and began bolting it down. Peter reached in the open window and grabbed the bone.

"Okay," he called, "I've got it." He walked behind the car to the rear of his Blazer, moving quietly so as not to alert Max. Lia pulled Max's leash from around her neck and took the clip in one hand. One cautious step at a time, she moved toward Max, waiting until she finished her feast. Peter reached into his car and pulled out a pair of brown paper grocery bags. He placed one over each end of the bone, overlapping them in the middle to fully contain the bone. He was putting the package in the back of his SUV when he heard Lia whoop.

"Gotcha!" Lia yelled, triumphant. Applause broke out at the fence line as Lia clipped a leash to Max's collar. Max looked up. Her bewildered expression morphed into betrayal when she realized her bone was gone and she was restrained.

The crowd at the fence broke up. Terry returned to his truck, where Jackson and Napa had been patiently waiting with their heads hanging out of the windows.

Lia turned to Peter. "What happens now?"

"I'm going to need your help. We've got to get Max to retrace her steps so we can find out where that bone came from. Do you have time for a hike in the woods?"

Lia crinkled her brow, considered. "I'll call Renee again. And I need to take everyone home and feed them first."

"You won't need to feed Max, she just ate a pound of hot dogs."

Max chose that moment to start heaving. She vomited hot dog chunks all over Peter's shoe. Relieved of her gastric distress, she looked up and grinned.

"Damn." Peter pulled a handkerchief out of his pocket and stood on one foot while he wiped off his defiled footwear. "She did that on purpose. It was revenge for taking her bone away."

"Seriously? She's just a dog. She doesn't think that way."

"Want to bet?" Peter watched Max lap at the disgorged pieces of meat laying on the pavement.

"Max, stop that!" Lia dragged her away from the mess.

"Take Honey and Chewy home and feed them. I'll hang on to Max. I'd rather she was hungry, It'll motivate her to go back to her find. I'll get someone from District Five to pick up the bone while you're gone. You still have that machete with your camping gear?"

"You think we'll need it?"

"No telling where she's been."

MAX WAS in no hurry to get anywhere. She moseyed, she meandered, she sniffed for clues and displayed no indication that she was headed for a particular destination. She dragged them through the underbrush, leaving Peter and Lia with a variety of scratches on their exposed skin despite Peter's vigorous use of the machete. Max descended the ravine behind the park, crossed the creek, headed upstream and eventually cut up the far side. She made her way over a couple more rises.

Peter didn't know what to think. On the one hand, he was not upset to have an excuse to dump the bottle bomb interviews off onto Brent for the time being. But hang it all, if that dog wasn't a royal pain in the ass, and becoming more of one with every passing minute. He was ready to suggest giving up. Yet, the thought of searching the entire forest with cadaver dogs kept him hoping Max would return to her find. Just a few more minutes–

The leash tugged like an impatient child. Max was straining, whining. There was nothing he could see that would draw Max's attention, except a pile of downed trees in the bottom of their current gully, the remains of a storm back in '93.

Max jerked on the leash, pulling Lia off balance. She fell to her knees and would have tumbled down the slope if Peter hadn't grabbed her arm. Max was a shrinking blur torpedoing downhill, her leash whipping behind her.

Lia got her feet back under her. She swiped her palms on her jeans. "Go after her. I'll follow. I'll be okay."

Peter handed her the machete, then moved quickly down the slope, momentum carrying him into a hard run on the uneven ground. He stumbled to a halt several yards after he made the bottom.

Panting, he leaned over with his hands braced on his thighs and wished he'd thought to bring water. Peter inhaled deeply and caught the scent of putrefaction, sweetish and sickening, heavy in the air. Underlying was the odor of urine. He steeled himself for a mess and wished he had his Vick's with him.

He rounded the end of the pile of logs and spotted Max pawing in a pile of decaying vegetation. Years of dead leaves had been disturbed, exposing the earth and the insects that liked to grub in the dark.

He took care now, examining each piece of ground before he stepped, moving quietly behind Max and planting his foot firmly on her leash. He bent over and picked up the tether. Max, intently focused on *something*, didn't notice him.

He moved closer, then pulled Max's head away from the ground. Max had been nosing at a hip bone.

"Lia! Don't come any closer!" He scanned the ground at the bottom of the gully, spotting random splashes of white. His eyes began to differentiate shapes in the crazy quilt of leaves and dead wood, picking out bits of blue and red. A skull materialized, perching on top of a rock. Bits of flesh and fine, white hair clung to the scalp. Peter was surrounded by a grisly expanse of bones and clothing.

He'd never seen anything like it.

Peter carefully made his way back to Lia, who was now sitting on a downed tree. She took Max's lead, wrapped it around a young tree, and clipped it to itself with her carabiner.

Her face was stoic. "What did you find?"

"More bones. Not sure what else is here." He pulled out his phone, called up an app and took a GPS reading. This he called in to the station. He tapped "end" and shoved the phone back in his pocket.

"They're going to bring out the crime scene folks and a cadaver dog. I've got to stay here to secure the scene. Can you find your way back?"

"Yeah, sure."

"If I give you my key, can you walk Viola and take her home with you today?"

She nodded. She looked exhausted. He knew the hike wasn't responsible. He tipped up her chin and kissed her lightly on the lips.

"I'll call later. If I get out of here in time for dinner, I'll bring pizza." He gathered her into his arms and hugged her tightly. "You done good, Babe."

"Babe," she muttered into his armpit, "is still a pig."

LIA HAD A HARD TIME CONCENTRATING. She rescheduled her appointment with Renee and spent the day puttering around her apartment, catching up on neglected chores while she worried about the bones they'd found in the park. Her artist's imagination had her conjuring gruesome scenarios. Cannibal bar-b-que. Satanic sacrifice. The newest installment of *Twilight*. The bone Max found seemed, for want of a better word, 'fresh.' Thinking about it made her shudder violently.

The phone rang with increasing frequency as the news spread. Lia briefly considered changing her outgoing message: "Yes, Max found bones at Mount Airy. No, I don't know anything else. Don't bother to leave a message. If you're my friend, I'll see you soon enough. If you aren't, I don't want to talk to you." The thought made her smile as she dutifully answered each call.

She removed calcium deposits from her bathroom plumbing, scrubbed the grout and washed windows. She repotted root-bound plants. She was eyeing Chewy's overgrown coat and reaching for her scissors when the phone rang again.

"Lia, it's me."

"Thank God, Peter. What's happening?"

"We're wrapping up here. Do you still want me to come over? I figure I can stop by Dewey's and be there in an hour. I'll tell you about it then."

VIOLA STARTED BARKING SHORTLY before 9:30. The others joined in, howling. A minute later, Lia heard a car door slam. She opened the door as a freshly showered and shaved Peter came up the walk carrying a pizza box from Dewey's with a bag on top. Frantic, Viola jumped on him and whimpered. He handed dinner to Lia, then stooped to pet Viola.

"What's in the bag?" Lia asked.

"Salad."

"Good man."

"I'm learning."

"Yes, you are." She leaned in, lingered over her 'hello' kiss. "Let's get you fed. Then I'll pry information out of you."

* * *

Peter leaned back on the sofa, propped his stocking feet up on the coffee table and tipped back a bottle of

Beck's. Having stuffed themselves on pizza crust, the dogs were spread out on the floor, napping.

"That was excellent," Peter said.

"I do agree. So, out with it. What happened after I left?"

"You can't share. Just the stuff that's public."

"Cross my heart," Lia said solemnly while she made the required swipes with her index finger.

"It looks like one skeleton, scattered around in pieces. Chris brought Boo to scent the area for other remains, but they didn't come up with anything."

"How do you think he died?"

"Brent found a crossbow bolt, so it's possible it was a deer hunting accident. I found a hunter's deer blind in one of the trees, something someone built out of scrap lumber. Permanent tree stands are illegal on public hunting grounds, so fat chance finding out who it belongs to. We think the shot came from there.

"Whoever he was, he died there. Boo found the spot where he bled out. It was recent. Not all the bones were clean."

Lia grimaced at the thought.

"What's really strange," Peter continued, "the area stank to high Heaven, like a corpse that has been kept in an oil drum for six months. We didn't find anything that would account for that. Then there's the question of why bones were scattered all over the place."

"How can you accidentally shoot someone and then not help them or call the police?"

"That's what we've got to figure out. We found the remains of clothing and something thick and plush, like a blanket. Could be he was asleep on the ground and the hunter didn't see him."

"Sounds unlikely, and it doesn't explain why there was nothing left but scattered bones."

"Yeah, that's what Brent and I think."

"So what's your next step?"

"The coroner's office should have a description and a time of death for the deceased by tomorrow. We'll check that against any local missing persons cases and see if we have a match. If we do, we get dental records and make a comparison. If not, we'll have to do a facial reconstruction and send it to the media. Meanwhile, we're pulling the names of all the bow hunters licensed for the current session of the deer cull at Mount Airy. Shouldn't be more than about thirty. If we don't get any joy there, we'll look at all licensed bow hunters in Cincinnati."

"Do you think there's a chance it wasn't a bow hunter?"

"There always is, but until we get evidence that suggests otherwise, we're looking for horses, not zebras."

"What do I get to tell everyone at the park? They know we found a human bone."

"We found a body and we're trying to identify it. The trails are closed to everyone, including hunters, until further notice."

"The hunters won't like being kept out of the woods."

"Nope, they sure won't."

2

THURSDAY, OCTOBER 10

Lia steeled herself for grilling as she strode up the park drive the next morning. She had all four dogs in tow, having agreed to keep Viola for a few days. Peter would be working long hours until headway was made on the case and would have little time for his dog.

The service road ended at a brick picnic shelter separating two fenced enclosures, one for large dogs and one for small. Lia noticed a middle-aged woman sitting at one of the tables, a polite expression on her face. She was of medium height and plump, dressed nicer than the usual dog park patron in tan knit pants and a green tunic topped with a heavy gold necklace that couldn't possibly be real. The conservative, chin-length bob of graying hair had clearly been styled at a salon. Lia thought she looked familiar, but couldn't place her.

Viola, who approached very few people, walked up to the woman, tugging on her leash. She sniffed at her, then lifted her head for a pet. The woman held her hand out for approval. Viola gave it a quick flick of her tongue. The woman stroked the top of Viola's head. Satisfied, Viola returned to her pack.

"Good morning," Lia said. "We don't normally get people without dogs."

The woman looked flustered. "I'm just waiting for someone."

"Who is it? I know most people who come here."

"I doubt you know him, but thank you." The woman angled away, signaling the end of their conversation.

Whatever, Lia thought.

She passed through the picnic shelter to the corral, released all the dogs except Max and headed for her favorite picnic table. Jim sat there, playing Draw Something on his Kindle. Fleece and Chester lolled beside him on the table top.

Lia seated herself on the table. Max settled on the ground. Viola jumped up, curling behind Lia. Honey and Chewy had abandoned her, hoping to find slow squirrels and evidence of deer incursions.

Lia peered over Jim's shoulder. "You ought to draw bigger. What are you trying to make?"

"It's a teapot. Think she'll get it?"

"That's a coffee pot."

"What's the difference?"

"Teapots are short, round, and have a long spout. Coffee pots are tall and have a short, triangular spout."

He held out the tablet. "Here, you draw it."

"You really want me to?"

"Sure, why not."

Lia handed Jim Max's leash, swapping it for the tablet and erasing the drawing. She started over, first laying down a background color of light tan, then a pale blue table cloth overlaid with thin, lavender stripes. Next, she selected the eraser and drew the belly of the pot, a sinuous spout and a curved handle in white. She drew a small knob on top. Then she selected a rose hue and decorated the pot with little flowers. Last, she switched back to the eraser and pulled wisps of steam coming out of the spout. She passed it to Jim.

"There you go."

He shook his head. "You're a terrific artist. Bonnie won't know what to think." He hit the send button.

"When do we get to meet this mysterious Bonnie?"

"One of these days."

Chester waddled across the table top and sat up on his hind legs by Lia. She turned to him and bent her face down so he could kiss her. Chester obliged, then tried to sneak his tongue up her nose. Jealous, Viola snapped at Chester.

"Eeeew. Stop it, Chester! Viola, Be nice!" She straightened up and looked back at the picnic shelter.

"That woman is still just sitting there. How long has she been here?"

"She was here when I arrived. I think that Nissan Altima in the parking lot is hers. I saw an Avis folder in the front seat. Guess she's from out of town."

"Or else her car is wrecked. Insurance will pay for a rental."

"True," Jim considered.

"She looks familiar."

"She's been hiking in the woods. I saw her head back there with someone last week. I can't remember who."

"In those clothes?" Lia raised her eyebrows.

"Takes all kinds."

"Hail, good people." Terry walked up with Bailey. Jackson, Napa and Kita chased circles around the picnic table, barely dodging their owners while Chester barked from his perch. "What's the story? Enquiring minds want to know. The news said your man found bones in the woods. Do we have a killing ground?"

"I don't know much," Lia responded. "It was just one body. They don't know who it is."

"And they found disarticulated bones? Not an intact skeleton? Terry asked.

"You don't need to be so happy about it," Bailey grumbled at Terry.

"I don't know anything about that," Lia evaded.

"There are many methods of removing flesh from bones. Dermestid beetles are the preferred method. They leave the skeleton in pristine condition. Unless someone cut most of the muscle mass away, it would take a significant amount of time to complete the process."

Lia looked at Bailey, whose throat was making tiny convulsive motions.

"Maceration also works. It requires containing the body in an enclosed space, preferably with water and enzymes of some sort. It's unpleasantly aromatic. Unlikely in this instance, since I'm assuming the bones were unarticulated, and you'd have to wonder why someone went to the trouble to move the bones to the woods.

"Boiling is the quickest method, but it makes for a brittle final product."

Bailey's face was turning green.

"... and all of these processes presume that most of the flesh has been stripped from the skeleton by some mechanical means first. I wonder, did they find any tool marks? That would indicate dismembering. If the bones have teeth marks instead ..."

Bailey backed away from the group with her hand over her mouth. Lia looked at Jim, who was drawing a were-wolf that looked like a collie on his Kindle. She looked back up at Terry.

"Scavengers must have gotten to it. It's the only thing that makes sense," Terry concluded.

"That's very ... *informative*, Terry. It's like watching CSI. I've got to walk Max." Lia stood up, and Max stood with her, stretching and yawning, then wagged her tail. Viola jumped down from the table and ran ahead. She looked back over her shoulder and barked. "Yes, Princess, I'm coming." A firm grip on the leash, she headed for the back of the park, where Bailey was tossing a ball for Kita, Honey and Chewy.

"You abandoned me," Lia accused.

"Sorry, it's my delicate sensibilities. I'm going to be off my feed for the next three days after that. How are you holding up?" Bailey asked.

"Once I got over the idea that I had a fresh, human bone in the back seat of my car, I was okay. Peter's the one who has to deal with it. Thank God, it doesn't have anything to do with me."

PETER CLOSED out the web page when he heard the distinctive clip of his partner's Ferragamo knockoffs entering the bullpen. He swung around in his swivel chair and leaned back, playing innocent.

"You may be fast, Brother, but your reflexes are no match for my eagle eyes. I must say, I cannot believe what I just saw." Brent Davis had blond good looks that were diligently maintained through grooming, wardrobe and exercise. The Atlanta transplant's magnolia-laced voice affected most women in an embarrassing way that had his fellow detectives shaking their heads when they weren't making bets. Peter found his courtly manners useful during interrogations.

"If you know what's good for you, you saw nothing."

Brent ignored the threat. "And on the people's dime, too. For shame. Does Lia know about this?"

"No, and she's not going to."

"She has to find out eventually."

"When I'm ready."

"Man, you must be dreaming. I don't think you'll ever be ready for the way she's going to react."

"I've got a workaround in mind."

"I hope you're not planning to give it to her for her birthday."

"Nope." Peter leaned back in his chair, folding his arms.

"You gonna slip it on her finger while she's asleep? Tell her it's just an odd skin growth? How will you explain the minister?"

"Ha. Ha."

"The usual way of these things is you let her pick out the ring after you've broached the topic of matrimony. That way you're not stuck with three K in dissed diamonds when she says, 'no.'"

"That is totally lacking in romance. In case you haven't noticed, Lia's not into the usual way of things."

"I have noticed. So why are you looking at the usual sort of ring?"

"Just getting a baseline. Anything wrong with that?"

Peter's phone rang. He grabbed the receiver. "Dourson … Yeah … We'll be right down." He hung up. "That was Jeffers. Time to go see a doctor about a corpse. You up for a ride to the University?" He headed down the hall, Brent behind him.

"This isn't over. It's my job to watch your back and right now, I'd say you're a train wreck waiting to happen. Lia ever suggest to you that she even wants to get married?"

"Marriage is what people do when they grow up. I know you're unfamiliar with adulthood, but maybe you've heard something about it?"

"You do know you're in the twenty-first century, don't you?"

They exited the building. As Peter turned left, toward his Blazer, Brent put a hand on his shoulder and redirected him to the right. "This way, my man. You're in for a ride."

"Meet Celeste," Brent said as he clicked his fob. A midnight blue Audi A4 obligingly flashed her lights and beeped. "She's my sexy new girl."

Peter let out a low whistle as he walked around the sporty sedan. "Isn't Celeste a French name? Shouldn't she have a German name, like Helga or Gertrude?"

"It may be a German car, but Audi is Latin. Celeste is Latin for heavenly. And that, my man, she is."

"If she didn't set you back a year's pay, I'll eat my badge."

"Start chewing, Brother. Even with the Bluetooth and

the iPod interface, the walnut inlay and those very snazzy wheels, I managed to skim under."

"That include insurance?"

Brent held open the passenger door and waved his arm. "I refuse to dignify that. Slide your manly rear onto that leather seat and Celeste will show you what she's all about."

Peter got into the car. Brent shut the door and headed for the other side.

"Did you get the sissy seat warmers?"

"No, I did not get the sissy seat warmers."

"Too bad, that could come in handy on a stake out."

"Celeste does not do stake outs. Celeste draws too much attention. Don't you, Baby?" Brent patted the steering wheel and started the car. "Hold on to your metaphorical hat." He pulled out onto Ludlow Avenue.

"So my Blazer is good for something then."

"You'll be ashamed to climb into that rolling pile of scrap metal after Celeste is done with you." He cut neatly through traffic and headed up the hill, toward University Hospital.

"Insult me all you want. My truck is paid for. While you're bleeding the equivalent of a house payment every month, I'm socking it away."

"House payment? You buying a house?"

"Not yet, but I've got my eyes open and I'm going to be ready when the right place comes on the market."

"Lia know about this?"

"I've been saving that money for years. No reason to talk to Lia about it until something interesting comes along."

"Rings and house payments. You do have it bad. I bet

she's perfectly happy with things as they are. You'd better have a chat with her about all this before you go any further down the road to Fantasy Island."

"There is no road to Fantasy Island. You have to take a plane. Don't you know anything?"

"I know trouble when I see it."

"You want to make love to your car. And you think *I'm* in trouble?"

PETER AGAIN SMELLED the scent of urine and putrefaction when he entered the morgue. Deputy Coroner Amanda Jefferson stood by a steel table holding an array of bones arranged roughly as a skeleton. The bones had been cleaned of all scraps of meat and sinew since Peter and Brent last saw them, revealing an abundance of gouges in the surface. There were a number of gaps where bones were missing.

"Gentlemen, meet John Doe. He was a Caucasian male, age somewhere between forty and sixty. He had white hair and he was five foot, six to five foot, eight inches tall. Clothing fragments found at the scene suggest he was wearing blue jeans, a red tee-shirt and a tan jacket. The only object found at the scene was a crossbow bolt with a three-blade hunting broadhead."

She picked up an ulna and held it so that Peter and Brent could see where it was riddled with triangular punctures. "These are bite marks from coyotes. The marks are of various sizes, indicating more than one animal. I haven't yet counted up how many coyotes feasted on John, but it looks like it could have been a whole pack.

"I found no specific marks on the skeleton to indicate cause of death. We can postulate that with the blood soaked area found at the scene along with the crossbow bolt, the bolt was the cause of death and that he bled out at the scene. The amount of blood in that spot suggests he bled out very quickly.

"It's likely the bolt struck a major artery, the carotid in the neck or the femoral artery in his thigh. It's doubtful he was struck in the head or the heart, as this would have been indicated by damage to the skull or the ribs.

"Due to the difficulty confirming cause of death, we're holding the remains until we can get a forensic anthropologist in to make an examination. This may take a week or longer.

"Our coyote pack went after John like a school of piranha. There was not much left for insects to chew on, but from the existing activity, my preliminary estimate is that death took place sometime on Monday. He's been dead approximately seventy-two hours."

"Why do you think the coyotes went after him like that?" Peter asked.

Amanda walked over to the next table and picked up a scrap of fabric from an array laid out like a quilt. As she brought it near, the reek grew stronger.

"What is that smell?" Brent asked.

"I've sent a sample over to the lab. It'll be days before we have an answer, but I suspect someone doused Mr. Doe here with scent lure. It would have drawn every coyote in the park. I bet they were fighting over the body like rabid zombies."

"Let's hope they did that after he died," Brent said.

BACK AT DISTRICT FIVE, Brent tackled their list hunters while Peter went to work identifying the victim. He pulled up the missing persons database and plugged in search options. There were three matches in the Ohio-Kentucky-Indiana region over the last year. He scanned them quickly for proximity.

One, a George Munce, lived less than two miles from Mount Airy Forest. This report was also the most recent, having been filed late Tuesday. He reviewed the other entries just in case. Neither were especially promising. He went back to George's file.

George was last seen by his wife on Monday morning before she went in to her job as a school counselor for Hughes High School. George worked evenings as store manager at the Dollar Hut on Colerain Avenue, and hadn't been discovered missing until he failed to show up for his shift that afternoon. He was most likely wearing jeans and a tan jacket. *Huh.* The family dog was also missing.

He glanced at the name of the officer taking the report. Hinkle. Peter snorted. That was why the report hadn't hit the news. It also explained why the interview was sketchy. Nothing like having to redo someone else's work. At least Hinkle remembered to put out a BOLO for the man's car.

How do you tell a wife that what might be her husband's body is in no condition to be viewed, and who is his dentist? Not a situation he'd ever faced before. It would be interesting to see how the likely widow reacted to news that her husband's body may have been found. He'd get Brent to tag along. Any excuse to power up his new toy would do.

THE WOMAN who answered the door was small and trim, neatly dressed with a cap of dark, salon-highlighted hair and a sprinkling of freckles across a small nose. Peter thought she looked like a pixie, except for the dark circles under her eyes.

Peter and Brent introduced themselves as they produced badges.

"Is this about George? Have you found him?" she bit her lip as her eyes pleaded for answers.

"We're not sure. We have some questions for you," Peter said. "May we come in?"

"Yes, please do. Can I offer you coffee?" Manners collided with nerves as she rattled on. "I have scones. I baked scones this morning. Please say you'll have one. I didn't have anything better to do, so I baked." She stopped talking suddenly and blinked, as if uncertain what to do next.

"Thank you, Mrs. Munce," Peter said. "It's not necessary. You don't need to go to any trouble."

"No trouble at all, it's already made." She led them into the kitchen. "Have a seat at the bar."

The kitchen was ruthlessly clean and organized. A fresh pot of coffee warmed on the brewer. A platter of scones studded with some kind of dried fruit sat on the breakfast bar. Next to the platter was a jar of clotted cream.

She pulled two pottery mugs out of a kitchen cabinet and set them on the counter. As she reached for a third, one of the mugs on the counter slipped and crashed to the floor.

"Oh! I'm so stupid!" She stooped and started picking up pieces, shaking her head. "I can't believe I did that. I loved that mug. ... I'll have this cleaned up in a jiffy."

Brent crouched beside her. "It's all right, Mrs. Munce. Why don't you let me take care of this while you sit down with Detective Dourson?" His voice whispered of Tupelo honey, soothing.

She shut her eyes for a moment, inhaled deeply, collected herself. "Let me get you coffee, at least."

"I see the coffee right over there. How about I pour some for you?" He took her by the elbow and gently raised her up, guiding her to one of the stools.

"I see you've got Splenda sitting out. Is that what you take in your coffee?" She nodded, surrendering to Brent's ministrations.

"There's half-and-half in the fridge. I'm sorry, I'm just so nervous. Please tell me you've found something."

Peter's eyes met Brent's. Brent handed her a cup of coffee, then went back to picking up the broken pottery. She clutched at the cup, rubbing her thumb over the clay ridges formed on the pottery wheel.

"Mrs. Munce," Peter began, "we may have a lead." Her hollow eyes bored into him. He plowed on. "We found a body, and we think it might be a match."

"A match? You mean it might be George? George isn't dead, he's just missing," she said inanely. "You're supposed to find him."

"In that case, we need to rule George out, make sure this isn't him."

"You want me to look at him? I gave you pictures, can't you tell?" Peter noticed a stridency in her voice that suggested she was getting angry.

"It's not that simple. The body was exposed to the elements. It's not recognizable. We're going to need dental records. Can you tell us who his dentist is?" Peter lowered his voice and spoke slowly, in the hope that she would also lower hers.

"He was just here, four days ago. How is it possible that he's not recognizable? Let me see him, I'm sure I can tell if it's him or not."

"I'm afraid we can't do that."

"Why ever not?" She demanded, escalating several decibels.

Peter changed the subject. "Mrs. Munce, this body was in Mount Airy Forest. Did your husband ever go there?"

"Yes, he liked to hike with Daisy. What does that have to do with identifying him?"

"Scavengers got to the body. There is little left to identify. That's why we need the dental records."

"You mean something *ate* him?" She set down the mug with a thump, slopping coffee over the sides. She stared at Peter.

"We won't know for sure until the coroner completes her report."

"How did he die?"

"That's undetermined at this time."

"Mrs. Munce," Brent placed a soothing hand over hers. "We're still not sure that it's George. One step at a time."

"I've been sitting here, waiting for him to come home, and he's dead?" her voice rose dangerously in pitch.

"Mrs. Munce," Peter interjected, "it may be George. It may not. If it is George, we'll have some questions for you."

"Oh, it's George all right."

Peter caught Brent's eye. Brent raised his eyebrows behind Mrs. Munce's back.

"Why do you say that, Mrs. Munce?" Peter asked.

"Because George wouldn't run out on me. Ask your questions. Go ahead and ask them now. I've had nothing to do all week but sit around and wonder where he was." She stood up and got down three small plates and placed scones on them. She slapped a generous dollop of clotted cream on each with trembling hands. The plates thudded as she set them in front of Peter and Brent. "You will have something to eat, won't you? It would be a shame for these to go to waste."

She busied herself in the kitchen, gathering cloth napkins and silverware with the grim determination usually reserved for military campaigns and root canals. The domestic routine appeared to soothe her. Peter watched as she willed competence back into her hands, rebuilding her facade bit by bit. When Peter and Brent were settled with coffee and scones, clotted cream and honey, she also settled.

A veneer of crisp efficiency firmly in place, she reseated herself at the counter and faced the two detectives. "What," she asked, "would you like to know?"

"This is premature, you understand?" Peter said.

"In my mind, it's overdue."

"Was George upset about anything in the weeks before he disappeared? Anything unusual going on?" Peter asked.

"Not upset, no. He *was* concerned about some issues with an employee at work, but he was in a good mood when I saw him."

"What does that mean," Brent asked, "'when you saw him'?"

"We work different shifts. I have to get up early because I'm a counselor at Hughes High School. I was often in bed when he came home."

"Did that bother you, never seeing him?" Peter asked.

"What does that have to do with anything?" Monica Munce's voice was no longer edging toward hysteria. Peter found her new, steely resolve no more reassuring.

"Please, Mrs. Munce, I need to have a picture of his situation. Anything could be important."

"We're settled married people, Detective, and we've got many balls in the air. I don't have to connect with him every day to know he's there."

Peter noted the use of present tense in her responses. "He have problems with anyone?"

"He was worried about that clerk, but I don't think it was anything serious. George was just George. He didn't like to make waves. He wasn't the sort to antagonize people. If he didn't like something, he usually kept it to himself." She was breaking off little pieces of scone that never made it to her mouth.

"Do you know the name of the employee?"

"Oh, I'm sure I don't remember. If it wasn't one, it was another. If you haven't noticed, the sort of people who work in those stores hardly have the best lives."

"What sort of trouble was he having with this employee?"

"I don't really remember. George didn't talk about work very much. It was just something he said in passing."

Peter observed a picture of a teenage girl on the window sill. She had dark, waist-length hair, conservative clothes and a serious expression.

"Is that your daughter?" He nodded to the photograph.

"Yes, that's Stacy."

"What was her relationship with her father?"

"George was Stacy's stepfather. They got along well enough. She's very busy with her studies and extracurricular activities. She's an honor student at Walnut Hills."

"She ever get into trouble?"

She shook her head. "Stacy is never a problem."

"What about drugs?"

"Not my child!"

"Begging your pardon, ma'am," Brent said. "We have to ask."

"What about financial trouble? Could anything like that have been bothering George?"

"We're not rich, Detective, but we're okay."

"Gambling?"

"George?" she sputtered. "He wouldn't do anything so tawdry. Let me explain something to you. Having a loving family was the only thing that mattered to him. He would never do anything to jeopardize us."

"I TELL YOU WHAT," Brent said as they pulled out of the Munce driveway, "that was like pulling teeth, getting the freaking dentist out of her. Couldn't you have just done that over the phone?"

"I wanted to see her reaction when she heard her husband might be dead. How would you describe state of mind?"

"Brittle? Histrionic? Then, for a minute there, I thought we were facing the reincarnation of General Patton." Brent said.

"Interesting shift of mood there. Like she was angry at him for dying."

"Shame about the mug."

"She said she loved the mug. Wonder why she never said anything about loving George?" Peter asked.

"Maybe she didn't, Brother. We get to come back this afternoon. I wonder how she'll act."

"We have to interview Stacy. Kids notice things."

"I'm looking forward to more drama. Fun city, Brother."

STACY HAD A QUIETLY defiant look on her face when Monica led her into the dining room that afternoon.

"Detectives Dourson and Davis have some questions they'd like to ask you, though I can't imagine what you could tell them," Monica announced.

Peter noticed Stacy narrowing her eyes behind Monica's back. *Something going on there.*

Stacy seated herself at the table, smoothing her skirt as she sat down. Her voice was excessively polite. "You don't have to stay, Mother. I'm sure I'll be fine."

"Don't be ridiculous. I wouldn't think of leaving you to face this alone."

Stacy's rolling eyes punctuated a long-suffering look. Despite the facial gymnastics, her voice remained calm and precise. "It's the police, not the Spanish Inquisition. If they pull out thumbscrews, I'll be sure to yell loud enough for you to hear me."

Monica ignored this. She looked pointedly at Peter and Brent. "What would you gentlemen like to know?"

Brent leaned forward. "Stacy, I'm Detective Davis, and this is my partner, Detective Dourson. He's in charge of the investigation into your stepfather's death. We're wondering what you noticed about your stepfather in the days before he disappeared."

"Noticed like what?"

"Anything unusual or different," Brent said.

"You mean like being happy?"

"Stacy! What are you saying?" Monica gasped.

"What? Like you think I never noticed how much you yelled at George? You think he *liked* that?"

Peter intervened. "What can you tell us about George's change in mood, Stacy?"

"I can tell you what caused it."

"What was that?" Peter asked.

"She caused it." Stacy's eyes darted sideways, gaging her mother's response.

"She?"

Stacy dropped her bomb. "His old high school girl-friend. From *Oklahoma*. He was having an *affair*. He was *happy*."

"Stacy! Go to your room!"

"Mrs. Munce, we are conducting an interview here. We will thank you not to interrupt," Brent said in his most polite Atlanta drawl.

"This story is preposterous!"

"It's the *truth*!" Stacy faced her mother, chin up.

"Mrs. Munce, are we to understand that you didn't know about this affair?" Peter asked.

"Absolutely not! George wouldn't do such a thing." She glared at Stacy, who looked back impassively.

Got her mother's goat, Peter thought.

"You want to know the best thing about it?" Stacy asked confidentially, her eyes gleaming.

"What was that?" Peter asked.

"She was *old*. And *fat*." She turned back to her mother. "You spend all that time at the gym doing Zumba, and he's running around with this dumpy looking woman."

Monica's eyes widened dangerously. Brent gave her a warning look.

"Stacy, how did you find out about this relationship?" Peter asked.

"It was on Kindle."

"I don't understand," Peter said.

"I picked up George's Kindle by accident one day, and when I turned it on, there was this paranormal thriller on the carousel. It didn't look like anything George would like, so I opened it up and read a few pages.

"I still didn't get it, so I checked the 'shared notes and comments' to see what people were saying about it, and there was all this stuff. They were writing to each other through their Kindles. Man, it was *hot*.

"He must have got the idea when I told him about kids using the *Oxford American Dictionary* to chat with since they aren't allowed to have their phones in school, but they can have e-readers."

"How does that work?" Peter asked.

"It's easier if I show you. Can I go get my Kindle?"

"Sure."

Stacy returned with her e-reader and turned it on. First she opened up the dictionary and showed the book to the detectives. Next, she tapped a little conversation bubble at the bottom of the screen and the page turned black. Comments appeared in white, with user names in red and icons in the margin. She handed it to Peter, who began scrolling through the entries.

"It's all random stuff," Stacy said.

Peter had to agree. The comments included such gems as "U R so tuf" to "EVERYBODY DANCE NOW!"

"Do we need George's Kindle to see his comments?"

"Nope. I bought the book so I could follow along on mine." She took the e-reader back and returned to the main page. She scrolled down through her favorites, then stopped at a book featuring a picture of a naked woman, waist-deep in a dark pool of water, facing away. This was juxtaposed against an enormous, evil looking animal eye and parallel red gashes that looked like claws had ripped into something. The word "Blood" slashed across the top of the cover in vivid red.

"I mean, this doesn't look like his kind of thing, you know? It was smart, the book is by this indie author and I don't think many people know about it. If I hadn't picked up his Kindle by mistake, no one would have ever noticed. I mean, anyone can pick up your phone and read your text messages." She gave her mother a scathing look. "But they'd never think to look here." She opened the book and clicked on the "shared notes" icon, then handed it back to Peter, who held it so Brent could see.

The most recent note was from "Buttercup," whose icon was a yellow flower. Buttercup said, "Baby, talk to me. I'm dying. Don't leave it like this." This was dated two days after George's disappearance. Under that, "Joe" said, "Sorry, we have to stop. Don't contact me anymore." This was dated the day George vanished.

"So you think George was this 'Joe'?" Peter asked.

"I know so. At first, I didn't think it was him, or

anybody I knew. I just thought it was high entertainment, all this sex talk. But he mentions Oklahoma, and Mount Airy Forest, and," she turned to her mother, "Daisy, who happens to be *missing*."

Stacy turned back to Peter and Brent. "And I noticed he was always in a good mood after 'Buttercup' posted a comment. There's all this sex talk about what they want to do to each other, and then they're planning to meet up. She flew all the way from Oklahoma to see him. They're like Elizabeth Barrett and Robert Browning or something."

"How far back can you scroll on this thing? Do the notes stay in there forever?"

Monica finally broke her silence. "Stacy, darling, why didn't you tell me about this?" Her voice was dangerously sweet.

"Why would I do that? *Somebody* should be happy around here."

"Ladies," Brent interrupted, "this is not a productive direction for this conversation. Mrs. Munce, I understand your consternation at these revelations. It's only natural. But please allow us to complete this interview. I'm sure whatever you and Stacy have to say to each other is much better said in private."

"Not hardly," Stacy muttered.

Monica sat back, lips clamped, the expression on her face an odd blend of mortification and rage.

"Stacy," Peter continued, "how do you know what this woman looks like?"

"I saw her once, from a distance. I was driving past the store and George was out in the parking lot with her."

"What did you see?"

"Not much. I saw her from the back. George was tucking her hair behind her ear. I just saw her for a second. Keeping my eyes on the road, you know." She gave what Peter thought of as a "Valley Girl" shrug, with her eyes rolled up and her head canted at a Hollywood angle.

"Can you describe her?" Brent asked.

"I dunno. A little taller than George. Wider." She smirked, looking at her mother from the corner of her eye. Monica's mouth gave minute, jerky twitches. "Her hair was light brown, more ash than blond. You know, that old lady color."

"What was she wearing?"

Stacy bit her lower lip and thought. "Looked like stretch pants. Some kind of tunic or cardigan. Grey pants, burgundy top? Can't say for sure. I was trying not to wreck the car."

"When did this happen?" Brent asked.

Stacy chewed on her thumbnail. "After school … a week ago? Ten days? I don't remember for sure."

"Mrs. Munce, I think we're finished with Stacy," Peter said. "We're going to need George's e-reader. I'd like Officer Davis to go with you while you get it."

"I'm sure I wouldn't know where it is. I have no idea where he kept it." She avoided Peter's eyes as she said this. She made no move to get up.

"That e-reader contains important information about George's last days. There's no telling what's on it. It's very important to this investigation. If you really don't know where to look, I can have Brent wait with you while I swear out a warrant and bring in a team to search for it. That will take several hours, of course."

Monica closed her eyes in an apparent effort to control herself. A tear escaped, signaling defeat.

"Mrs. Munce," Brent said, "we understand the contents of this e-reader are quite personal and potentially embarrassing to you. We will do everything in our power to keep private anything that is not germane to the investigation."

"Mom," Stacy said in a gentler tone than she'd used before. "I can show Detective Davis where to look."

"It's quite all right," Monica said stiffly, "I'm sure Detective Davis and I can find it."

"THAT IS ONE ANGRY LITTLE GIRL," Brent said once they were back in his car. "Remind me never to have kids. Either that, or drown them before they become teenagers. Speaking of angry–" He pointed his chin several houses down. "Check it out."

Peter saw a tall man– or was it a boy– at the open hood of an old Toyota. Instead of busying himself with the motor, he just stood there, scowling at them. Peter held his eyes as they drove by. The boy turned his head and spat.

"Spooky," Peter said.

"You got that right. He won't need a costume for Halloween. What about Mom? You think she really didn't know about Buttercup?"

"I think she's a terrible liar. She couldn't look me in the eye when she said she didn't know where the e-reader was. She took you right to it, didn't she?" Peter asked.

"She did pretend to dither a bit, but yeah, she knew

where it was. How about you? If your old man wrote hot letters to his floozy, would you read them?"

"My dad's favorite floozy was a cow." Peter had a quick vision of his father talking dirty to Flossie as he was milking her. Flossie was wearing a red satin garter belt edged with black lace and fishnet stockings. It was a disturbing image. He shook his head, as if what had been seen in his mind's eye could be dislodged that way.

"You boys from Kentucky sure know how to pick 'em. Cynth is going to have fun with this. I think after she pulls all the posts off this book, I'm going to ask her out for drinks. She might be needing some company."

"You leave her alone. You toy with her affections, and we'll be blackballed down in IT. We need her skills. She's not your type, anyway."

"Don't know about that. Take off those glasses, unbraid that hair, you don't know what you'll find. Could be interesting."

"It could," Peter said, "make our lives a living hell. Not *your* life, *our* lives. You go near her, and I'll tell her you were a bed-wetter up into middle school."

"That's a dirty, filthy lie, and it's beneath you."

"And it'll be all she ever thinks about when she looks at you. Wonder if she'll be able to keep it to herself?"

"Blackmail is against the law, Brother."

"Go ahead, press charges. I want to see you explain it to Roller," Peter said. "We've got to find that woman."

"Buttercup? You think we can get Amazon to give her up?"

"Maybe, but that will take more time than I care to think about."

Maybe she was caught on the security tapes at Dollar Hut."

"Why don't we head over there and find out?"

LIFE HAD SUCKED the marrow out of Carleen Thomas and was unlikely to give it back. She was hard and stringy for a woman in her thirties. The chipped state of her pink pearl nail polish suggested that the inches-long, dark roots snaking through her hair were neglect masquerading as fashion. Flecks of black mascara peppered her cheek-bones. Her store smock was stained and her lips were pinched. She reeked of cigarette smoke.

"I really liked George. I can't believe he's dead. We didn't know what to think when he didn't show up for work Monday."

"I'd like for you to remember back to the week before he disappeared," Peter said. "We're looking for a woman who may have visited him here at the store. She would be a little taller than him, and overweight."

"You mean regular fat, or Cincinnati fat?"

"What do you mean by 'Cincinnati fat'?" asked Brent.

"Can she find clothes at Walmart?"

Brent looked perplexed. "I guess so."

"Then she ain't Cincinnati fat."

Peter gave Brent a look. Brent stifled his snort, turning it into a cough.

"We're guessing maybe thirty, forty pounds over-weight," Peter said. "Light brown hair. Conservative dresser. But we'd be interested in hearing about anyone who came to see him recently."

Carleen snapped her gum. "Nope, nobody came to see George, not that I saw. Hey, Shondra," she called to a young black woman. "Come talk to these police officers."

Shondra had cornrows braided into extensions that were gathered loosely in a long tail. She wore green nail polish with red rose decals and cheap tennis shoes. The light that had gone out of Carleen still burned brightly in her. Whoever Carleen had met on the road, Shondra had yet to make his acquaintance. "What?" she inquired, smiling at Brent.

Peter introduced himself and Brent and explained their mission.

She shook her head. "Can't think of anyone."

"How about your relationship with George?" Peter asked. "How did you get along?"

She shrugged. "He was nice, for a boss, but we didn't have no relationship."

"We understand he was concerned about one of his employees. Would either of you have any idea who that would be?" Brent asked.

The two women looked at each other, shrugged.

"He was always helping somebody out," Shondra volunteered. "When they screwed up Maria's food stamps last month, he took her grocery shopping." She nodded at Carleen. "He helped Carleen find a divorce lawyer a while back. Could have been anybody."

"He have a problem with anyone here at the store?" Peter asked.

"George was nice to everybody," Carleen insisted. "He didn't play favorites, and nobody gave him trouble, except for maybe not showing up on time for work." She looked pointedly at Shondra.

"Whatever," Shondra said. "Now we got you instead of him. He could have used a favorite if you ask me."

"How so?" Peter asked.

"Man seemed sad, a lot. He was always nice, but just kinda down."

"How about lately?" Peter asked.

Shondra shrugged. "Now that you mention it, I did see him smiling some last couple weeks. You notice that, Carleen?"

"I don't know. Maybe."

"Maybe he got that favorite after all."

* * *

Peter and Brent talked to Maria and an older man named Duane, discovering nothing. Carleen gave them the number for Dollar Hut's head of security for the district. They could have copies of the video files for the past two weeks, but it would take at least twenty-four hours to pull and copy them.

"That gives us twenty-four hours to figure out a way to dump that chore onto someone else," Brent said. "You suppose we could lay this on Hinkle? He's not bright enough to wiggle his way out of it."

"He's covering the bottle bomb interviews at Hughes High School for us."

"I guess we should be grateful. If not for your girl-friend's dog, we'd be running down teeny-bombers right now."

"Besides, it would be pointless to give the tapes to him. Our girl could do the Harlem Shake naked in front of the camera and Hinkle would miss it," Peter said.

"I'm not sure what good reviewing the tapes will do. We won't catch Munce laying a big wet one on Buttercup in the parking lot. He knows where the cameras are. How will we know who it is? Do you know how many overweight, middle-aged women with medium length, greying hair there are in Cincinnati? It's at least fifteen percent of the population."

"She'll be the well-dressed one," Peter said.

LIA HAD NEVER heard anything like it. The sound emanating from the living room was definitely canine in origin. It was a rhythmic groaning that rose and fell like a car engine trying, and failing, to turn over. She walked into the room and spotted Max with her tailbone pressed against the lower edge of the futon couch frame, rubbing her sacrum back and forth across the wood edge. The noise, apparently, was ecstasy.

Lia sighed. Max looked up and grinned sheepishly, caught in the act. Then she resumed her gyrations and her indecent orations.

"Whatever floats your boat, girl," Lia told her. "At least you aren't into humping legs." The phone rang.

"What, on God's green Earth, is that noise?" Peter asked when she picked up.

"That," Lia said, "is Max, committing a bizarre form of self-gratification against my furniture."

"You're letting the children see this?"

"Their innocence is lost forever. Do you think Brent wants a dog?"

"Wreck his carefree bachelorhood? Doubt it."

"Do you suppose if we snuck her into his car when he wasn't looking that he'd keep her?"

"Lia, if you don't want the dog, just take her back."

"I can't do that. I don't know where she'll end up."

"So, how's my girl?"

"She's fine. I don't know how she can sleep through this racket."

"I meant my best girl."

"I thought Viola was your best girl."

"How about my best two-legged girl?"

"She's good, too. I managed to hook up with Renee today."

"What mad scheme does your favorite patron have up her sleeve now?"

"She wants a larger-than-life portrait of Dakini. She says that's to make up for her curator friend backing out on the sculpture commission the museum was going to give me. Last time she spoke to them, the curator dithered something about one of their biggest donors and her latest boy-toy artist. Apparently her nepotism outranks Renee's nepotism."

"What's Renee need a painting of her dog for? She's got Dakini right there, all she has to do is look at her."

"Philistine."

"You can't be talking about me. I've never been near the Middle East."

"Hick."

"Keep abusing me, and I won't come over."

"Promises, promises. You bringing dinner?"

Peter dug his chopsticks into a bowl of pad Thai while Lia delicately nibbled the end of her spring roll.

"Thai is perfect. How did you know I was in the mood for pad grapao?"

Peter leaned over and wiped a bit of plum sauce off the corner of her mouth with his index finger. "I'm a detective. They pay me to know these things."

"Uh-huh, knowing my secret cravings for Asian cuisine really goes a long way toward keeping our streets safe."

"There are times when that's all that stands between order and chaos."

Lia snorted at Peter's earnest expression. "I refuse to dignify that remark. What's going on with the bones we found? Do you know who it is yet?"

"We think so. We're waiting on a dental comparison, but the timeline fits and he liked to hike in Mount Airy. I wonder if you knew him."

"That's a gruesome thought. Bad enough to find the bones of a stranger. I hate to think the coyotes were chewing on someone I knew."

"I have a picture. Brent and I are going to show it around tomorrow, after we get confirmation. See if anyone remembers him. Would you mind looking at it?"

"ID-ing dead people over dinner. You sure know how to show a girl a good time."

"You brought it up."

"Yeah, throw that in my face. It's okay. Hand it over."

Peter pulled up a photo on his phone and handed it to Lia. She blinked as she took in the piercing blue eyes that belied middle-age bloat, the receding white hair, the full lips quirked to one side in an ironic half-grin.

"That's Daisy's dad. I can't think of his name."

"George Munce?"

"Yeah, that's it. That's who was in the woods?"

"That's what we believe."

"Geezelpete. That's who she was waiting for. No wonder he didn't show up. Poor woman."

"Who are you talking about?"

"There was this woman at the park today, waiting for someone in the picnic shelter. She didn't have a dog. Didn't want to talk. Dressed too nicely for the park. Jim remembered seeing her before, heading into the woods with someone. He couldn't remember who."

"Did you get a good look at her?"

"I was about six feet away. Why?"

"We've got to find out who she is. I need to set you up with a police artist so we can get a picture." He reached for his phone.

"Relax, Wonder Boy. I can draw my own damn picture." Lia went into her home studio and brought out a drawing pad. She flipped to a clean page and swiftly blocked out a sketch of a heavyset woman sitting at a picnic table.

Peter watched, fascinated, as a face evolved from Lia's brisk lines, features emerging from nothing. At first the lines were vague, an approximation. Lia went back in with her pencil and overlaid her sketch with authoritative marks. She shaded under the nose and chin. She used her eraser to pull highlights out. He noted the hint of anxiety in the eyes of the fleshy woman, the nervous tapping of her fingers on the picnic table, the short, neat nails.

"This is great. You're so talented."

Lia sniffed and drew herself up. "I'm a professional," she announced in a lofty tone.

Peter chucked her chin. "We still need to talk to the police artist. He'll take you through a process that will refine this to a photographic likeness."

Lia narrowed her eyes.

"Don't get huffy. He's going to love having your drawing to work with. We still need to have an E-FIT composite that meets departmental standards."

"Departmental standards, my ass," Lia grumbled.

"THIS IS REALLY GOOD," Officer Foreman said.

Lia smirked at Peter. He rolled his eyes. Andy Forman laid Lia's drawing down next to his computer.

"So we're looking for a middle-aged woman with light, chin-length hair, squared face, heavy build. That right?"

"It lacks poetry, but those are the basics. Are you going to ask me about her nose now?"

"That won't be necessary," Andy said. "We gave up the 'Mr. Potato Head' approach recently. This is far superior. Now we work with evolutionary algorithms to morph into the correct likeness holistically."

"Excuse me?" Lia wrinkled her brow, she turned her head, and caught Peter looking too innocent. "You," She growled as she poked him in the chest, "Are not supposed to snicker at witnesses." She turned back to the computer screen. "Okay, how does this work?"

"Just watch. I love this program." Forman keyed in the basic data. Nine different images popped up on the screen. "Look at the faces and tell me which one is most like the woman you saw."

Lia scanned the array, pointed to the middle image on the top row. "That one."

"Now look at them again and tell me which two faces look least like her."

She considered, then selected two more faces. "Why do you want to know what she doesn't look like?"

"It feeds into the algorithm." He entered her choices. A new array of photos popped up, all variations of the first photo she selected. "Same thing. Which looks most like her?"

Lia selected three more faces. They went through this process several more times. Each time the faces offered looked more like the woman in the park. Finally Lia said, "That's it. That one. It doesn't have the emotion, but that's her."

"Shame we don't have a program yet that can overlay feelings onto the likeness."

"This is amazing. It's not at all stiff like the sketch I saw on television last year of the Blue-Eyed Rapist. What do you do with the drawing now?"

"Andy," Peter nodded at Officer Forman, "is going to generate some copies. Brent and I are going to spend tomorrow running them around to all the motels within a five-mile radius of the park. If she's an out-of-towner, we've got to catch up with her before she takes off. Do you think Jim's still awake? It would help if we had a description of the vehicle. Once we get that, we can hit the rental agencies."

"What if it turns out the body isn't George?"

"We still want to find her. A stranger at the dog park,

waiting for someone who doesn't show, no dog, inappropriately dressed. Maybe her friend didn't show because he couldn't. Even if she wasn't waiting for our dead guy, she's been hanging around the woods. She might have seen something."

"Do you think she killed him?"

"I don't know. She's an anomaly, and cases are built on anomalies."

3

FRIDAY, OCTOBER 11

"Brother of mine, we are not taking your ten-year-old Blazer. Apart from being embarrassed to be seen in it, there's always the question of when its poor, worn out engine is going to drop on the road." Brent walked past Peter's SUV and clicked his remote key-fob. Brent's Audi beeped and flashed its lights.

Peter gritted his teeth. "My engine is fine. I had it rebuilt last year. You just want an excuse to show off your new car."

"That I do."

"You have to promise to obey all traffic laws."

"You just want to ruin all my fun, don't you?" He got into the driver's side, waited for Peter. "You know, you could trade in your Blazer for an Escape. Every time you transported a suspect, you'd be making an ironic statement."

"That truck is going to live at least another ten years."

"It's a car, not a marriage. Where to?"

"We've got a choice. There's the Comfort Inn up on Mitchell Avenue. A middle class lady would feel comfortable there. Or there's that string of older motels down on Central Parkway. We could hit all of them in the time it would take for us to go up to Mitchell and back."

"Isn't that like looking for your car keys under a street lamp because the light's better? Some of those places are really run down."

"What's closest to us is also closest to the park," Peter pointed out. "They're small, and chances are that if she's staying at one of them, the clerk on the desk would know it. Comfort Inn, she could be staying there and unless she stood out, which our girl doesn't, they might not remember her. More employees to interview, too."

"She might be staying in one of those bed and breakfasts in the Gaslight District."

"I'm betting not. From what Lia said, she was uncomfortable with being questioned. A place like that, they like knowing everything about why you're in town and what you're doing."

"Central Parkway it is, then. Fasten your seatbelt and prepare for takeoff. This is a short flight, so we will not be serving any refreshments."

The first place they stopped had a mostly empty parking lot and a gum chewing desk clerk sporting a nose ring. She looked as tired as the motel. Peter smelled burnt coffee. There were a pair of unappetizing glazed donuts on a chipped plate by the coffee maker. The girl glanced at the photo. "Nah, ain't seen her." She snapped her gum for emphasis.

"Thanks for your time, Miss," Brent said.

She snorted.

Back in the lot, Brent unlocked his car. "Did you see those donuts? If they'd showed me those at the police academy, I would have had second thoughts about becoming a cop."

"You and your doughnut fetish."

"A man has to have a hobby."

They checked the $37 Interstate Motel just for form. The motel's iconic sign had overlooked the highway for decades. It was hard to tell if the exterior paint was supposed to be that ugly gray, or if time and neglect had drained the color out of it. They were known to rent rooms by the hour, catering to participants in sordid couplings, mercenary or otherwise. Peter was certain the mystery woman with the carefully coifed hair would never lay her head on these pillows.

"Comfort Inn looking better?" Brent arched an eyebrow at Peter on their way out.

"I haven't given up yet."

"I bet you tomorrow's doughnuts she's not on this strip."

"You're on."

The third place showed signs of care with neatly trimmed privet hedges and a recent paint job. It was modest in appearance, with the parking lot hidden behind the building. It occurred to Peter that this feature prevented passersby from noticing who was there.

The lobby furniture was old but sturdy. The aroma of fresh coffee scented the air. There was an array of bagels, orange juice and cold cereal set out on a table for breakfast. Peter imagined they didn't go all out because there was a Big Boy with a daily breakfast buffet nearby.

A jowly man with a greying military haircut identified

himself as the manager. He put on the reading glasses that hung around his neck and peered at the photograph.

"Yes, I've seen her. Far as I know, she's still here. She doesn't look dangerous."

"We don't think she is. We just need to talk to her," Peter explained.

He turned to his computer, clicked through screens. "Her name is Kate Onstad. She hasn't checked out … reserved the room for three weeks. She still has four more days. Room 227. Would you like me to ring her room?"

"That's okay, we'll go knock on her door. Do you have a description of her car?" Peter asked.

The man scanned the rest of her registration. "Blue Nissan Altima, Kentucky plates V39- 795. Oklahoma driver's license."

"That's very helpful. Thank you," Brent said. They stepped out of the office and scanned the parking lot.

"No blue Altima. She's probably not here."

"It's still early. She might be down the road, getting breakfast."

"Let's knock on her door, just in case. Then we'll check."

They were on the metal exterior stairs leading to the second floor when Peter's phone rang.

"WHEN ARE you going to let Max off her leash? She learned her lesson. You won't run away, will you, Max?" Jim spoke to the dog from his usual perch on the picnic table.

"When pigs fly."

Max gave Lia a disgusted look and turned pointedly away.

"Hold on," Lia said. "Whose car is that? Do you recognize it?" Lia nodded at the blue Altima pulling into the lot.

"Looks new. Could be your mystery woman. They were silent as they waited for the car to pull into a spot. The driver sat inside for a few minutes. Lia clenched her teeth, mentally willing the driver to step out. Eventually the door cracked open. A pale head appeared.

"Is that her?"

"I can't tell from here. Let's walk closer so we can get a good look at her when she comes up the drive." They headed up to the front, trailing six dogs.

"What are we going to do if it is her?"

"I'm going to call Peter. You're going to move your car and block her in."

"Me? Why do I have to block her in?"

"Because you've only got two dogs to handle. I've got four. Yours won't howl in your ears while you sit in your car."

Jim grunted.

The stocky figure came around the curve in the drive, appearing on the far side of the picnic shelter.

"It's her."

"You want me to go now?"

"Hold on, let's see what Peter says."

She pulled her cell out of her pocket and punched his number on speed dial.

"Hey, Babe," Peter said. "We already got an ID on the car. Tell Jim thanks anyway."

"I'm not a farm animal. And you might have an ID, but

we have the car. We also have the driver. What do you want us to do?"

"What's the situation?"

"She just sat down in the shelter. I assume she's going to wait, like she did yesterday. I thought maybe Jim could block her car in so she can't leave."

"It'll take us about ten minutes to get there. I don't want you to spook her. Can she see the lot from the shelter?"

"Nope."

"Have Jim wait in his car. Keep an eye on her, and if she starts to leave, call Jim and have him block her in."

"Do you want me to try to talk to her?"

"No, and don't let her know you're watching her. We don't want things to get complicated. We're on our way."

She clicked off the phone. "Guess we're supposed to act casual." She sent Jim down to the lot, then climbed on the table closest to the gate. Max, still on her lead, jumped up beside her.

Lia put her arm around Max and scratched behind her ears. Honey, jealous, butted her knee. Viola jumped up on the table and gave Max an evil stare for taking her favorite spot. Max gave Viola a bland look. Lia stroked Honey absently on the head and angled so she could observe the woman while appearing to watch Chewy prowl the fence line.

Bailey banged in through the corral with Kia.

"Hey, what's up with Jim? He's just sitting in his car."

Lia widened her eyes and made a face. Bailey scrambled up next to her.

"Did I do something? Why are you looking at me like that?"

"Keep it down," Lia hissed. "We think that woman in the shelter knows something about the bones in the woods. Peter's on his way. Jim's ready to block her in if she tries to leave."

"Who, her?" Bailey said, looking at the shelter.

"Don't look over there!"

Something drew the woman's attention. She alerted, much like a hound on a scent trail, head up and sitting very still. Then she stood up and hooked her purse over her arm.

"Dammit, I think she's leaving. Why would she leave? She just got here!" Lia fumbled with her phone. She started pushing buttons, dropped the phone. "Quick," she told Bailey, "run down to the fence and get Jim's attention. She's just headed around the curve, so she won't be able to see you. Go!"

Bailey took off while Lia continued to punch buttons, finally pulling up her directory. She located Jim's number and heaved a relieved sigh as she hit 'send.'

Jim answered on the second ring.

"Why is Bailey waving at me? She looks like a windmill."

"The package has left the shelter."

"Huh?"

"She's coming! Get a move on!"

"All right, all right. You don't have to yell."

Lia squeezed into the corral, dragging Max with her and leaving the other dogs behind. She hurried down the drive, arriving in the parking lot just in time to see the woman approach Jim's Dodge Caliber, where it was parked behind her car. He rolled down the window.

"Will you be moving soon? I need to get out," the woman said.

"I can't just yet."

"Can't you just move over a bit so I can squeeze out? There's plenty of room."

Jim looked helplessly at Lia. His shoulders sank in resignation. "Ma'am, we'd like you to wait here. There's someone who wants to talk to you, but they're not here yet."

"Is it George? Why didn't you say so!"

"No, Ma'am, it's not George."

The woman looked perplexed. "I don't understand. Who needs to talk to me?"

Jim looked pointedly at Lia.

"Excuse me," Lia said. "Two detectives are on their way. They think you might have seen something when you were back in the woods."

"No, I haven't seen anything. What would I have seen? I really would rather not get involved with the police. I have to leave. Please let me out." She clutched her purse in front of her chest. For protection? White knuckles betrayed agitation despite her reasonable tone.

Lia said nothing. She looked up and saw Chewy, Honey, Kita and Viola, all lined up at the fence next to Bailey. They chose that moment to start howling for attention. Max barked in response and sat on the woman's foot. Fleece and Chester joined the hullabaloo.

Cornered, the woman looked around her, desperate for a way out. Tears began rolling down her face. Grim faced, she got into her car and sat, facing forward as if it would all go away if she couldn't see it. Lia, Bailey and Jim looked at each other and shrugged.

Lia sighed in relief when Brent's Audi pulled into the lot. The car parked next to the trapped Altima. The two detectives got out.

"What part of 'Don't let her know you're watching her' didn't you understand?" Peter asked.

"Unfair, Dourson."

He walked up to the driver's window.

"Smooth, Anderson," Brent said. "Jim, you can move your car."

"Good. I'm going home."

"Traitor," Lia hissed. She stalked back up the drive, dragging Max behind her.

✦

"Kate Onstad?" Peter asked.

"Yes, what's going on? Why am I being prevented from leaving? I feel like a prisoner."

"I'm very sorry about that. I'm Detective Dourson, and this is my partner, Detective Davis. We'd like very much to talk to you. We can go back up to the park if you'd be comfortable there, or we can go to the station."

"I don't want any of those crazy people listening in. Isn't blocking me in a form of kidnapping?"

"I'll make sure they keep their distance." Peter ignored her question and hoped it would go away.

Kate got out of her car. "What's this about? Should I have a lawyer?"

"We're just looking for information. If you feel the need for a lawyer, we can go back to the station and you can contact one."

"That sounds like a lot of trouble."

Peter and Brent escorted Kate back up the drive and into the small dog park, where a lone picnic table stood in the back.

"Will this be private enough?"

"It'll be fine. What's this all about, Detective?"

"Before we get started, I'd like your permission to record this conversation. This ensures that we have an accurate record, and protects you as well as us. Is that okay with you?"

Kate looked apprehensive but nodded her assent. Peter set up his little digital recorder and read in the date, time, location and participants, as well as stating that the taping was being done with Kate Onstad's knowledge and consent. After these preliminaries, he began.

"Are you acquainted with George Munce?" Peter noted her deer-in-headlights expression.

"Yes," she said carefully.

"When was the last time you saw him?"

"Why are you asking, Detective?"

"We're very sorry to tell you this, Ms. Onstad," Brent said. "A body was found in the woods two days ago. It's just been identified as George Munce."

Kate Onstad blinked several times. She chewed her lip. "George is dead?"

"Yes, Ma'am."

"I don't understand."

"Neither do we. We thought you could help us out. When was the last time you saw George?" Brent asked.

"Five days ago, Sunday."

"Where was that?"

Kate continued to chew her lip. She looked at Brent,

then at Peter. "In my motel room. He came by before he went in to work."

"Ms. Onstad," Peter asked, "what was the nature of your relationship with George Munce?"

Kate appeared to crumple. Her eyes shimmered as tears trembled onto her cheeks. She cried silently, her mouth open and quivering. Peter and Brent waited while she gathered herself.

"George and I knew each other in high school. We reconnected on the internet a few months ago and fell in love. I hadn't seen him in thirty years. I took time off from work so we could figure out how far we were going to take this thing. We were talking about getting married." She smiled sadly. "I can't believe he's gone."

"Did anyone else know about your relationship? Anyone at all?"

"No one. I didn't dare confide in anyone. None of my friends would have understood me taking up with a married man. My high school friends would have died if they knew I was in contact with George. He was a bit of a hoodlum when we were in school. Tell you the truth, it's a relief to be able to talk about it now. I can't believe George told anyone. He worked so hard, he had so much at stake."

"What was at stake?" Brent asked.

"George hadn't been happy for a long time before we found each other again, but he had a family to think about. He didn't want to hurt Monica unless it was absolutely necessary. She wasn't always … stable.

"He was willing to let things go on the way they were until we met by accident on Facebook. He said if he got a divorce, neither of them would have been able to keep the house. It would have meant uprooting his stepdaughter. I could have helped him with the mortgage, but forcing Stacy to accept a new stepmother right away would have been too much.

"There was also the risk Monica would take Stacy and move away. He was concerned for Stacy's welfare, if Monica had to deal with being a single parent. Such a mess. All we wanted was to be happy. Didn't we deserve that?"

Such a loaded question. Peter decided to dodge that one, too.

"Ms. Onstad, you came to the park yesterday, and you came back today. Why?"

The sad smile flitted across her face. "George loved the woods. We met up here several times to hike with Daisy. He said when we were here, he could believe there was no one else in the world but us. We had a little spot where we could be alone … and just talk." Her rising blush suggested to Peter that "talk" was euphemistic.

"Were you aware of the deer cull? Hikers aren't permitted in the woods except on Tuesdays."

"Oh, well, that. George said there was no need to concern ourselves since any deer hunter who knew anything wouldn't hang around in the middle of the day. We weren't the only ones in the woods. That woman who told me you were coming, I've seen her back there with those dogs, down in the gorge."

Peter winced.

"Yesterday and today," Peter reminded her.

"I was supposed to meet George here Monday morning. I'm staying over on Central Parkway, by the Big Boy. I went there for breakfast. When I came back, my tire was flat. I tried calling George, but his phone was off. Then I got a message from him saying that it was over. I sat in my motel room for three days and cried.

"Yesterday I woke up and decided I wasn't going to be brushed off like that. I figured if I waited here, I would catch him next time he brought Daisy to the park. I thought I deserved to know why."

"You were only here a few minutes before you decided to leave. What happened today?" Brent asked.

"I sat out here for three hours yesterday. Today I started feeling self-conscious and pathetic. I realized that if George showed up, I might humiliate myself. So I decided to forget about it and just go."

"We'd like to believe your story, but another officer went through Mr. Munce's phone records, and she didn't find any unknown numbers."

"Oh, well. George was very concerned about how he might come out in a divorce if it were known he was having an affair. He had another phone, one of those prepaid ones. He called it his 'burner.'"

"What kind of message did you get from him? Was it voice or text?"

"Neither. We liked to trade long messages sometimes. We had this system. It's something the kids do. We used our Kindles."

"How did you do that?" Brent asked, feigning ignorance.

"We used the public notes function on our Kindles as a sort of chat room. It's a lot less cumbersome than texting." She explained the process, much as Stacy had.

"Huh," Peter said. "Are the notes still there?"

"They should be. I was thinking about deleting mine, but I wasn't ready to do that yet."

"Ms. Onstad," Brent said, "that flat tire bothers me. Are you absolutely certain no one knew about your relationship with George?"

"I don't see how they could."

"Where did you and George go, here in town?" Peter asked.

"We had dinner at that lovely Italian place up on the hill, the one with the view. George said he didn't know anyone who ate there, and he would have said something if he saw anyone."

"Where else?" Peter asked.

"Just here, at the park, and my motel room. We, uh, ate a lot of carryout."

Peter and Brent exchanged glances.

"Surely people saw you with George, here at the park?" Brent asked.

"I guess, but we never talked to anyone, we just went into the woods. We usually used that path off the parking lot so we didn't run into many people."

"You saw Lia in the woods."

"Well, yes, but George just knew those people to nod at. They didn't know anything about him. For all they knew, I was his wife."

"You saw George Munce nowhere except your motel, this park, and one dinner at Prima Vista?" Peter asked.

Kate pressed her lips together and furrowed her brow. Her eyes widened. Peter raised his eyebrows and waited.

"I did stop by his store a few times when he was working. I can't believe anyone there knew there was anything between us."

Peter mentally rolled his eyes. *Only the entire staff,* he thought. *Whether they admit it or not.*

"Did he ever call you from work?"

"Yes, most evenings."

"Ms. Onstad, we're done for now, but I do have a favor to ask of you before you go."

"Yes?"

"Will you let us search your car?"

"Will that help your investigation?"

"It will help us rule you out as a person of interest."

"You go right ahead, then."

PETER DIDN'T KNOW what he was looking for. Mostly, he wanted to gauge Kate Onstad's reaction to having her car searched. He stood with her at the rear of the Altima while Brent examined the interior. He watched as her eyes followed Brent while he riffled through her glovebox and felt under her seats. Her eyes wandered to the park. He saw the flush creep up her face when she realized the patrons had gathered at the top of the hill and were taking in the show.

"This is so embarrassing," she said.

"It will only be a few more minutes."

Brent backed out of the car and shook his head. "The inside is clean."

"Open the trunk," Peter said.

Brent reached in and popped the latch. Peter pulled the lid up.

LIA, Terry and Bailey stood among the watchers as Brent

closed the trunk and Peter pulled the woman's hands behind her back and handcuffed her wrists.

"What do you suppose was in the trunk?" Bailey asked.

"Perhaps she kept a bone as a souvenir," Terry offered. "A tooth she could have made into a key ring. A finger she could enshrine in a reliquary. A tibia to use as a—"

"Stop being so gruesome," Lia admonished.

"She seemed so harmless," Bailey said. "Did you see the look on her face? I don't think she knew there was anything in her trunk."

"It does beg the question," Terry said. "I don't imagine they had a search warrant, so why would she allow them to open her trunk? A guilty conscience, perhaps?"

"I'm with Bailey," Lia said. "Whatever was in that trunk, I don't think she had a clue it was there. This feels wrong."

"You should have seen her," Lia told Renee as she adjusted the settings on the camcorder. "She looked like she should be selling cookies at her church bazaar. Then they searched her car, and Peter and Brent just handcuffed her and hauled her off like her trunk was full of dead babies."

She looked up, checked the direction of the sun against the placement of the agility jump in the park Renee called a yard. Renee and her perfectly groomed Collie, Dakini, waited on the far side of the jump. "Okay, I'm ready. We're rolling. Go!"

Renee took Dakini over the hurdle several times. Lia zoomed in on the jump and recorded the Collie from the front, hoping to catch exhilaration on Dakini's face. Lia then moved off to the left and recorded several more jumps from an angle. Finally she shot the jumps from the side, tracking the graceful dog as she soared effortlessly through the air. "Okay, that's enough. Let me check the file to make sure I got enough source material."

"Source material," Renee commented. "That's a fancy phrase for taking movies of my dog. How do you plan to use the footage?" Renee Solomon was a fit brunette with a glossy, spiraling bob. She and her husband, Harry, had worked their way up from blue-collar roots. She was an enthusiastic woman who both appreciated and enjoyed her wealth, and managed to do so without arousing enmity. Lia adored her.

"I'll run the digital file through the film editor on my Mac. I'll be able to click through, frame by frame to catch the perfect shot of Dakini in motion. I'll export it as a still and use that to paint from. The quality of the photo won't be great, but it's much more certain than attempting to catch her at the perfect moment while shooting stills."

"When I commissioned a portrait, I thought you'd just have her sitting pretty. I didn't think we'd be doing all this."

"Wait until you see the stills I pull. They'll be very dynamic. This will really energize your den. That is where you're going to put this, isn't it? I can see it over the mantel. Dakini's coloring will fit so well with your fieldstone fireplace."

"That's what I love about you, Lia. You don't just give me what I ask for. You give me what I never knew I wanted. Let's go inside and you can see the den. I'll call

Esmerelda. I think we could use something to drink after all that exercise."

Something turned out to include iced pomegranate tea for Lia and Renee and a bowl of water for Dakini. The dog sprawled on the sofa with her head on Renee's knee. Renee stroked Dakini as she and Lia huddled over the camera's tiny screen.

"Is this okay?" Lia asked. "We could upload it into your computer. You'd be able to see it better that way."

"This is fine for now. Aw, look at my baby," Renee cooed. "Isn't she gorgeous? I love how her fur is flying. How did you ever come up with this?"

"I saw how excited Max was when she jumped the fence the other day. Then I remembered that Dakini had her MACH in agility. I thought it might be more fun than the usual pet portrait."

"I'm thinking you thought right. Are you going to paint all of her, or just her face?"

"I don't know yet. I want to take a couple pictures of this space, think about what size and scale would work best here. If we go large and just do the face, you might feel like you've got 'Oz the Great and Powerful' staring down at you. You ever been in the same room with a Chuck Close?" Lia asked, referring to an artist famous for oversized faces.

"I see what you mean. Still, this room is big enough that it might work just fine. I'm going to leave the details up to you. You did such a wonderful job with our last project that I think I'll just step out of your way.

"Enough about business," Renee continued. "I want gossip. Must have been something awful interesting in that trunk. What do you suppose it was? Surely not dead babies."

"I have no idea. Unless it was a big sign that had 'I killed George Munce' written on it in blood."

"You sound like you're not happy with Peter right now."

"I'm not. I'm the reason he arrested her. I just thought he wanted to talk to her. I let Peter know she was there. I even had Jim block her in so she couldn't leave."

"Didn't you say Peter already knew where she was staying? It would have happened anyway, don't you think?"

"True, but I wouldn't have been involved. She was so shocked when they popped that trunk. I can't believe she did anything wrong. Viola liked her. Viola's very picky. She wouldn't like a criminal."

"Maybe not. If it's a mistake, they'll release her soon enough. Poor woman. I wonder ..." Renee looked over at her garage. "If they let her go, I imagine they won't want her to leave town right away. I doubt she'll want to be stuck in that motel where anyone could come knocking on the door. I've got that little apartment over the garage. Think she'd like to stay here?"

"You just want to get all the dirt first, but she'd be foolish to pass up the offer. Aren't you concerned about taking a possible killer into your home? You've only got my say so that she's harmless."

"Yours and Viola's. I trust animals more than I trust people, in most situations. But if she is guilty of something, I suspect she'd be on her best behavior while everyone's got their eyes on her.

"Tell you what." She said, reaching down to stroke her

beloved darling's head. "I'll have a lawyer look into the situation, and she can make the offer if she thinks it's okay. Then, if Dakini doesn't like her, I'll make some excuse and put her up in some hotel. My girl wouldn't let anyone near me who was dangerous."

"What's Harry going to think? Peter won't like it, either."

"Esmerelda's going to like it even less. They'll just have to put on their big girl panties and deal with it. It doesn't hurt that Harry's out of town this week, even if he is used to my little adventures. I'm thinking, the less everyone else knows, the better. I'm going to make a quick call to Martha Culler. She's a criminal attorney, a good one. I'm sure that poor woman could use some counsel." Dakini got up and followed her mistress out of the room.

Lia hoped Esmerelda wouldn't blame her for the incursion of a stranger. The cook might wind up putting ground glass in her next omelet.

PETER STRODE through the door to Lia's apartment and plopped down on the couch. He leaned his head back and stared at the ceiling, saying nothing.

"Um, hello to you, too?" Lia said, sill holding the door.

Viola jumped at Peter in a fruitless bid for attention. Finally, Lia shook her head and, realizing the door was still open, shut it.

"I don't know why I'm letting you in if this is the way you're going to be. Shall I just ignore you and go about my business, or am I supposed to fetch you a beer like a good little woman and go back to the kitchen where I belong?"

"Sorry, Babe. It's been one hellaciously long, frustrating day."

Lia softened. "If I fetch you that beer, will you tell me about it?"

Peter scrubbed his face with his hand. "I could use a good ear."

Lia ducked into the kitchen, returned with a Dos Equis. Peter took the bottle and held it against his forehead, then tipped it for a long swig.

"Spill it, Kentucky Boy," Lia primed the pump. "There must have been something awful in that trunk for you to arrest her right away like that. Terry said she probably kept a finger bone to make into a keychain."

Peter shook his head, snorted. "She might as well have. She had everything else in there."

"She had bones in there?"

"Nope. A crossbow, a real pro job. Bolts with hunting tips that matched the one we found with the body. A bloody bandana. George's wallet. His primary cell phone. And an empty bottle of homemade predator lure."

"What's predator lure?"

"If it's the same stuff that turned up on George's clothes, and it smells the same, it's some kind of rotting animal corpse mixed with coyote urine."

"Eeew." Lia grimaced.

"Not exactly Chanel Number 5."

"I don't get it. She gave you permission to look in her trunk, right? I know you have to have permission."

"Yep, she sure did."

"She looked so shocked when you opened it up. I don't think she knew what was in there. We could see that from the top of the hill. Are you so sure she's guilty?"

"If that wasn't the murder weapon in her trunk, I'll eat my badge. I don't know what to think. The cross bow was wiped, but whoever did it, they didn't do a good job. We found a couple partials, and they weren't hers."

"Then somebody else put it there. I don't believe she hurt anyone."

"That's what her lawyer keeps saying. She also pointed out that there wasn't a cocking device with the bow, and there's no way Onstad could have used the crossbow without it. We had to let Onstad go. Martha Cullers may look like Sally Field, but she's a pit-bull. They say she used to butcher hogs on her family farm when she was a kid.

"But," Peter continued, "if someone planted the bow, who knew about her? Who knew enough to plant it? She swears nobody was aware of her affair with George."

"So they *were* having an affair!"

"You don't know anything about it. Remember that when Bailey starts asking questions."

"I still don't believe she did it."

Peter set down the beer and looked at her a long time. "Lia," he started. "I don't know how to say this, but your judgement isn't the best. The last person you said would never hurt anyone nearly killed you."

"That's so unfair." Lia tilted her chin up, challenging. "Asia said she was psychotic, and the chances of running into another person like that were extremely rare. She's an expert, she should know."

"And what kind of person do you think shoots someone with a crossbow? Have you thought about asking your expert therapist that?"

"Then what was she doing, waiting for George at the

dog park? If she killed him, she knew he wasn't going to show up."

"Murderers aren't always rational. Especially if she didn't mean to do it."

"How can you not mean to shoot someone when you're pointing a crossbow at them?"

Peter took Lia's hands in his, chafed her palms with his thumbs. He pleaded with his eyes, eyes a deep, not quite indigo, blue. Blue as the sky after sunset when the stars begin to appear.

Forget the gun. He should have to register that look. It's a lethal weapon. She pulled her hands back, clasped them in her lap, looked away.

"Lia, please don't get caught up in this. If I could, I'd keep you a hundred miles away from this case."

"I set her up for you. Jim and I held her there until you could get to the park. I need to know I did the right thing."

"We had her motel room. We would have gotten her. Not as soon, but we would still have her today. You just speeded things up."

Lia's shoulders sagged. "I guess you're right. There is one thing I want to do, though."

"What's that?"

"I want to find Daisy."

"Daisy? The dog?"

"George loved her. Everybody thought George took her when he ran off, right? But he didn't run off. So that means Daisy's on the loose."

"Really, Lia, I don't think you should be getting involved."

"I'm just looking for a lost dog. I'll get a picture from Mrs. Munce and put up some posters, call a few shelters.

Jim and Bailey will help, I'm sure. Terry, too. I'm not going to mess with your investigation."

"That's all you're going to do?"

Lia nodded solemnly. "That's all I'm going to do."

"Cross your heart and hope to die?"

She drew her index finger across her breast. "With a pinky swear on top."

4

SATURDAY, OCTOBER 12

THE WOMAN WHO ANSWERED THE DOOR LOOKED distracted. "Can I help you?"

"Hi. Mrs. Munce? I'm Lia Anderson. I knew George from the dog park."

"This isn't really a good time."

"I don't mean to intrude, but it's just, well, are you doing anything to find Daisy?"

"Daisy? I lost my husband! I have too much to deal with to worry about his damn dog," she snapped.

"I'm sorry." Lia took a startled step away from the woman's sudden vitriol. "I didn't mean to imply anything. I just thought some of us from the park could look for her."

Monica Munce closed her eyes, inhaled audibly in a way that suggested forbearance, or perhaps an effort to regain control of herself. "Of course." She enunciated the words carefully. "That's very kind of you. I should not have flown off the handle. I just got off the phone with the coroner's office. They are being very difficult."

"Do you have any pictures we could use? I'd like to put one on the poster."

Monica rubbed one temple. "George posted plenty of pictures of Daisy on Facebook. I'm sure you could pull whatever you need from there. I hope you plan to use your own phone number on the poster. I really can't handle anything else right now. Now, if you don't mind, I've got to figure out how I'm going to keep my house with George gone."

The door shut before Lia could utter a word in response. *With a wife like that, no wonder he was having an affair ... Okay, be nice, Anderson, she just lost her husband. She has a right to be testy.*

BAILEY JIGGLED the handle to the door of Northside Grange. She stepped back. "It's locked. Why would he be shut down in the middle of the day?"

"I see Jerome inside. I bet the door's just stuck." Lia shifted Max's leash to her other hand, pressed the latch and shoved hard. The door gave.

Max led them into the turn-of-the-century storefront housing the urban farming and pet supply store. Decorative garden spikes paraded among pumpkins in the window. More pumpkins lined the wall. Fifty pound sacks of Amish chicken feed were stacked on a pallet next to a rack of doggie adventure wear. Sacks of pet food filled the wood shelves and baskets were filled with exotic dog treats, from elk antlers to duck feet.

Jerome Wilson stood behind the counter. He was a tall, slender man, prematurely bald, with round, wire-rim glasses and an amiable face. Lia thought he needed only a white apron to complete the quintessential shopkeeper look.

"Hey, Lia," he said. "I see you brought Max. See, Simba? Max is here."

Simba, a handsome young German Shepherd, jumped up and propped his legs against the gate that penned him in behind the counter. He gave two sharp barks. Max barked back and strained her leash. Jerome unlatched the gate and Simba bolted out. Lia dropped Max's lead and the dogs fell into a friendly tussle.

"I'm glad you brought her. Simba's been feeling restless today," Jerome said over the sound of canine play-growls. "What can I do for you? Need any kibble?"

"I'm good for now. I'll be ready for another bag of the grain-free in a couple weeks. It's done wonders for Honey's skin. She's finally stopped scratching."

"Glad to hear it. So what's up?"

"Jerome, this is my friend, Bailey. We were wondering if you could hang a poster in your window. We're looking for a dog that went missing when her owner was murdered in Mount Airy Forest. Did you know George Munce?"

"I don't think so." He shook his head.

Bailey wordlessly handed him a flyer featuring a grinning Daisy. Jerome held it toward the dogs. "Look, Simba! She looks just like you." Simba popped his head up, gave the paper a quizzical sniff and went back to wrestling. "I guess a dog on the floor is worth more than a flyer in the hand," Jerome shrugged. "I haven't seen her. I'd notice her because she looks so much like Simba. I'll post the flyer and keep an eye out."

"Thanks, Jerome," Lia said.

"That's your new neighbor?" Bailey asked after they left the store. "He's cute. Why haven't you introduced me before?"

"Isn't he a little young for you?" Lia asked.

"I'm barely in my fifties. That means I'm still in my sexual prime. He looks like an intelligent young man who would appreciate experience and enthusiasm in a woman."

"What about John?"

"Please, forget I told you his real name. As far as you know, he's 'Trees.'"

Though Lia thought the subterfuge silly, she figured as long as she was involved with a cop, it was best to humor Bailey about the hacker's identity.

"I do love him," Bailey continued. "But as long as he lives in Tennessee and I live here, we have a don't ask, don't tell arrangement."

"Did you two talk about this?"

"He hasn't asked, and I'm not telling. He's free to do the same."

"Uh-huh." Lia was skeptical.

Bailey waved an elegant hand in the air. "Oh, you know me. I wouldn't really do anything. But I can dream, can't I?"

LIA SAT AT HER COMPUTER, pulling frames of Dakini jumping. She stopped the video feed whenever the dog reached the hurdle, then clicked through individual frames to find the ones where her fur flew and her eye lit up with excitement. Then she moved back and forth, seeking the image with the most tension and movement, the peak moment of the jump. These frames she exported as JPEGs. She had a dozen contenders to show Renee when Viola ran to the door, barking excitedly. "Your dad must be here," she said.

She opened the door before Peter could knock.

"Hey, Babe," he said, leaning down to ruffle the fur on Viola's head. Chewy and Honey crowded around, seeking attention. Max affected boredom, sitting on her haunches and scratching behind one ear with her hind leg, eyes slitted.

"Oink," Lia replied.

He kissed her briefly. "How about I call you *mon petit couchon* instead? It's French."

"That's promising. What does it mean?"

"My little piglet." He smirked as Lia huffed and rolled her eyes, handing her a plastic bag. "Kale from Alma's garden. She told me to pick some, since she can't eat it all."

"Tell her thank you. I can sauté this with some garlic. It'll go with the black beans I have in the crock-pot. I'll put on some brown rice, too."

"Black beans again?"

"They're good for you. They lower your cholesterol, regulate blood sugar and keep your intestines moving. And they taste good."

"Says you."

"Please?"

"I said, you're the cook, you choose the menu."

"I have to make up for all the junk you eat when you're roaming the streets."

"It's so sweet that you care."

Lia put a pot of water on to boil for the rice. She filled one half of her sink with cool water, then dumped in the greens. She laid a clean towel on the counter, then swished individual leaves around in the water, lifting them out and laying them on the towel. When she was done, she pulled out a bamboo cutting board and set about chopping up the greens with her favorite ceramic knife.

Peter pulled a beer out of the fridge and leaned against the counter, relaxing as he watched her work. "This is so homey. Have you given any more thought to us living together again? I mean without the stress of a serial killer on the loose?"

Lia laid down her knife and hugged Peter. She kissed him on the cheek. "You want to drink beer and watch me cook every evening? That just makes my heart go pitter-pat."

"I don't think you should have to cook for me all the time. I just like the idea of coming home to you."

Lia turned to the stove and poured a cup of rice into the bubbling water, stirred it briefly, covered the pot and turned down the heat. She selected a garlic bulb from the pile in the wire vegetable basket hanging by her sink and started breaking off cloves. She stared intently at the garlic. "Peter, I love you."

"I love you, too."

"But."

Peter paused, his beer halfway to his lips. "But?"

"I think I see where you're going, and I really don't want to go there. I like what we have. It works. We don't ever have to resent each other. We're together when we want to be together and we're apart when we need to focus on something else."

"Don't you suppose your family has given you a warped view of what marriage is?"

Lia smashed the garlic with the side of a steel knife, then started popping the cloves out of their peels. She took a moment to consider her words. "My mother married every single time for love, and it never worked. It wasn't enough. Watching her taught me a lot about what marriage is.

"It's about chores and wanting the same things and figuring out what to do with money. All of a sudden, my time, my money, it's not mine any more. All of a sudden, I'm not free to do what I want to do, unless my partner is okay with it. And the same goes for you. Suddenly, the pettiest things become a reason to be angry. Do you really want that to happen to us?"

"It doesn't have to happen. My grandparents have been married for fifty years and they're very happy together. I wish you could meet them. You'd see what a good marriage is all about."

"They married at a time when most women did not expect to be in control of their lives. I'm sure that had something to do with it."

"Marriage is work. I know that. I don't expect you to be the little woman."

"Yet you expect to protect me from my own judgement. You'd be happier if I wasn't looking for Daisy, admit it."

Peter set down his beer. "There's something off about this case. Serving up a dead body to a pack of coyotes is not the act of a sane person. You nearly died last year. You still have a bullet hole in your leg. Is it so wrong for me to care about your safety?"

"Why don't we look at this case? An unhappily married man trying to relive his youth while he violates his marriage vows." Lia pulled her largest skillet out of the oven, poured in a dollop of olive oil and turned on the gas. She retrieved her garlic press from the gadget drawer and pressed several cloves into the heating oil, stirring them with a wooden spoon.

"I can't argue that, but we're not them. I'm not George, you're not Monica, and you're not your mother, either." He ran a hand through his hair in frustration. "What *do* you want for us, then? Do you even want there to *be* an us?"

Lia picked up a large handful of chopped greens and dropped them in the hot skillet. She stirred the kale, added more as it wilted. She lowered the heat and turned to him, wrapped her arms around his waist. "Of course I do. I just haven't figured out how to keep us from becoming like so many other couples."

He hugged her back. "Maybe you shouldn't be trying to figure it out by yourself."

"I need you to trust me more. Tomorrow I'm going to see Renee, and I imagine I may run into Kate Onstad. I need you to be okay with that."

"I wish there was a way around that." He tucked a loose strand of hair behind her ear. "Can't you meet Renee somewhere else? Why don't you meet at your studio?"

"This is my job, just like chasing after criminals is your job. I don't ask you to give up your job, and I'm not going to insult my best client by refusing to go to her home. I can't believe that Kate Onstad has the strength to load a crossbow and the skill to kill a man with one."

"Yeah, her lawyer did point that detail out to us." He rubbed his neck. "I'm trying to see this from your side. All my life, I've been told it was my responsibility to do the right thing and take care of those who were weaker than me, and I grew up around women who want that protection. It's that whole Adam's rib thing. It's hard to set it aside."

"You're going to have to bend those principles if you want us to make it, Kentucky Boy." She gave him a squeeze. "Let me finish making dinner. Let's give this a rest for right now, and you can tell me all about your squirrelly case while we eat."

Peter forked up the last of his greens and rice, chewed, swallowed. "The crossbow is a Barnett Zombie. It's a serious crossbow with a 175-pound draw. It does take a lot of practice to handle, especially without a laser sight. We have the same concern about Kate Onstad, that she's unlikely to have the ability to pull off a kill shot, especially if she used that hunter's blind. Hard enough to imagine her climbing that tree, even with the rungs nailed into the trunk. Still, even if she didn't do it, she's attracted the attention of the person who did. Please be extra careful around her."

Lia suppressed a smile. "Yes, Daddy, I promise. What will you do now? Can you trace the bow to its owner?"

"Crossbows aren't registered like guns. We used the serial number and went to the manufacturer. The owner never registered the warranty but the manufacturer traced the shipment to a local store, over a year ago. They're unhappy someone used one of their bows to kill a person, so they're reviewing their records. If it was bought with a credit card, we'll have him.

"Since the package cost around six hundred dollars, it's unlikely he paid cash. Too bad the sale took place so long ago. If it was recent, we'd be able to use the time stamp on the receipt to pick our guy out on the store's surveillance videos.

"They had several of this model. They'll track down all of them for us, if they can. Then we get to sweat the guys who bought them, match them against hunters licensed for the deer cull."

"You think it was a hunter who did this?" Lia asked.

"They didn't buy the bow to kill George, then wait a year to do it. That doesn't fly. They had the wrong arrowheads on the bolts for target shooting. So they bought it to hunt with. There are a couple hundred bow hunters licensed for this year's cull, but only thirty had permits to be in Mount Airy Forest when George was killed."

"Thirty is a lot of suspects, isn't it?"

"George typically didn't head for the park until after nine. Most of these guys were at work and will have alibis. It's still plenty to go through, and there's no guarantee that our man had a legitimate license for that period. He'll show up somewhere on the registry, though. You don't spend that much money on a bow unless you intend to use it."

"What else is happening with the case?"

"I reviewed Munce's phone calls. He was talking to a divorce lawyer, so we'll need to interview him. It looks like Munce was planning to be a different kind of statistic. Enough about work. How did you do today with the flyers?"

"Bailey and I hung up at least fifty flyers around the park. I imagine, if Daisy is still there, she'd be near the picnic areas because that's where she'd find people and food. I'm thinking about taking Honey up there and walking around. Daisy knows her. I'm hoping if she's still in the woods, she might smell Honey and come out."

Peter winced inwardly at the thought of Lia up near the killing ground. He reminded himself that the woods were still closed to all hunters as well as hikers, stifled the impulse to lecture. "That was smart thinking. It might work."

"No one we talked to has seen her, but we're getting the word out. Someone is going to spot her and call."

5

SUNDAY, OCTOBER 13

"What's this?" Jim asked as Lia pinned a poster to the bulletin board at the park. Chester sat up on his haunches in front of Lia. She knelt so that he could give her a kiss. Viola and Fleece eyed each other, as if to say, "Show off." Jealous, Honey leaned against Peter, who was along for his weekly visit to the dog park. He stroked her head.

"Bailey and I are looking for George's dog. You know Daisy, don't you? Hasn't Fleece played with her before?"

"Sure, I recognize her."

"We spent yesterday afternoon putting up posters. There's so much to do still."

Jim studied the flyer, scratched his beard. "What can I do to help?"

"Next on our list is contacting the rescues. That might be time consuming. You can only get some of them by email, and with the others, you rarely get a live person on the line."

"That's all right, I'll take care of it. Just tell me what to do," Jim said.

"Great. I've got to work today. I wouldn't have been able to get going on this until tomorrow afternoon or later." She handed him a poster. "Here's the information." Jim folded the poster in quarters with the picture on the inside, then pulled out a stumpy pencil. Lia listed a number of rescues he could contact, which Jim wrote on the back of the poster.

Terry walked up. "Greetings! What's the word?"

"The word is that George's dog got lost when George was killed and we're looking for her," Lia said. "Would you mind calling around to the vets in the area?"

"The lovely Daisy has gone astray? I'm happy to help. I can also send a notice to the Northside newsletter. I'm sure *Bits 'n' Pieces* will run it. They may even do it as a special notice."

"That's a great idea. Can you check the internet for 'found' notices, while you're at it?"

"Milady, I am at your service."

"Thanks, Terry. I owe you one." She handed him a poster.

"Lia! Just the person I want to see." Jose approached Lia's table with Sophie ambling at his side. Sophie walked up to Lia and presented her backside. Lia leaned over and gave it a good scratch.

"Hitting on my girl, Mitsch?" Peter was sitting next to Lia with the rest of the group around them.

Lia elbowed Peter. "Hey, Jose, what's up?"

"Nah, nothin' like that. I know you carry a gun." He winked at Lia, then reached into one of the cargo pockets on his pants and pulled out a phone. He passed it to her.

"What's this for? Am I supposed to call someone?"

"You can call anyone you like, as soon as you activate it with your number."

"You're *giving* it to me?"

"I got a new one. I thought, I can trade this one in for next to nothin', I can mess with selling it on eBay to some stranger, or I can give it to a friend who doesn't have a smartphone. It's only a first generation Android, but it has a camera and you can do things you can't do on the phone you have now."

"You mean like playing Draw Something with Jim while he's sitting here right next to me?"

"There's GPS, taking pictures, looking up stuff on the internet—" Jose enthused.

"Spending more money on phone bills—" Lia added.

"Butt dialing—" Bailey said.

"Well," Terry said. "The accidental pocket dial is certainly a danger with older models. I always carry my phone in a pocket on my vest. It prevents such mishaps."

"I'm not going to wear a concealed carry vest just so I won't call Peter by accident. I look terrible in camouflage. Thank you, Jose. This will be fun."

"Stick it in a cargo pocket," Jose said. "That'll fix it."

"I don't know," Peter said, rubbing his chin. "Maybe I want her butt to call me."

6

MONDAY, OCTOBER 14

"I don't know what to do, Bailey." Lia and Bailey were tossing balls in the back of the dog park. Lia had Max on a leash to keep her close. Max kept giving her hurt looks, then walking to the end of her lead, as if she wanted to chase the balls. Lia knew better. Max would use any excuse as an opportunity to escape.

"What's the problem?"

"Peter brought up living together again. We tabled the subject, but I know he won't forget it."

"You don't want to wake up every morning next to that handsome hunk of man-flesh?" Bailey's amazed expression made Lia laugh.

"I can do that now, anytime I want. That's not the issue."

"What is it, then?"

"I'm barely surviving as an artist. I'm only managing because I make sacrifices. If I move in with Peter, I'll have to upgrade my standard of living and I'll wind up splitting the cable bill. Then it's no longer feasible for me to support myself and I wind up financially dependent. I hate cable."

"Living with Peter could make things easier on you, couldn't it? Wouldn't he be willing to pick up the slack?"

"Maybe, but what will he expect in return?" Lia threw a hand up in the air. "Right now he's unhappy that I'm going over to Renee's because Kate Onstad is staying there. He can't create too much of a fuss about it because we're not living together. What if we move in together and he starts telling me what I can and can't do, the way Tom did? What if he expects me to put him before my painting?

"Then I've given up my place, which I love, and I'm stuck starting over. A nice, inexpensive two-family in Northside is hard to come by. It took me a year to find the place I have now. I don't want to go through that again." Lia looked at Bailey helplessly as her rant ran down.

"I see what you're saying. I have an idea."

"What are you thinking?"

"Have you ever heard of synastry?" Bailey asked.

"What's synastry?"

"That's what they call it when you compare charts in astrology, to see how two people are going to get along together."

"Astrology? Seriously, Bailey?"

"Synastry is what convinced me that astrology works."

"How is that?"

"I took my chart, and I compared my planets to each of my ex-boyfriends' planets, and the result was the story of our relationship," Bailey explained.

"Seriously?"

"Seriously. It took a weight off my shoulders. It showed me that I didn't do anything wrong. Things were meant to be the way they were. Like when you add bleach to ammonia. You always get chlorine gas. No amount of self-help books will ever change that."

"I don't know, Bailey ..."

"It can't hurt to let me try. Do you know what time you were born?"

"I can find out, but won't you need that information about Peter, too? You want me to ask Peter when he was born so you can tell me if our stars align?"

"That would be best. I can still tell a lot with just his birthday."

"Ha! I can just see telling him I'll consider living together if he'll let you run an astrology chart on him."

"You never know. He might go for it."

"I HOPE YOU BROUGHT AN APPETITE," Renee said as she led Lia to the breakfast nook. "Esmerelda is making her special potato pancakes. I thought Kitty could use some comfort food."

Despite what she'd said to Peter, Lia had been hoping to avoid Kate, since she was the one who ratted her out. *It was bound to happen. Best to get it over with.*

Kate Onstad was seated at an oak pedestal table set in front of a bay window with a view of Kentucky hills on the other side of the river. She looked up from her paper and smiled hesitantly.

"You must be Lia. Renee tells me you're responsible for

me having a good lawyer and a quiet place to stay. Thank you."

Lia relaxed, relieved. "I'm so glad you're okay. I had no idea Peter was going to arrest you. I feel so bad about that." She took a seat and poured coffee from the carafe, added cream.

"You didn't know what was in my trunk. I didn't either. I was the one who let them look in my car."

"I imagine that was quite a shock," Lia said.

"I didn't understand what it was at first, because it was all black and jumbled. I've never seen a crossbow before. It looked like a child's toy rifle with this contraption on the barrel."

"Should you be talking to me about this? You do know I'm in a relationship with the detective in charge of George's case, don't you?"

"Renee explained that to me. I suppose my lawyer wouldn't approve, but I honestly can't think of anything I could tell you that would make my situation worse."

"How bad is it?"

"Well, I knew George, and I knew where he was going to be. The crossbow and his wallet were in my trunk. But I also had that flat tire the day he died. The tire couldn't be fixed because someone stuck a screwdriver in the sidewall, and you can't patch that. It took hours before they were able to get me into a new car so I could get back on the road.

"They won't find my fingerprints or DNA on anything in that trunk. I never got into it. Of course, I don't have a motive. I loved George."

"Martha thinks they'll have a hard time making a murder charge stick," Renee said. "And they'll think twice about trying, with her as your defense attorney. Our best bet is that they look in another direction and find the one who did it."

Lia was charmed. The woman who was so diffident at the park was now warm and compassionate, exuding gratitude when many would be bitter. "What do you think happened? Do you mind me asking?"

Esmerelda interrupted with plates bearing potato pancakes and fried eggs with crisp bacon on the side. The three women busied themselves with the food while Kitty considered her question. "I hate to point fingers, you understand. I know so little about his life here in Ohio. I wonder if his wife found out about us. She was supposed to be at work, but maybe she got someone to do it for her?"

"It wouldn't surprise me," Lia said once she'd chewed her bacon and swallowed. "That woman is a piece of work."

"Oooh, do tell," Renee urged.

"I don't know much, but she went off on me when I asked about Daisy. Then she was totally unconcerned when I offered to look for Daisy, like she couldn't care less that her dog was running around, lost and traumatized. You know, in all the time George came to the park, no one ever saw her with him. What kind of woman doesn't want to walk in the woods with her husband?"

"She doesn't sound like a romantic, that's for sure," Renee said. "Maybe she had to work?"

"Not in the summers, she didn't. She's a school counselor."

"Oooh, good point," Renee said. "So what was her motive?"

"Besides George wanting to divorce her?" Lia clapped a hand over her mouth. "Oops, I should not have said that."

"He did?" Kitty asked. "How do you know?"

"Well, I guess the milk's already spilt. Peter said he had several calls in to a divorce lawyer on his phone. That's not proof, but it's suggestive, isn't it? What if Monica knew he was going to leave her and didn't want to split the assets?"

"I don't know, but I'm so glad you told me." Kitty wiped a tear from her eye. "He said he wanted us to be together, but you never know if a man really means that kind of talk or not, especially when all you've had is the internet."

"Please don't mention this to your lawyer. Peter will never tell me anything ever again if it gets out I told you."

"I imagine Martha will find out soon enough through discovery, don't you think?" Renee said.

"That's quite all right." Kitty said, smiling, mistily. "You have no idea how much this means to me."

"Kitty, how did you and George meet?" Lia asked. "I hope I'm not being too nosy."

"I don't mind, and please, call me Kitty. I met George back in high school. It was very *West Side Story*, or maybe *Grease*. He was from the wrong side of the tracks. George was really smart, but he never showed that to anyone. He was always doing this Elvis sneer." Kitty's smile told Lia the memory was a fond one.

"Then one night, he rescued me from this party after I caught my boyfriend making out with another girl. George took me for a drive out in the woods to cool down, and he was so sweet. I just fell in love with him."

"Oh, my," Renee said, patting her chest. "Be still my heart."

Kitty bit her lip, looked at them with a gleam in her eye. "I lost my virginity in the woods that night. It was the most amazing night of my life. All those hormones, all the newness, and George treating me like I was a goddess."

Renee fanned her face. "Whew, is it hot in here or just me?"

"That's quite a story," said Lia. Breakfast forgotten, she leaned forward, chin propped up on her hands. "What happened?"

"Like I said, he was from the other side of the tracks and he a rough life. I didn't know this until recently, but he'd decided we wouldn't work out as a couple, so he might as well end it while the memory was a good one. I didn't see him for several days, and then when I did, he acted like we didn't know each other. I was so crushed."

"I imagine," Renee said.

"What brought you back together?" Lia asked, riveted.

"George was so unhappy. He tried to hunt me up on the internet, but couldn't find a way to contact me. Turns out we had a mutual friend on Facebook. Neither one of us had any idea. Then one day, he saw a comment I made on our friend's page.

"He pursued me after that. I was so suspicious. It had been thirty years and I'm no prize these days. He said it didn't matter, that our night together changed things for him. It took a while, but I came to believe it would be worth the risk to see him again."

Renee's neglected coffee sat cooling as she placed a hand on Kitty's. "Was it worth it?"

"Something in me broke that day when he ignored me.

Coming here healed me in ways I'm just now beginning to understand. We had less than two weeks together, but we were happy. I'll always be grateful for that. I'll never forgive myself if it turns out I was the reason he died." She sniffed and dabbed discretely at her nose with her napkin.

Lia took Kitty's other hand, looked directly into her eyes. "No matter why someone says they killed him, the only reason he's dead is because a murderer made the choice to take a human life. Whatever you and George were doing, there were other options. Don't let them victimize you."

"Thank you for that. Renee says you're an artist, and you're painting a picture of Dakini. Will you let me see what you're working on?"

"Sure thing. Let me fire up my laptop."

AN HOUR LATER, Renee walked Lia to her car. "So what did you think about Kitty's story?" she asked.

"I thought it was very romantic, but I'm not married," Lia said. "What would you do if Harry left you for a high school flame?"

"Oh, I'd kill him. There's no question about that. A crossbow sounds just about right for the job. But I'd also walk in the woods with him. There's no excuse for allowing a marriage to grow empty like that."

"And yet it happens all the time."

"It's work, keeping a marriage going. But it's worth it."

"I wonder about that. Peter wants more out of our relationship, but I'm scared it will spoil everything."

"I don't know all the answers, but I do know it's

important to be with someone who is willing to work things out with you, who listens and takes your feelings seriously. And you both better be able to laugh at yourselves, because there will be times when that's the only thing left to do.

"It's best when expectations are clearly stated. So many people get married with this picture in their head about how things are going to be and their partner doesn't know anything about it. That's one thing Harry and I got right. We made sure we understood what we each wanted from marriage before we got engaged."

"I moved in with a boyfriend right after I got out of college," Lia admitted. "Once I signed a lease with him, he started expecting things. I was supposed to be a little *hausfrau*, and my painting was never as important as whatever he had going on. It was like he was on good behavior the whole time we dated, until I signed for that apartment. Then the real him came out."

"It didn't last long, I take it?"

"Longer than it should have. It took me a while to recognize what was happening, and then it took me a while to realize it wasn't going to get any better. When the light finally came on, I couldn't get out of there fast enough."

"I can see why you'd be nervous now. Have you thought about talking to a professional about this? Something like premarital counseling might help you and Peter figure out if you're on the same page, or even reading the same book."

"That's like religious counseling, isn't it? A church thing? I don't know if I want to do anything that has the word premarital in it, unless we're talking about sex."

"Where have you been while I've been tracking down hunters?" Peter asked as Brent set a cardboard box down on his desk. "Out showing off your new girlfriend?"

"I talked to Munce's lawyer, then I decided to do some detecting. I detected that bow hunters for the deer cull are required to pass a marksmanship test with the exact weapon they will be using while hunting. Being a smart detective, I wondered if there was a record of applicants' tests that included their weapon. I wondered that over the phone to the park board and they put me on the trail of the original hard-copies. I hope you didn't have any plans for this afternoon."

Peter smiled. "Sometimes I think you almost deserve that shield."

"Thank you, Brother. I shall take that as a compliment."

Peter eyed the box, dubiously. "That many hunters applied for the deer cull this year?"

"That's from the past two years, since our weapon was shipped out from the factory. It occurred to me that our man may not have applied this year. So I got the previous year to avoid making a second trip."

"Huh."

"How about I pick up a pizza and we sit here and run our man down. What's that kind you like?"

"Dewey's," Peter said absently. "Edgar Allen Poe."

"That can be your half. I'd like a Green Lantern with olive oil instead of red sauce on my half, thank you very much. Phone it in and I'll head on down there to pick it up. Don't forget to pay for it," he called over his shoulder.

"Hey!" Peter yelled after him, but Brent was gone, his leather heels clipping down the hall.

"That, Brother, was a dirty trick," muttered Brent as he set the hot pizza box down on Peter's desk.

"Expecting me to pay for the whole pie was a dirty trick," Peter responded.

"You're lucky I had a few dollars in my wallet. Celeste is an expensive mistress."

"Then you shouldn't have suggested an expensive lunch. Give me a plate. I'm starving." He deftly disengaged the largest slice from his side of the pie, and slid it onto the paper plate Brent handed to him.

"How far did you get while I was gone?"

"You wanted me to start? I'm sorry. You should have said so. Oh, but you couldn't. You were too busy high-tailing it out of the station so I couldn't tell you to pay for your own lunch." Peter shrugged and took a large, satisfying bite out of his pizza.

They hunkered down, each pulling a stack of hand-written records out of the box. They scanned the cards in silence for several minutes.

"Jackal, Inferno Fury, Predator, Ghost, Wildcat, Cobra … These bows all sound like code names for the members of some wet work team in a Russell Blake novel," Brent said.

"Russell Blake? Who's that? What happened to J. K. Rowling and Harry Potter?"

"Russell Blake is this Kindle millionaire who can spit

out a new thriller in less time than it took for your first experience of carnal knowledge."

"Nice. You've got to get a real woman. Playing with your Kindle and talking to your overpriced car are doing strange things to you."

"Maybe so, but at least I now know twenty-three ways to kill a man with my pinkie. Lookie here, I think we have a winner." Brent held out the yellow card. Peter took it and squinted at the blue scrawl. "Looks like it says 'Zombie' to me," Brent continued. "Too bad they don't include serial numbers."

"That would have been expecting too much," Peter said, laying the card to one side. "What do we know about Scott Estep?"

"It's your computer, Brother."

"Right." Peter turned to his keyboard and pulled up Scott's driver's license. He checked the record. "Looks like a solid citizen. A few speeding tickets. No arrests, no warrants. We'll put him on the list and keep going. According to the manager of the sporting goods store, there's more than one Zombie in the area."

Their second hit was Mike Heekins, who had a commercial operator's license and an ancient arrest for public intoxication. Hit number three was a Bill Stryker.

"I wonder if he's related to the guy who invented the Stryker saw. What does Hal say?" Brent asked.

"Name your own computer. Leave mine alone. Mr. Stryker looks interesting. A DUI, some D and D's, and a Domestic Violence charge. Also a restraining order filed by one Colleen Stryker."

"Interesting, indeed. I say we need to go have a talk with

Mr. Stryker, once we finish looking through the rest of these." They continued reviewing the cards in silence. Finally, Brent replaced the last one in the box. "That appears to be it. Three matches. Are we going on a field trip?"

"We taking your girlfriend?" Peter asked.

"I think, if we're going to see a man with a known temper, we should go in your car. Just in case."

"Where was that address, again? Brestel? Isn't that off of Baltimore Avenue?"

"Didn't a meth lab blow up over there last year?" Brent asked.

"If it didn't, it wasn't for lack of trying."

"Good thing you're driving. That's some incline over there. Doesn't bode well for our interview that he tucked himself away on top of that hill. Folks up there are clannish."

THEY TURNED onto a side road that led, as Brent predicted, up a lumpy asphalt road that took two long switchbacks before climbing a hill that was too steep for most cars and hadn't been paved in too many years. The weeds on the side of the road were taller than a man and could be hiding … anything.

Echoing Peter's thoughts, Brent said, "If there's a militia presence in Cincinnati, this is where they do maneuvers. We could be surrounded right now and we'd never know it."

Peter wondered how the residents got in and out in the winter. Probably didn't. Probably just stayed put and lived off their Armageddon rations and the occasional unlucky possum.

The road flattened out at the top of the hill and ran a short distance before it stopped dead. It wasn't a proper cul-de-sac. The asphalt gave way to gravel and dirt, the tail end surrounded by four one-story brick houses in various stages of disrepair. There was a weedy vacant lot where a fifth house, possibly the ill-fated meth lab, once stood.

Woods encroached all around. Several stacks of old tires sat in patches of dying grass. Peter imagined the tires collected water in the summer and became a breeding ground for mosquitos. Boxes of beer and whiskey bottles sat on one porch, while another house was fronted by a sagging sofa. A stained mattress lay in a yard. Several of the windows were boarded over. A rail thin pit-bull strained the chain that tethered him to a porch and snarled.

"What do you suppose they have all those tires for?" Brent wondered.

"Good question. Maybe target practice."

"Just what we want. A man with a known temper and skills."

The man who answered Peter's firm knock stood five foot, nine. He was muscular, straining the seams of an undershirt that might have once been clean. A hairy navel peeked out from under the hem of the shirt, with jeans riding low. A red scalp showed through his military buzz-cut. He held onto the doorknob with one hand while gripping the probable mainstay of his diet in the other, a bottle of Hudy Delight.

Obviously a man of taste and refinement. Peter schooled his face. "William Stryker?"

"Who wants to know?"

Peter and Brent flipped out their shields. "I'm Detective Dourson, and this is Detective Davis of the Cincinnati police. We'd like to talk to you for a few minutes."

"Did you find it?"

"Did we find what, Mr. Stryker?" Brent asked.

"My goddamn Zombie. Isn't that why you're here? My crossbow?"

"Yes, we're here about a cross bow–" Peter started to say.

"Well, well, whaddya know. From the way the moron you sent was talking, I didn't expect to ever hear from you again."

Peter and Brent looked at each other. "Which moron would that be, Mr. Stryker?" Brent asked.

"Some guy named Hinkle. Don't you guys talk to each other? Isn't his name on the report?"

"We're not aware of a report–" Peter said.

"I reported that bow stolen over a week ago. If that's not why you're here, then what do you want?"

"We understand you own a Barnett Zombie crossbow. Is that true?" Brent asked.

"It was until some rat bastard took it."

"Do you have the serial number?" Peter said

"I gave it to that other guy. What's this about?"

"A Zombie crossbow was used recently in a crime. We're trying to determine who owned the bow," Peter said. "May we come in?"

"What was my bow used for?"

"Homicide," Peter said.

Stryker glared at Peter. "That bow was stolen, you have it on your report. And you're not getting in here without a warrant. You want to talk to me, you do it right here where all the neighbors can see. I want witnesses." He looked around, raised his voice. "Y'all hear that? They think I shot someone with that crossbow what was stolen out of my garage."

Peter thought about looking around to see who Stryker was talking to, but felt it prudent to keep his eyes on the man. He attempted to suppress an image of an armed militia emerging from the woods dressed in camouflage, black greasepaint slashing their faces. In his mind's eye, they turned into a flash mob while "Dueling Banjos" played in the background. In that fraction of a second it occurred to him that he might never call Lia 'Babe' again.

"We don't think anything, Mr. Stryker," Peter said. "We're just trying to find out what happened. At this point, we don't know for sure that it was your bow."

"Whatever. Who is it you think I killed?"

"The deceased is a man named George Munce," Brent said. He pulled the photograph out of the inside pocket of his jacket. "Have you ever seen him?"

Stryker glanced down at the picture, curled his lip. "Nope. When'd he die?"

"Last Monday. Can you tell us what you did that day?" Peter said.

Stryker snorted. "I was working on my truck. Right there. Pulled the transmission." He pointed at a greasy patch in the gravel. "Plenty of people saw me, including the mailman, if you don't trust my neighbors."

Peter jotted a few words in his notebook. "What time was that?"

"Late morning, early afternoon."

"What about the rest of the day?"

"Right here. You want to try that hill with a bum transmission?"

"Did you spend any time hunting deer at Mount Airy in the past month?"

"I was scheduled for the first round. Last time I was there was October third. Thursday. Haven't been back since my bow was stolen. No reason to go until somebody gives me back my goddamn bow, which would be nice, since my session isn't over yet."

"Have you ever seen this woman?" This time Brent showed him a photograph of Kate Onstad.

"She dead, too?"

"Not at all."

"Are you employed, Mr. Stryker?" Peter asked.

"Not since those bastards at Hudepohl fired me."

"When was that?"

"Back in July. You got any more questions for me? Want my shoe size? It's 10C. And in case you need to know, I'm circumcised." A flush spread up Stryker's face during this tirade.

"That'll be all for now," Peter said. "We'll review the report you made and get in touch with you if we have any further questions."

Stryker grunted and slammed the door.

"THAT WAS FUN," Brent said once Peter's Blazer was creeping back down the steep grade. "Think he did it?"

"Don't know. I wouldn't mind having a search warrant for his place, if it turns out to be his bow. Not likely to get it, unless we can prove some connection between him and Munce."

"Know what's peculiar? Hudepohl fires him, and he's drinking Hudy Delight beer. What do you want to bet one of his friends at the brewery pushed it off the back of the truck?"

"I don't take sucker bets, Brent. You know that."

"So, Boss, what's for the rest of the afternoon?"

"First we pull that report and see if the serial number matches. Then we start canvassing hunters, see who saw whom when they were in the woods. According to Mr. Stryker, he was nowhere near the woods when Munce died. But he could have seen him wandering around the woods earlier. Next time we talk to him we should take a map of the forest and get him to show us where he hunted. I wish I'd thought to bring a map today."

"Sounds like a plan."

"By the way, what did the lawyer tell you? You never said."

"George was pondering the wisdom of divorce and the financial ramifications. He received the best and worst case scenarios and was taking a little time to fully consider same before he made his decision."

"He was putting his wallet before the love of his life?"

"Not so much that, more worried about the situation a divorce would create for the girl, his stepdaughter. He was very concerned about her welfare. To hear the lawyer tell it, that marriage was deader than the roadkill on Donald Trump's head."

PETER DECIDED that expecting Lia to cook after the 'little woman' business the night before was a dangerous idea and instead offered a trip to Pleasant Ridge for Ethiopian. Lia enjoyed African cuisine, though they rarely made the trek across town for it.

An olive branch wasn't really called for. They hadn't exactly had a fight, but they'd certainly skirted around the edges of one. Still, Peter liked to be proactive whenever possible.

Lia insisted that they toss the ball for the dogs for a while before abandoning them for the evening. Peter tossed, Honey chased the ball, and Chewy and Viola chased Honey. Max backed up against the lip of one of the wood steps and ground her sacrum against it. Peter could see where her fur was worn down. The dog grunted and moaned, producing sound effects straight out of a cheap porno.

"She's going to take the paint off that step if she keeps it up."

Lia sighed. "It's either that, or scratch her myself. I'd rather lose a little paint."

"You sure there's nothing wrong with her?"

"The rescue took her in for a full physical. They checked for impacted anal glands. I'm afraid she's just deviant."

Peter held a tennis ball up to her nose. Max sniffed it, then turned back to her grinding. Peter bounced the ball on the walkway to see if he could engage her interest. No dice. "Isn't there anything else she likes? Besides this?"

"There's food. Running away. Finding dead bodies. Speaking of which, how is your dead body coming?"

"We know where the bow came from."

"You found the owner of the bow?" Lia asked. "Then that must mean Kate is off the hook. Have you arrested him yet?"

"Not so fast. He reported it stolen two days before George died."

"Maybe he knew he was going to kill George and just said it was stolen."

"I don't think he's that smart. He also has an alibi. We still have to check it out, but if we can verify it, it clears him. And we don't have a connection between him and George Munce. Or Kate Onstad."

"Well, that stinks."

"One step at a time. Cases aren't built in a day. We made progress and that's important."

Honey ran back with the ball and dropped the slobbered orb at Peter's feet.

Peter stared at the Honey's offering. "I bet the Chucker was never intended for throwing balls further. I bet it was invented so people wouldn't have to pick them up covered in dog goo."

"A big, manly guy like you, afraid of a little saliva? Chicken." Lia picked up the ball, tossed it again, sending the trio rampaging after it. Max just groaned and grinned sheepishly when Peter and Lia stared at her.

"How is this progress if you don't think he did it?" Lia asked.

"It's still part of the picture. If he didn't do it, he was

still in the orbit of the perp. So now we know that our perp not only crossed paths with George, he was also aware of Kate and knew Stryker kept a crossbow in his garage."

"You think it was another bow hunter?"

"Doubtful. Bows aren't like guns. They don't leave forensic fingerprints so there'd be no reason not to use his own. Just get some bolts in a brand you don't use. Buy them out of town and pay cash for them. We checked Hinkle's report. This guy used Stryker's bolts. Even Stryker isn't that dumb."

"But your perp has to be able to handle a crossbow. That's kind of odd, isn't it? Someone who would have the skill to use the bow but not own one?"

"True." Honey brought the ball back to Peter. This time he picked it up, tossed it, then pulled a white handkerchief out of his pocket and wiped his hand off.

When the dogs returned, Lia opened the door and the pack made a mad scramble up the steps and into the kitchen. She found them milling by the counter where she kept dog biscuits in a cookie jar.

"Sit," Lia commanded. Three butts plopped on the floor. Lia gave Max a stern look. Max turned her face away and slowly, as if obedience would kill her, lowered her hindquarters until they barely touched the ground. Lia reached into the jar and handed each dog a treat.

"That dog is just contrary," Peter said. "Do you always give them a treat each time you leave?"

"Every time. It lets them know I'm leaving. I like to think it eases any separation anxiety, but I don't know if that's true or not."

They climbed into Peter's Blazer. Peter turned on the

ignition and put the car in gear. "What do you think of my truck?"

"What do you mean?"

"Would you rather be riding in something stylish, like Brent's A4?"

Lia laughed. "I asked my mechanic about Brent's A4 when I took the Black Beauty in for her oil change last week. He says they're over-engineered, expensive to fix and demand frequent dates with their mechanics.

"Stan said, given the choice between my twenty-year-old 240 and a brand new A4, he'd take the 240. I bet Brent will begin to rethink his love affair with Celeste before he's had her six months. Seriously, don't you have better things to do with your money?"

"Well, uh …"

"You think I'm going to run off with the first guy who drives up in an expensive car?" she teased.

"I was just wondering." He shrugged.

"Yeah, it gets me all hot and bothered, sitting down at Stan's and drooling over those expensive, busted cars he works on. I'm just dying to hook up with a guy who has enough money to burn on one." She rolled her eyes. "Seriously, don't you know me better than that?"

"Uh umm …"

"Stan, I might run off with, if it wasn't for that wife of his."

"Excuse me?"

"Except I have you and I don't need anyone else. You gonna quit asking me stupid questions, Kentucky Boy?"

"That wasn't why I was asking."

"No? Why were you asking?"

"I didn't want to make a big deal out of this. Last night

you said marriage is about money and wanting the same things, and there's a lot of truth to that. My former fiancé dumped me because she figured out my income bracket would never be up to her standards."

"Leaving aside She-who-will-not-be-named, a car's a car. It gets you where you want to go. I'm practical about things that involve money. Right now I have to be, but that wouldn't change if I had more of it, and I don't think it's your responsibility to provide an endless supply of it. Did I pass?" She batted her lashes.

"How was your day, darling?"

"Do I detect evasive action?"

"You do."

"It was fine. Renee oohed and aahed over the pictures I showed her. She picked the one I like best, with Dakini's fur flying and her eyes all wide while her tongue is hanging out. It's a bit goofy. Renee wants a big canvas so it will reign over her den like portraits of Chairman Mao in China, back in the sixties."

"Did Renee put it that way? About Chairman Mao?"

"She did. You know I wasn't alive back then."

"How big is this going to be?"

"I've got to go back to measure her fireplace to be sure, but I'm thinking three by four feet, maybe four and a half."

Lia and Peter sat in a quiet corner of Emanu Ethiopian Restaurant. Lia tore a bit of injera off the layers of spongy flatbread lining their platter and used it to scoop up a bit of stewed vegetables.

"So what's next with the case?" she asked, popping the morsel into her mouth.

Peter chewed thoughtfully. "We're going to give Stryker a good hard look, make sure the alibi holds up. Find out where he did his hunting in the woods, who knew about his bow, ask the neighbors if they'd seen anyone strange around the neighborhood. If you could call that a neighborhood. We're not looking forward to going back."

"Was it that bad?"

"It's like another country up there, isolated from the rest of the city like it is. We're also going to continue checking in with hunters to find out who's been where in the forest, and what they've seen. It's tedious, but it's our best shot at finding a witness. There's a good chance they don't realize what they saw."

"What about other suspects? Wouldn't the wife have a motive?"

"She was at work."

"She could have gotten someone else to do it, don't you think? A hit man or a boyfriend? Couldn't she have gotten wind of his plans to divorce her? Maybe she didn't want to split the assets. Maybe she felt angry and humiliated."

"I don't think she's hired anyone. We went over the family financials a couple days ago. No signs of a large amount of money being moved. Only a really stupid hit man would do the job without getting an advance."

"Or maybe a really smart one who knew that's the first place you would look. Maybe someone has some reason to believe they could count on getting paid."

"Like what?"

"I don't know. I'm just tossing it out there. Maybe she handed over collateral."

"What kind of collateral could she give him?"

"You're missing a car, aren't you?"

Peter nodded thoughtfully. "It could work. He gets the car as the first part of his payoff, sells it to a chop shop or otherwise disposes of it."

"What about a boyfriend? If he was cheating, she could be cheating, too."

Peter tried to imagine Monica with her freckles and her Martha Stewart home ushering the meter reader in the back door while wearing a neon red negligee trimmed with dyed marabou feathers. It didn't play. "We talked to her neighbors, also her co-workers. We couldn't find anyone she was especially close to. No sign of a boyfriend, not that anyone knows about. According to them, it goes against type."

"Doesn't mean there isn't one."

PETER OPENED the passenger door of his Blazer for Lia.

"You don't have to keep doing that," Lia said. "My fingers work perfectly fine."

"I do if I want to sneak a peek at your ass without you noticing."

"Men." She climbed into the truck, turned, and caught his line of sight. Peter shrugged, whistling as he walked around the SUV to take the driver's seat.

"You never mentioned if you saw Kate Onstad today," Peter said as he pulled out onto Montgomery Road.

"She had breakfast with us. She was so nice. I was

afraid she'd hate me for turning her in, but she was grateful I hooked her up with Renee."

"Huh." Peter turned south on Ridge Road.

Lia turned to look at him in the darkness. "She told us this story, about how she hooked up with George the first time, back in high school."

"Oh?"

"It was very romantic. She gave him her virginity out in the woods."

"Really?" Peter gave her a speculative look.

"You ever make love outside like that?" she asked.

"A gentleman never tells. Would you like to?" He took his eyes off the road to gauge her reaction.

She bit her lip, hesitant. "Well … it's, I don't know … it's an interesting thought."

He whipped the SUV into the nearest parking lot and turned around, heading north on Ridge Road.

"Where are we going?"

"French Park. You keep thinking about losing your virginity in the woods while I drive."

"It's chilly out."

He patted her thigh as the car inched over the speed limit. "I'll warm you up. I promise. Who are we? Captain of the football team and hot head cheerleader? Hoodlum and honor student?"

"That's what they were. He was a hoodlum, she was studious. Maybe we could go in a different direction. Tramp and virginal jock who is also an altar boy."

"Depends. Do you want to be swept away or powerful and in control?" He entered the park, drove up the hill, parked in the lot beside the now vacant caretaker's cottage.

"Here? In a parking lot?"

"Oh, ye of little faith, where is your trust?"

"I want high school petting rules. No hickeys on the neck, and you're going to have to make me desperate for you before you get to peel any of my clothes off," she bargained.

"Why do I have to do all the work?"

"You're the gas and I'm the brakes. Woody Harrelson said so in a movie."

He grabbed a blanket out of the back and opened Lia's door for her. She slid out, into his arms as he leaned over to kiss her.

She placed an index finger against his lips. "Not so fast, Kentucky Boy. What's with the handy blanket?"

He ducked her finger, nipped her neck. "Emergency first aid. Shock victims, that sort of thing. But you can look for semen stains if you like." Nibbled some more. "What's your name tonight? Vanessa? Kelly? Maybe a sweet, wholesome Sue? Did I get you drunk first?"

She stared over his shoulder, at the stars, considered. "Your name is Kirk. You're a star basketball player, and you were about to flunk out of English before the coach hooked you up with me for tutoring. He really needs you for the state championship. My name is … Natalie. I'm very protected and inexperienced, and I'm saving myself for marriage. You've been sitting really close to me for months and we keep exchanging looks. Oh, and I'm the coach's daughter. Dad said it was okay for you to take me out for a milkshake since you passed your midterms. He trusts you."

She stepped out of Peter's embrace and turned wide

eyes on him. "Kirk, I thought we were just getting a milk shake. What are we doing here?"

"I just thought we'd go for a walk." He shrugged, faking indifference. "It's a pretty night out. You don't have to be back yet, do you?" He dabbed the corner of her mouth with his finger, grinned. "You had a bit of chocolate there."

"I guess it's okay, but I'm a little chilly."

"Here," he said as he took off his jacket, slung it around her shoulders. "Warm enough?"

"Oh, Kirk, your letter jacket. This is almost like being your girlfriend."

"Would you like to be my girlfriend?"

"I-I thought you were going steady with Sally."

"Nah, we just went out a couple times. It's not anything."

"She's so much prettier than I am."

He took her chin in his hand, tilted her face up. "It's all makeup and big tits. You're prettier than her any day."

"You mean it?"

He bent over and pressed his lips against hers. She kept her lips closed, like a proper virgin. He kissed his way over to her ear, sucked on the lobe. A thrill shot through her. "Open your mouth for me," he whispered against her skin.

Lia parted her lips and Peter covered them with his own, slipping his tongue inside her mouth. She jolted. "What are you doing?"

"Sweet Natalie, haven't you ever been French kissed?" His warm breath feathered her cheek. He slid a chilled hand under the hem of her blouse, startling her as it met the warm skin at her waist. "You want to be my girlfriend, don't you?"

"I … I don't know." She edged away, dislodging his hand. "Someone could come along and see us. Dad would kill me."

He winked at her, nodded toward a copse of evergreens with heavy boughs sweeping the ground. "Let's go in there. I bet it's totally private."

She said nothing as he led her toward the circle of trees, then ducked between the branches, disappearing in the shadows. She felt her way along, following the pull of his hand. "Kirk, I can't see you. I can't see anything."

"It's okay. Let's sit down." He tugged. She sat on the blanket with a thump, bumped into him.

"Oops, I'm sorry. Did I hurt you?" She felt around, trying to get her bearings in the dark. Her hand collided with his chest. She snatched it back.

"Nah, I'm fine. Let me put my arm around you … There, are you warm enough?" His hand brushed the outside of her thigh in a time-honored, faux-casual encroachment that sent shivers through her.

"Uh-huh. Kirk?"

"Yeah?"

"Will you kiss me again?" she asked, shyly. "I can't do anything else, but I-I like kissing you."

7

TUESDAY, OCTOBER 15

"Are you ever going to let her off that leash?" Bailey asked.

Lia eyed Max from her perch on the picnic table. Max was giving Lia dirty looks from the other end of the twenty-foot training lead. "Nope."

"Aw, she wants to be free, don't you, Max?" Jim said. "See, she wants to run around with the other dogs. Look at how much fun Honey and Viola are having."

Honey and Viola, Lia observed, were laying in the grass, doing nothing. Just like Fleece and Chester. "She doesn't give a damn about the other dogs. She wants to be on the other side of that fence."

"You don't know that," Jim said.

"I do know it, just like I know that the minute she's over the fence, you're going to remember that you're late for an appointment to get your colon irrigated."

"Poor Max," Jim said. "Nobody loves you." Max

wandered up to Jim and gave him a sorrowful look. He scratched behind her ears.

"I wish I could let her off lead. As it is, I have to take an extra walk every day to give her some exercise."

"How did it go at Renee's yesterday?" Bailey asked. "Did she like your photos?"

"You know Renee. She's so easy to work with. I wish I could clone her. She invited George's mystery woman to have breakfast with us."

"Really?"

"Poor woman." Lia paused to consider her ethics, then decided she could share some of Kitty's confidences. "She came all the way up here to be with the guy she crushed on in high school, only to have him murdered and her a suspect."

"I'm sorry he died, but I don't condone adultery," Jim said.

"I don't think she's responsible for the issues George was having with Monica," Lia said. "I think meeting her again gave him the courage to face the problems that were already there. She said he was talking about getting a divorce."

"Leaving someone is not facing your problems," Jim said.

"It sounds like he was being a swinging monkey to me," Bailey said.

"What's that?" Lia asked.

"That's a guy who won't let go of the woman he's got until he has the next one lined up, like Tarzan swinging from vine to vine in the movies."

"Women do it, too," Jim said. "It's no better when they

do it. Are you sure you should be friendly with that woman? She did have a crossbow in her trunk."

"You sound like Peter. I don't believe she did anything. You should have heard her yesterday. She needs all the friends she can get. She's over a thousand miles from home, stuck here while they sort things out. I'm glad Renee is helping her."

"Here, hold this." Lia nodded to the end of the inch-wide tape measure, which she pinned to the edge of the stone fireplace with one hand. Renee took over and Lia walked the tape out to the other side of the masonry column. Dakini lay on the floor, sphinx-like, supervising this operation.

Lia eyed the markings. "Eight feet, give or take a half inch to allow for irregularities in the stones." She walked the tape back and took the end from Renee. "How high is the ceiling?"

"Fifteen feet, at this end."

Lia measured from the top of the mantel to the floor. "Five and a half. That gives us nine and a half feet by eight feet to play with. We'll want a roomy margin of stone all the way around, at least two feet."

"I want her to look like she's jumping over the heads of everyone in the room," Renee said. "The grandkids will love it and it'll make Harry's business associates nervous, just the way he likes them. You can make it look like she's going to pop right off the canvas can't you?"

"I'll do my best," Lia promised.

"I'm sure it will be wonderful. I trust your judgement. Now have a seat and let's discuss other topics."

"Don't you mean gossip?"

"Well, if you want to get all technical about it."

Lia sat on one end of the leather sofa. Renee poured coffee from the thermal carafe Esmerelda had brought in earlier. Lia accepted the cup, added half-and-half. Renee sat down by her. Dakini jumped up on the sofa next to her mom.

"Where's Kitty?" Lia asked. "How's she holding up?"

"Poor thing. Not so well, I'm afraid. She puts on a brave front, but I think she's just devastated. Wouldn't you be? I talked her into letting my massage therapist come and give her a session in the guest apartment. I thought that would be best. I wanted to talk to you in private."

"Oh?"

"She needs some help, and I think we should give it to her. You know that stick of a wife has to be behind George's murder, even if she didn't do it herself. Who else would want him dead?"

"She does seem like the obvious choice, but what can we do about it?"

"We need some good intel. I don't know the woman, so that leaves you."

"Me? What do you want me to do about it?"

"Just talk to her and be sympathetic. I know you can handle that. You dealt with Catherine, and she could be a real witch."

Lia leaned back, furrowed her brow. "What exactly do you have in mind, Renee?"

"Oh, nothing onerous, I assure you. The family is grieving, aren't they?"

"I suppose so."

"What do you do when a family has a loss? You take them food, of course. Then she has to be polite and invite you in. You just get her talking and see what falls out of her mouth. Notice things in her house, that sort of thing."

"So you want me to make her food, then take it to her and pump her for information."

"Exactly, but you don't have to cook anything. I've got Esmerelda putting together a lasagna for you to take over there."

"You want Peter to kill me?"

"What's the harm? George was a regular in your park, wasn't he? Isn't this a natural thing for a caring person to do? And if you happen to see or hear anything interesting, well, you don't have to tell Peter about it, do you? But it might give Kitty's lawyer something to work with. You can get in there where a private detective is stuck outside, staring in the windows."

After her previous experience with Monica, Lia thought it unlikely the widow would invite her in. She supposed she could deliver a casserole, just to make Renee happy. "This is just a one-time thing, right?"

"Well, I was thinking, she's not likely to spill her guts the first time you drop by, but if you went a few times and became more of a presence, she might relax a bit. Don't you worry, though. I'll have Esmerelda make up your care packages. The dog park really ought to be making a show of support, don't you agree?"

Lia shook her head, amused. "You railroad Harry like this often?"

"All the time."

"I'll take the lasagna, but I'm not promising anything

after that. And I won't keep secrets from Peter. We made a deal about that."

LIA TOOK A DEEP BREATH, then rang the doorbell. A deep, melodious chime sounded within. Monica Munce answered the door wearing neat camel-colored slacks and a boat-neck, business-casual tee. Both had been ironed. The pants had knife-edge creases.

"It's kind of you to drop by. As I said over the phone, it really isn't necessary. Will you come in and have a cup of coffee?"

Lia agreed, hoping she wasn't going to float away after all the coffee she'd already had. She followed Monica through a spotless living room to the breakfast bar that fronted the kitchen. Everything was perfectly arranged, except for a stack of library books on a table by the door. She was certain the decorating scheme had been copied out of some paint store color guide, if not from Martha Stewart's magazine. Monica looked ready for Dame Martha herself to drop in.

She looked, but could not spot a dog hair anywhere. She hadn't known George very well. Still, she couldn't feel his hand in the house. His presence had been relegated to a montage of family photos on the hall wall.

"Who's into Suzanne Collins?"

"Sorry?"

"I saw *The Hunger Games* in your living room."

"Oh, that's my daughter, Stacy. All the girls want to be Katniss now. I hope you don't mind sitting in the kitchen. It's where I do everything."

"It's lovely. You have such a beautiful home."

"Thank you. Let me take that. You really shouldn't have gone to so much trouble, but Stacy and I appreciate the effort. I do enjoy lasagna. If it wasn't for the carbs, I'd have it all the time. What's in this one?"

Lia stammered mentally while Monica put the lasagna into the fridge, then poured coffee in sunny yellow mugs that matched other decorating accents.

"Family secret?" Monica asked when Lia didn't answer.

Lia smiled and shrugged. "You know how it is."

"I certainly do." She handed one mug to Lia. "I've got skim, if you want it. I'm afraid I don't have any whole milk or cream."

"Skim is fine." She topped the coffee using a small pitcher with a sunflower motif. "How are you getting along?" she asked once Monica was settled.

Monica gave her a tremulous smile. "I don't know if you've ever lost anyone. One day I'm okay and the next I fall to pieces again." She sipped her coffee. "Then there's the funeral.

"I have to apologize for the other day. I'd just gotten off the phone with the morgue. They won't release George until a forensic anthropologist has a chance to examine him, and it's got me very upset.

"It's not like me to be so rude, especially after you've gone to so much trouble to find Daisy. Are you having any luck?" Monica gave her an open look that suggested interest. Lia failed to sense any genuine concern beneath the polite expression.

"Not so far, but I'm hopeful. Some of the other people at the park who knew George are helping out. We're contacting every vet and rescue organization and spreading her picture everywhere we can think of. Hopefully, we'll get a call soon. Daisy is such a sweet dog. I hate to think about her running around, lost and frightened." There was no dog dish on the newly waxed floor. Lia wondered where it went.

Monica murmured noncommittally and sipped her coffee.

"Do you have any idea when the funeral is going to be?" Lia asked. "Some of us at the park would like to pay our respects."

"Not yet. The coroner's office has been giving me the run-around for almost a week now." She gave Lia a thin, tight smile. It didn't reach her eyes. "Everyone has questions, but nobody has any answers."

"So the police haven't found out anything?"

"Not that they'll tell–"

A knock at the kitchen door interrupted. Monica opened the door for a tall, good-looking young man wearing a hoodie with the sleeves shoved up and his hands stuffed into the pockets of his low-riders. Lia guessed he was eighteen. Maybe nineteen. Dark hair. Dark eyes under heavy brows held adult awareness. He bore the intense physicality of male hormones in overdrive, sauntering in without being invited as if he had the run of the place. Lia imagined she would have swooned over him in high school. And regretted it. He gave a little jerk when he saw her sitting at the counter.

"I've got company, Jacob." Monica still held the doorknob. "It's not the best time."

"No sweat, Mrs. M. I'll just get started on the, uh, leaves then." He ran a strong hand with well-defined knuckles through errant bangs, shoving them out of his face. Lia wanted to paint his hands, his forearms. She imagined them gripping … clenching … *something* … a branch, a hammer, free weights? Something that would have those lovely muscles contracting, his tendons, popping, saying so much with just those strong young arms.

"Thank you, Jacob. I'd appreciate that." Monica closed the door behind him and sat down. Lia noticed she was a little flushed. She followed Monica's gaze out the back window, where Jacob was stripping off his hoodie, revealing a long lean torso. He dropped the jacket on the patio table.

"A friend of Stacy's?" Lia asked.

Monica flushed. "Jacob lives in the neighborhood. He's a student at the high school where I work. He takes care of some things around the yard for us, that's all."

"That's considerate of him," Lia said.

"THAT WAS A BUST, and not of the recreational substance sort," Brent said as he steered his Audi out of the parking lot of the auto parts store, onto Cheviot Road. "How many hunters have we interviewed today? Eight? Ten? What have we got? Zip. Zilch. Zero—"

"I wouldn't say that," Peter said, checking the next name on his list.

"What would you say, Kemosabe?"

"We're getting a picture. So far, nobody has seen any strange cars and no one spotted the Zombie. No strange hunters. No one saw Stryker after he reported his bow missing. These guys see each other, year after year at the marksmanship exam and in the parking lots and out in the woods. They know each other's blinds, and we've got them marked on the map. It would have been hard for our man to be in the woods without either him or his car being seen by someone, if he was there during the usual hunting hours.

"From what they say, that jury-rigged tree-house we found has been in the woods for years. Park maintenance was supposed to pull it down, but they haven't gotten around to it. Nobody knows who built it, or when. It may never have been intended as a blind, since the word we're getting is, that area is not very productive for hunting deer. Which is also why nobody spotted the deceased before Max did."

"Like I said. Nothing," Brent repeated.

"Nothing is something. So far everyone alibis out for the time period we have for the shooting, which is late morning to early afternoon. Everyone who was in the woods that day was gone before nine a.m. That means our perp was never there to shoot deer, and didn't show up until the hunters were gone."

"How does that help us?" Brent asked.

"We put that together with the report Stryker filed on his stolen crossbow. What else was missing from his house?"

"Some crossbow bolts. Nothing else."

"Exactly. Nothing other than what our perp needed to kill Munce. Nothing else disturbed. Does that sound like your typical housebreaker to you?"

"No. He'd grab anything that had monetary value."

"Everything suggests that our perp specifically went after that bow to use as a murder weapon, that he knew exactly where Munce would be in the woods and when he would be there. It's tedious, but what we're doing is ruling out the possibility that Munce's death was a crime of opportunity. There's nothing random about this. It narrows the field."

"Kate Onstad is the one person we know for sure knew George was going to be in the woods that day," Brent said.

"How'd she know about the bow?" Peter asked.

"I'm working on that."

"What about her tire?"

"She had an accomplice?"

"Ah, the ever-popular unknown accomplice," Peter said. "Whoa - pull in here."

Brent turned the car into the next parking lot. He saw the sign over the store's glittery display window and groaned. "Don't do it, man. No good will come from this." He scrambled out of the car after Peter, followed him into the jewelry store, caught up with him at the ring counter.

The glossy woman behind the counter smiled at Peter. "What can I help you find today?"

"I'm just looking. I'll let you know if I need help. But thank you," Peter said. Her smile drooped a little and she moved off to the side.

"What part of 'I love you, Peter, but I need my space' did you not understand?" Brent hissed.

"I understood it. I just don't think it has to be a deal breaker. Why does all this stuff look like it came out of a gum-ball machine?" He turned away from the display of engagement rings and wandered over to a case containing estate jewelry. "I like this much better."

He eyed a ruby surrounded by small, rectangular

emeralds. "I like this one, but it's not quite right for Lia. Too big."

"The question isn't whether you think it's a deal breaker. The question is whether she thinks it's a deal breaker."

The pearl with diamonds was pretty, but too … conservative? Bland? Snooty? … for Lia.

"I guess it's up to me to show her that it's not."

"You think a big, fancy ring is going to do that?"

"No, she doesn't like big and fancy. I think the right ring will help. It will show her that I understand her. And none of these are the right ring." He held up his hand in an abbreviated wave to the woman behind the counter and walked out.

IT WAS after ten when Viola ran to the door. Lia put aside her book and let Peter in. When she opened the door, he was leaning against the jamb, his eyes closed.

"Beer?" Lia offered.

"You have to ask?"

"I guess not. You look beat. You should have gone home."

"My two best girls are here." He leaned down and gave Lia a kiss, then got down on the floor to rumple the fur around Viola's neck. She jumped up and kissed his face with light, happy flicks. He sat on the floor and let Viola, Honey and Chewy climb on him, petting whichever head was nearest each hand. Max snorted and lay her head on her paws.

"She misses you," Lia called from the kitchen.

"Can't be helped. Until we get a handle on this case, I'm not going to be available much. How'd it go at Renee's today?"

Lia handed a bottle of Beck's down to Peter. He stopped petting Chewy to take it. Chewy head-butted his hand, causing a bit of beer foam to spill out the top. Peter grimaced, then shrugged.

"It was fine. We squared away the details. Taking the pictures was the easy part. Now I get to paint it. She asked me to take a lasagna to Monica and Stacy Munce." Lia held her breath, waiting for Peter's reaction.

He shook his head. "I know Renee is the soul of compassion, but something tells me this is about something else."

"You know Renee, anything for a bit of good gossip." Lia reached out a hand. Peter grabbed it and stood up, shedding the trio of furry four-paws.

"And did you find any good gossip?"

In the light of Peter's scrutiny, her discoveries seemed silly. She decided to avoid ridicule and not mention Stacy's reading proclivities. "I don't know. One of the neighbor kids is hanging around. He seems to have a thing for Monica."

"Seriously? What does he look like?"

"Tall, broody, dark hair."

"Brent and I saw him the day we went by. You think the very proper Mrs. Munce goes for bad boys less than half her age?"

"She was blushing. But she doesn't have to go for him. She just has to be willing to manipulate him, don't you think?"

"True. So the high school counselor is willing to

destroy a young life by making this kid a party to murder? And another thing. I know this kid thinks he's a bad-ass, but I bet Stryker would eat his liver before he ever got close enough to him to even know about his bow."

"So you think whoever stole the bow has to be a brute?"

"Just try driving a Honda Fit up there and see what happens. It's not a place for civilized folks."

"Now you've got me curious."

"Promise me you won't go digging around up there, no matter what Renee says."

"Relax, Kentucky Boy." She brushed his hair out of his eyes. "I don't even know where 'there' is."

8

WEDNESDAY, OCTOBER 16

Renee was at the park with Dakini, waiting on the far side of the corral as Lia and Bailey walked up the drive. "Well, how did it go?" she called through the fence.

"How did what go?" Bailey asked.

"Hello to you, too, Renee." Lia let the dogs in the corral. Glancing over at Bailey, she said, "Renee drafted me for undercover work. She has me spying on the Widow Munce. What brings you here, Renee?"

"Why wouldn't I be here? This is a lovely park. Oh, look, is this Max? What a handsome girl. Your mom tells me you've been very enterprising lately." She put her hand up to the fence and let Max sniff her palm. Dakini turned her head, a canine version of rolling her eyes.

"Uh-huh." Lia poked her tongue in her cheek.

"Well, I thought it might be better if I talked to you here instead of possibly disturbing Kitty. I don't know how she'd feel about our little investigation. You have to tell me how it went. Don't keep me in suspense."

Lia unclipped Honey, Chewy and Viola, and opened the inner gate. The three dogs bolted for the back of the park. She swung the coiled training lead off her shoulder and hooked Max into it before releasing her walking leash.

"You're not taking any chances with that one, are you?" Renee asked.

"Not at all. Let's get back to our table and then I'll give you a full report." The three women crossed the park and settled themselves on top of the old picnic table. Lia reflected on how different this setting was from the antiseptic kitchen she'd visited the day before.

"How was she?" Renee primed.

"Very polite. Much nicer than she was when I stopped by to ask about Daisy. Well put together. She irons her tee shirts."

"Seriously?" Bailey asked.

"And she waxed her floor recently. I could practically see myself in it."

"Well, people react to grief in different ways," Bailey said.

"I don't know how much she's grieving. She looks like she's grieving, but it feels kind of put on, as if that's how people expect her to act. There was something creepy about it, like she was getting off on the attention."

"You mean, like Munchausen by proxy? That would be really weird if she killed her husband just to get sympathy," Bailey said.

"So, besides being an able housekeeper, what else did you notice?" Renee asked.

"One of the neighbor boys has a crush on her, and she knows it."

"Really?" Renee drew the word out, adding an extra syllable. "How about that. How did you figure that out?"

"He showed up at the back door and walked in like he lived there. Then he fumbled when he saw me. She hustled him out, and she over-explained why he was there. She was blushing."

"Well now," Renee said. "I wonder if Monica's young swain has himself an alibi? What do you think, Lia?"

"He's fit enough to climb a tree and shoot off a crossbow. Peter pooh-poohed the idea, but I wouldn't be too hasty. Another thing. Someone in the house is reading *The Hunger Games*. Monica said it was Stacy."

"Why is that significant?" Bailey asked.

"How many teenaged girls do you know who have read that book and *didn't* want to pick up a bow and arrow?"

"So we need to look at Stacy and Jacob," Renee said.

"I'd like to take a look at Jacob. Was he hot?" Bailey asked.

"Wes Bentley hot," Lia said. "Very broody looking, like he was in *American Beauty*, except without the knit cap and the unibrow. He's still in high school. I wonder if she knows him in her professional capacity as school counselor. We could be looking at a very improper situation."

"Wes Bentley? I thought that was Jake Gyllenhaal," Bailey said.

"Motive?" Lia asked. "What do you think, Renee?"

"Our young Lothario either wants the widow for himself, or he is avenging her honor, or both," Renee said.

"And Stacy?" Lia asked.

"Maybe she felt betrayed by the affair? Because George was going to leave?" Renee pondered.

"Could they have been in it together?" Bailey asked.

"It's possible," Lia said, shrugging. "But then the motive becomes murkier."

"How so?" Bailey asked.

"I doubt Stacy is going to help Jacob in pursuit of her mother. That's just too disturbing to think about. It would have to be Jacob helping Stacy for Stacy's reasons. And if she has the attention of Jacob to the extent that he would commit murder for her, why would she care what George was up to?" Lia explained.

"What if they're sick, twisted adolescents, acting out their nihilistic fantasies?" Bailey suggested.

"Did you get a look at Stacy? She seem to have nihilistic fantasies to you, Lia?" Renee asked.

"I only saw pictures of her. She seems like a straight-arrow, studious type."

"We have a problem," Lia said.

"What's that?" Renee asked.

"We need to connect the bow with someone. Peter and Brent found the owner of the bow, and it came from a very dubious neighborhood. Not a place middle-class sorts would care to go, and not people they would care to associate with."

"If they identified the owner, why wasn't he arrested?" Bailey asked.

"The bow was reported stolen before George died," Lia explained.

"And I'm sure they were telling the absolute truth," Renee pouted. "So where is this dubious neighborhood?"

"I don't know. Peter wouldn't tell me, just that it's dicey. Anyway, I have to draw the line there. It's one thing to take food to the Munces. That's something I'd do, anyway, that is, if I actually knew George. Which we don't, really. But we have no business being anywhere near the guy who owned that bow."

"Well, pooh." Renee made a moue. "Maybe you'll find out more when you go back today."

"Am I going back today?" Lia asked.

Renee patted Lia's hand. "Of course you are. I have today's offering in the car."

"ALMA, how do you stay so limber? I know people half your age who aren't as fit as you are." Peter took a drink from his morning Pepsi as he watched his tiny octogenarian neighbor pick kale from her garden.

"Daily yoga, and fresh greens keep my hair black. It's so nice that kale grows on into winter. I can have home-grown greens almost year round." She handed the bag to Peter. "Take these. I bet that girlfriend of yours knows what to do with them." She pulled another plastic grocery sack out of her pocket and resumed pruning the older leaves.

"Yeah. She makes me eat them."

Alma chuckled. "You listen to her. You may think you can eat anything—" She gave his Pepsi a scathing look. "—and get away with it, but you're not too far from the day when your body will rebel. So, when are you going to marry that girl?" She stood up and looked him straight in the eyes.

Amused, Peter quirked up his mouth and looked straight back. "I'd marry her tomorrow, but she's a hard sell. She likes things the way they are."

"Why do you want to marry her? You're getting the milk for free, aren't you?"

Peter sputtered. "Alma! You know it's not like that."

"Okay, let's look at it a different way. You want a wife. She doesn't want a husband. Why don't you look elsewhere? You're a handsome young man. You've got a job and you don't hang out with low-life types. I don't think it would be too hard for you to find a wife."

"I don't want a wife, I want Lia."

"Because?"

"Well … because she's the most amazing woman I've ever met."

"That's good then. To make a marriage work, she has to be your hero. Of course, you have to be hers, too. Are you her hero?"

"Um, I don't know. That's not exactly something that comes up in daily conversation."

"Think of it like respect. Do you respect each other."

"I think so."

"I mean, do you like her exactly as she is, or do you think marriage is going to change things somehow?"

"I guess I thought we'd buy a house, make a home together."

"Uh, huh, and who's going to iron your shirts?"

"Nobody irons my shirts. They don't need it."

"That's good. Too many men think of wives like their cars. Something they need that makes their life easier and hopefully looks good; and that they take care of to keep from whining but mostly ignore."

"That's insulting!"

"Just making sure you're not expecting Lia to be your housekeeper-sex goddess."

"You're harsh, Alma," he scolded.

"Marriage is serious business. Too many young people jump into it thinking it's going to fix their lives, when it's likely to make things harder. If you want a good marriage, first you have to have respect based on admiration, trust, and then friendship. You have to have all three things, and you have to have them on both sides, or it won't work. "

"You left out love."

"You're going to have love at the start of every relationship, but love isn't enough to make a marriage, or even keep itself going. Lots of things kill love, and you can love someone but not be able to stay married to them."

"That's a lot to think about."

"If your girl is balky about making a commitment, then you need to be building on those three things, you and she both. So what's missing?"

THE DOOR OPENED. Lia noted the questioning look in Monica's eyes, as if she were uncertain why Lia was there. The look vanished, replaced by a hesitant smile, very proper for one who is grieving. "More gifts? You are too kind. Please come in." Monica ushered Lia inside. "We still have plenty of lasagna. It's lovely, by the way."

"I brought salmon croquettes today."

"Aren't you the cook."

"It's just a hobby," Lia demurred. Monica took the covered dish, poured coffee.

"You really don't have to keep bringing us food," Monica said.

"It's no trouble. I wish there was more we could do. George was well liked at the park."

"I never realized. He never said."

George hadn't said, because we barely knew him. If we had, we would have missed him and called. Not that I'm going to tell Monica that.

"How is Stacy handling things?" Lia asked.

"Stacy's a trooper. She's my pillar of strength. I don't know what I'd do without her. I just hope this doesn't send her grades into the sewer. She's shooting for Stanford. I suppose we can forget about that, with George gone." She sighed. "It's not like the old days, when you could work your way through school."

Monica looked at her watch. "I'm sorry, I'm expecting my brother and his wife any minute now. I hope you'll excuse me. They're driving in from Indianapolis to help out with the funeral." She stood up.

"Has the coroner released George, then?"

"Not yet, but they said the anthropologist would be here this week, and then they would release him. So we're having the funeral next Tuesday. We're going to finalize everything after they get here. I hope you'll come, and bring George's dog park friends."

She ushered Lia to the door. "Thank you for the croquettes. I'm sure they'll make a lovely dinner. Please don't trouble about us for tomorrow. We'll be going out to eat."

A teenaged girl with dark hair down to her waist came up the walk. "Stacy, darling," Monica called. "This is Lia. She made that lovely lasagna we had last night."

Stacy's mouth stretched in a parody of a grin. Proforma acknowledgment with ironic undertones. She slipped inside without saying anything.

LIA RENDEZVOUSED with Bailey and Max around the corner from the Munce's house. Bailey opened the back door and Max jumped in. She slid into the front seat beside Lia.

"How come you got to sit inside and drink coffee while I had to walk Max? She's your dog."

"Monica knows me now, so she might tell me something. She doesn't know you at all. Max needs the exercise, and you needed an excuse to loiter." Max jumped up and propped her forepaws on top of the seat back so she could lean over and lick Lia's ear.

"See, she missed you. She kept looking at the house, wanting to follow you. I kept telling her she was going to give us away, but she didn't care."

Lia gave Max's head a scratch. "Sorry about that. Did you find anything out?"

"I saw a Wes Bently clone coming home from school. I'm sure it was Jacob. I was able to get his address, and I texted it along with Stacy's info down to Trees. He should be able to get back to us within a day or so. Then we'll know if there's anything off about Stacy or Jacob, like any criminal or psychiatric history.

"By the way, you're right. He's a hunk."

"A very young hunk."

"Spoilsport. Did you find out anything about Stacy?"

"Monica claims Stacy is the perfect daughter. Excellent grades, thoughtful, et cetera, et cetera. The princess made her appearance as I was leaving and showed a shocking lack of manners. I don't think Stacy is as perfect as Monica wants everyone to believe."

"Jacob drove home. Stacy pulled up about the same time. They didn't acknowledge each other. So either they don't like each other, or else they don't want anyone to know they like each other."

"Well that's clear as mud."

"HI, GORGEOUS." Brent flashed Cynth a perfect, practiced smile as he sat on the edge of her desk. "How's our little project coming?

Cynth looked over the top of her black frame glasses and rolled her eyes. Peter winked at her. She flipped a heavy, wheat colored braid over her shoulder and pressed a hand to the full and well-formed bosom lurking underneath her baggy golf shirt. "Oh Brent," she said breathily. "I've just never seen anything like this. I never imagined men and women would write such things to each other. It is positively scandalous."

Was that a little Scarlett O'Hara Peter detected in her voice?

Brent leaned forward, crowding her personal space. "So when are you going to let me have a look at it? I just want a little peek."

She leaned back and fanned her face with a small stack of pages. "I really don't know if anyone should be seeing this. Why, looking at it has me quite … flushed."

"Is that it?" Brent nodded at the papers.

"Oh, this?" She looked at the pages she held as if she

hadn't seen them before. "You want this?" She held the pages out, then pulled them back as Brent reached for them. She held them close to her face and adjusted her glasses. "I believe these are for a Detective Dourson. Is your name Dourson?"

"Cynth, don't make me beg."

"I kinda like making you beg. I know that's a rare experience for you. Peter, do you want these? I'm sorry it took so long. They had me pretending to be a teenager on Facebook, looking for comments about the bottle bombs at Hughes High School." She handed the pages to Peter. "These are rated for mature audiences, so be sure to keep them away from Junior, here."

"Why don't you come over to my place?" Brent said. "We'll see who makes who beg."

"Oh!" She pressed her hand to her breast again. "My heart is all aflutter."

"You know he's going to show it to me," he told Cynth. "Women," Brent muttered to Peter on their way out of the IT department.

Peter heard Cynth snort.

"No COFFEE, Esmerelda, I'll float away," Lia said as she sat down on the leather sofa. "Thanks, though." Max lay down on the floor beside her and pretended there was no leash restraining her.

"I didn't expect to see you again so soon," Renee said. She bent down to pet Max. Dakini nosed in, jealous. "What happened? Did you find anything out?"

"I wanted to talk to you before you put Esmerelda to

work for the cause. We're not exactly busted, but I got a strong hint or three from Monica that further culinary goods were not desired."

"Drat. What if we send someone else? Someone from the park?"

"Who would you send? We can't send Bailey, Stacy saw her walking Max today, so she might wonder why this person who was on her street is now knocking on her door."

"I see what you mean," Renee said, tapping her chin. "What about Jim?"

"I'm not sure how Jim would feel about what we're doing. I can't imagine Monica telling him anything significant, can you?"

"You may be right, though he has such a kind look about him. I remember Catherine saying how much she loved talking to him. It wouldn't hurt to ask, would it? What were you able to accomplish today? Anything good? Did you find out when the funeral is?"

"Funeral?" Kitty stood in the doorway, her eyes bleak. Her clothes were bagging. Lia wondered if she'd lost weight. "Is there going to be a funeral? I'd wondered, after what you told me about the condition of the body."

Lia and Renee exchanged glances.

"It's being scheduled," Lia said. "I don't know the exact time or any of the details, but she said Tuesday."

Kitty perched on the edge of a chair. She sat straight, with her hands clasped in her lap, hope battling with nerves. Her eyes darted between Renee and Lia, uncertain. Max stood up and wandered over to Kitty, at the limits of her leash. She sniffed at the woman's fingers. Kitty responded reflexively, stroking Max's head. "I would love to say good-bye to George. If you find out where it is, maybe I can visit the grave after the service is over." Lia let go of the leash. Max laid her head on Kitty's knee and sighed.

Renee waved dismissively. "Don't be so cliché, Kitty. Nobody knows who you are, except a few people at the dog park. I think you should go. Lia can take you. You're going, aren't you?"

"Well, I, uh …" Lia said as Kitty continued petting Max.

"Of course you are! Doesn't the killer always go to the funeral? You have to be there, and there's no reason not to take Kitty along."

Kitty's mouth trembled, hinting at a smile. "Do you think I could go? It would mean so much to me."

Lia saw the tiny spark appear in Kitty's eyes. *I'm doomed. Totally doomed.* She shoved the thought aside as a brainstorm occurred. "Max seems to like you," she said.

"… I cleared it with the rescue, so for the time being, Max is staying with Kate, and Renee's going to show her how to do basic obedience with Max. It'll give Kate something to do, and provide Max with attention I just can't give her right now. I'm hoping Renee's rescue and my rescue will rescue each other." She and Peter sat on the back stoop, watching their dogs nose around the yard. The sun had passed behind the trees and the air chilled. She leaned against him for a bit of body heat.

Peter tapped her cup of tea with his beer bottle. "Pure genius. Have I ever told you that I think smart girls are sexy?"

Lia laughed. "Oh, really?"

"Really. Seriously, you seem much more relaxed now that you don't have to worry about Max escaping."

"It's true. So how was your day, Dear?" She fluttered her eyelashes teasingly.

"A lot of i-dotting."

"Sorry?"

"Dotting i's, crossing t's. Brent and I have been chasing down hunters to find out if any of them saw anything. Brent's making eyes at Cynth in IT."

"Cynth? Isn't she a little … umm … *geeky* for Brent?"

"I think he's having sexy librarian fantasies since we gave her the job of tracking down George and Kate's love-notes to each other. He says he wants to be handy in case reviewing their communications sends her into a fit of unbridled lust."

"Why that opportunistic cad!" Lia huffed, outraged.

"I wouldn't worry about it. Cynth likes the IT stuff, but she can take care of herself out on the street. She excelled in hand-to-hand in the academy, and she takes off every year to play sword mistress at the Renaissance festival. Brent is no match for her. Near as I can tell, she finds him amusing. I haven't shared that with Brent. It's too much fun to watch."

"You should be ashamed of yourself."

"They're both adults. They can handle it." He took a deep breath. "Have you given any more thought to our conversation the other night?"

"About living together?" Lia examined his face in the failing light. "Peter, why do you want to live with me?"

"You sound just like Alma. She grilled me about the same thing today."

"Oh? You ask her to move in with you, too? And I thought Brent was a cad." She made a disgusted sound.

He shoulder bumped her. "I confess, I'd dump you for her in a minute, but she says I'm not old enough. Yet."

"Cute. So answer the question, Dourson."

"We don't have to live together." He searched for words. "It's just, my place seems lonely without you. I think of things I want to tell you, but you're not there. I like my place a lot. At least I used to. I don't enjoy being by myself as much as I did before we started seeing each other. It feels like my life is over here, with you."

"Oh, Peter." She leaned against him, wrapped her arms around his waist. "I know I have issues. Part of it is trust. You've never done anything for me not to trust you. I just find it hard to rely on someone else. But only part of it is trusting you. The rest of it is trusting me."

Peter beetled his brows. "What are you trying to say?"

"Look, I like people to be happy. That's one reason why I like doing commission work. It allows me the pleasure of giving someone what they want. But I get to go home at the end of the day, and so it balances out. Do you see?"

"I'm not sure I get you."

"When I'm in a relationship, I want the other person to be happy. Sometimes I do too much to make them happy and forget about myself. I'm so much better with you, but I don't know if I've figured out how to balance it out yet."

"There you go, trying to figure things out by yourself again."

"I do that, don't I? I guess I do that to make sure I'm not being influenced by anyone else."

"I can see that. I wish you trusted me to have your

needs at heart. I'm not totally selfish, am I?" He wrapped an arm around her.

"No, you're not, not at all. You're the sweetest, most generous man I've ever dated," she admitted, leaning into him.

"I think we could build a life together. I'm not sure what it would look like. We have to deal with two demanding careers. I'm not saying it has to start tomorrow. I'm just wondering if you can start thinking about what it would take for us to do that, and if that's something you might want. Not today, not tomorrow, but sometime."

"Wow. You sure know how to blow a girl away. Bailey wants to do synastry on us," Lia blurted out.

"Bailey wants to do what?"

"Synastry. Compare our astrological charts to determine our relationship potential. She thinks she can tell us how we are in a relationship, and how to make it work."

"Sure, why not."

"Huh?" Lia blinked.

"It'll be interesting."

"I can't believe you're going for this nonsense."

"You're calling it nonsense? She's your friend."

"That doesn't mean I believe in all the stuff she gets into."

"C'mon. It'll be fun. Besides, I already know what she's going to say."

"What's that, Kentucky Boy?"

He tapped the dent in her chin with his index finger. "That we're meant for each other."

"You're that confident, are you?"

"Yep. Who knows, she might say something useful.

And if it's all a crock, I think we're smart enough to let it go. One condition. She has to tell both of us what she finds at the same time."

Lia's mind raced, looking for an out. She hadn't expected Peter to go for Bailey's offer. She should have remembered about his granny, the one who claimed to have "the sight." She was stuck, she admitted to herself, and it was her own fault for bringing it up. Philosophically, she acknowledged defeat. "Okay, I'll tell Bailey. So you look up your birth certificate and I'll look up mine and we'll let Bailey do her woo-woo act on us. Agreed?"

Peter kissed her to seal the deal. "Agreed."

9

THURSDAY, OCTOBER 17

"Did you lose Max? I don't see her anywhere." Jim was sitting at the usual picnic table, Chester at his side. Lia clambered up on the table next to Chester. Chester sat up on his haunches, showing off for a pet. Viola jumped up and sniffed noses with Chester. She snapped at him, then lay down, satisfied that she had sufficiently clarified her proprietary rights regarding Lia. Honey and Chewy meandered away.

"Viola! Be nice!" Lia admonished. "I left Max with Kate. I thought they needed each other."

"That was sneaky."

"I guess I'm a sneaky kind of girl. Can I ask you a personal question?"

"Depends. How personal?"

"You and Mary were married all your lives. What do you think made it work?"

Jim scratched his beard and pondered. "You have to cooperate. You both have to adjust. You adjust, he adjusts.

It doesn't work if the other person isn't adjusting, too. Neither one of you can say, 'that's the way it's going to be and that's it!'"

"Doesn't that mean that neither one of you gets what you really want?"

Jim scratched his beard again. "I never thought of it that way."

"Did Mary work?"

"She did before Jim, Jr. was born. Then she tried going back to work, but that didn't work out."

"What happened?"

"I was really unhappy about dropping him off at daycare every day, so we had a talk and she saw that staying at home was worth more than the extra money she'd bring in working."

"What if she had really wanted to work? What then?"

"Well, uh, I don't know about that."

"Uh-huh. You're not helping."

Bailey walked up with Kita. "What's on today's skull-duggery agenda?"

Jim gave Lia a betrayed look. "You're up to skullduggery? I thought I was your skull-whatsis partner."

Lia shrugged. "Renee thinks George's wife is behind his murder and Peter's not looking at her. So she's been sending me over with food to check her out. I had Bailey on surveillance yesterday." She turned to Bailey. "I think I've worn out my welcome with Monica. I need to get some painting done, anyway."

"I can deliver food just as well as anyone," Jim volunteered. "I can make a crazy cake. I can be just as dupla … duplia … duplis …"

"Duplicitous?" Bailey offered.

"Duplicitous. What you said."

"You want in on this?" Lia was amused. "I'm not sure how much we can find out by snooping around Monica. By the way, Bailey, did you hear from Trees?"

"Stacy's a straight A student, a member of student council and an all-around busy girl. No disciplinary issues. Jacob, on the other hand, has precarious grades and a handful of substance abuse and truancy related suspensions. No police record on either of them. Trees said he had a vision of a dog, a German Shepherd."

"Bailey, surely you don't believe–" A faint wolf-whistle emanated from the vicinity of Lia's hip. Viola and Chester pricked up their ears.

"What was that?" Bailey asked.

"That has to be Peter," Lia said, reaching for her phone. "I must have sat wrong. Hey, Kentucky Boy."

"As much as I love your ass, it doesn't have much to say."

"Sorry. I've got to figure out how to carry this thing so it doesn't happen so much."

"I enjoy getting these random peeks into your life. It's like surveillance without the guilt. I gotta go. Love you, Babe."

"Babe is a pig," Lia told the dead phone.

"How long do you think he was listening?" Bailey asked.

"I don't know, but he already knows about the food offerings. I think he finds our investigation amusing."

"Speaking, of," Jim said, "what are you looking for?"

"I'm not sure, exactly. Just trying to get a sense of Monica and her daughter, the dynamics. I think it's kind of a fishing expedition."

"Don't forget the hunk down the street," Bailey added.

"We think he's crushing on Mrs. Munce," Lia explained, "and she seems to be crushing back."

"After school, then," Bailey added.

"What's after school?" Terry walked up with Napa and Jackson.

"We're skulking," Bailey announced. "You want to be a skulker?"

"Are detectival pursuits afoot? I presume we are after the killer of the unfortunate George Munce? Who is the quarry? Suspects! I must have suspects!"

"Well, there's–" Lia began.

"Don't tell me, I'm cogitating. Obviously, you don't believe it is the scheming mistress, or you would just leave this to the police."

"Kitty is *not* scheming," Lia protested.

"That leaves the recently bereaved Mrs. Munce. Am I right?"

"She's at the top of the list, but her alibi is a problem. She was at work," Lia said.

"We think she had an accomplice," Bailey added. "Maybe the kid down the street. He looks like he could pull it off."

"Intriguing." Terry stroked his chin, pursed his lips. "I must pay my respects to the widow and put my ratiocination skills to work."

"You can't go before I take her my cake," Jim said.

"Wouldn't the owner of that dust mop you call a dog be upset if she found out you were visiting other women? I should take the cake," Terry announced.

"Make your own damn cake," Jim said. "You're not getting mine."

"Children, children!" Lia scolded. "Terry, it won't hurt for more dog park people to stop by. You're just going to have to find your own comfort food for the Munces."

"Tell me again why we're returning to the scene of the crime?" Brent asked.

"Because they always do it in the movies," Peter deadpanned. "It's supposed to inspire us."

"Sweet bleeding Jesus." Brent's head swiveled as a chrome car pulled onto the road in front of them. "If that isn't slicker than frog spit in August." He patted his steering wheel. "Celeste, Baby, would you like to look like that?" He turned to Peter. "How much do you think it would cost to have that done?"

"Chrome plating isn't much, but taking the car apart and putting it back together again will cost you. I bet that's a car wrap. You could do it yourself for around five hundred dollars."

"What's a car wrap?"

"It's vinyl with adhesive on the back."

"Contact paper for cars? On my Celeste? Oh my everloving Lord, I think I'm going to puke. I've never heard of anything so absolutely *tacky*. Pun intended." He stroked his steering wheel. "I apologize, Baby. Don't you worry your little head-gasket about it. I'd sooner trick you out in fuzzy dice and spinners."

"Justin Bieber has a chrome car," Peter said, straight faced.

"Tell me you made that up."

"Would I lie to you?" Peter's expression mingled mock-hurt with astonishment.

"I was lusting after the Bieber-mobile? How will I live with myself?"

"You'll manage."

"I think I need to pluck out my eyes."

"We've got eye wash in the first aid kit if you need it. Turn here."

BRENT PEERED up from the ground. "Are you communing with the essence of murder yet? Are you inside the killer's head? Thinking his thoughts?"

Peter looked down from his perch in the makeshift tree stand. "Wander over by that pile of downed trees, will you?"

Brent made his way to George and Kate's love nest. "What am I doing over here?"

"Giving me a chance to think. Say something in a normal tone of voice. I want to see if the sound carries."

Brent began to recite the *Pledge of Allegiance*. Peter listened with half an ear as the sound floated up. *Who are you? Why were you here? George and Kate only met after the hunters were gone for the morning. You weren't hunting.*

He caught a whisper of something, a scent that had been masked by the overwhelming reek of predator lure during his last visit. He leaned over. Sniffed. Whiskey, soaked into the wood. *Were you drinking up here?* He pulled out his pocket knife and a baggie, scraped up a small pile of the alcohol infused wood fibers and tucked the sample away for later testing.

"Come on back, Brent." He scrambled down from the makeshift aerie. "I think I know who our man is and what he was up to."

"Do tell."

"Stryker was hunting and brought along a bottle. Got drunk enough up there to spill some of it. Maybe he passed out, maybe not. He hung around long enough to catch the George and Kate show, listened in on their plans to meet again. He realizes he has an opportunity to kill Munce, but he doesn't want to get caught. He goes home, reports his bow as stolen and then pulls the tranny out of his car. The big question is, why did he shoot Munce? I think we have some more digging to do on William Stryker. We've got to find a connection to George Munce and break that alibi. We also need to come up with a plausible scenario for how he got down off that hill without his car."

BRENT POPPED the last onion chip into his mouth and looked at the empty slider boxes scattered across Peter's desk. "Remember, you promised. You cannot tell anyone I eat this stuff."

"I took a picture with my phone when you weren't looking. I'm going to send it to Cynth and tell her that's what she has to look forward to on your first date."

"You do that, and I'll tell Lia you've been drinking Pepsi again."

"That's low."

"Speaking of low, what could a low-life like Stryker

have to do with George Munce? Munce ever work for Hudepohl?"

"Munce managed that Dollar Hut for almost five years. I don't know what he did before that, but I can't imagine Stryker waiting that long if he had a grudge, can you?"

"No, I guess not. So where do you want to start?"

Peter pulled up Bill Stryker's police record, scanned it. "I say we start with the ex-wife, Colleen." Another search revealed that Colleen Stryker now went by her maiden name, Thomas. Peter tapped a few more keys to pull up her driver's license.

"Hel-lo."

"What is it?" Brent rolled his chair over by Peter so he could see the computer monitor.

"Look familiar?"

Brent narrowed his eyes, cocked his head to one side. "Let's see. Dump a gallon of peroxide on her head and put a red smock on her, and I think we have the lovely Carleen from Dollar Hut. Now isn't that a surprise?"

"Do you suppose he offed Munce because Munce helped her get away from him, or do you think he did it so she would get a promotion?"

"Could be, it's a twofer. Maybe he thought that was the way to get his punching bag back."

"Murder is a real romantic gesture. What do you want to do first? Talk to Carleen or pull him in?"

CARLEEN SMILED when they walked into the store. Peter noticed her front tooth was chipped. He wondered if the dental defect was courtesy of Bill Stryker.

"Back again? Did you find what you wanted on those security tapes?"

Peter mentally smacked his head. They hadn't even looked at the video files. "They were helpful. Thanks for getting those to us. Ms. Thomas, we have a few more questions for you. Can you take a break? Is there somewhere we can go?"

"Sure, we can go to the office."

Carleen informed the cashier on duty that she would be off the floor for a while. Then she led them through a door in the back of the store which opened into a small hallway. This, in turn, led to the stockroom. The employees' restrooms were on one side, a time clock and a rack of time cards on the other. Next to that was a tiny office.

The office held a small desk with an aging secretarial chair. Two stackable chrome and plastic chairs were against the side wall. A pair of battered file cabinets were against the rear wall.

Carleen had apparently started to make the space her own. The desk and the tops of the filing cabinet were decorated with chipped and broken knick knacks, probably salvaged from damaged merchandise. Her taste leaned toward cringe-worthy-cute ceramics that Monica Munce wouldn't decorate her garbage can with. On one filing cabinet, a struggling snake plant grew in a pot decorated with Halloween jack-o-lanterns and black cats. It was surrounded with a schizophrenic jumble of decorative objects. Peter imagined the antiseptic and oh-so-tasteful Mrs. Munce attacking the display while wearing a hazmat suit.

Carleen nodded to the two chairs, then sat at her desk. She swiveled her chair around, facing them. Peter sat. His chair rocked slightly. He leaned forward and rested his elbows on his knees to put his weight on the front legs.

Carleen looked at them expectantly.

"We'd like to ask you a few questions about your ex-husband," Peter began.

"Is this about Billy?" She gave them a confused look. "I thought you were here about George."

Peter ignored the question. "How long have you been divorced, Ms. Thomas?"

"Please, call me Carleen."

"About that," Brent said. "Your driver's license says your name is Colleen."

"Oh, everybody calls me Carleen. My baby brother couldn't get my name straight, and it stuck. I've been Carleen since I was in grade school. Why do you want to know about Billy? We've been divorced for six months. He hasn't done anything, has he?"

"We don't know," Peter said. "Shondra said Munce helped when you were having trouble with your husband. We were wondering how your ex felt about that."

"We were fighting a lot back then. I came in with a black eye and George was upset about it, and he kinda pushed me into leaving Billy."

"Did your ex-husband ever say anything about George?" asked Peter.

Carleen fidgeted. "No man likes it when someone interferes with their business. Billy wouldn't do anything about it. He was all talk."

Except when it came to planting his fist in your face.

"We're very concerned, Carleen," Brent said. "We believe your ex-husband's crossbow was used to kill George."

"His bow? His bow was stolen. He told me so."

"When did he tell you this?" Peter asked.

"Right when it happened, after he called the police. He called me, bitching about not being able to pay child support. He said someone took his bow right in the middle of his session of the deer cull and he wouldn't be able to give us any venison because of it. Last year he took a deer. It fed us all winter.

"Billy didn't kill George," Carleen insisted.

Peter did not note any of the usual signs of deception when she said this, or during her previous responses. Whether or not Bill Stryker killed George Munce, Carleen wholeheartedly believed he hadn't done it.

"Why do you think his bow killed George?" Carleen asked.

"We found the bow," Brent said, "with George's wallet and phone."

"You did?" Carleen's eyes went wide with fear.

"We find the coincidence interesting," Brent said. He pulled the photo of Kate out of his breast pocket. "Have you ever seen this woman?"

Carleen glanced at Peter, looked at the photo. She shrugged. "Maybe. I might have seen her in the store a time or two."

"Have you ever heard the name Kathleen or Kate Onstad?" Brent asked.

She shook her head, looked down in her lap. "Is that the woman you were looking for? Is she dead, too?"

"No, she's alive," Peter said. "We were wondering if there might be some connection between her and your ex-husband."

"I wouldn't know about that."

"THE FIRST THING out of Bill Stryker's mouth when he opened his door was 'I want a lawyer.'"

Peter was chopping onions while Lia tended to a pot of quinoa. She turned on another burner to heat a larger pot with olive oil in the bottom. "Put those in here." She gestured to the pot with a wooden spoon. Peter obliged. The onions began to sizzle. Lia stirred them with the spoon to keep them from burning. "You think Carleen called him?"

"I'm sure she did."

"Did you get anything out of him?"

"Nothing worthwhile. But we were able to get a warrant based on his connection to Carleen and probable motive, along with his ownership of the crossbow. Guess what we found."

"A dead body."

"Well, there was that."

Lia turned from the stove, her mouth gaping. "No!"

"Of a sort. He makes his own predator lure by closing up a raccoon carcass in a five-gallon bucket with water until the remains liquefy. Then he adds coyote urine for good measure."

"Ugh! Kitchen? Food? Did you have to tell me that when we're about to eat? Hand me the spinach."

Peter handed her a bag of pre-washed, organic spinach. She dumped enough to loosely fill the pot, then began stirring it so it would wilt without scorching. She lowered the heat and placed a lid over the greens. "Okay, fish."

Peter handed her two foil packets, each containing a

marinated tilapia fillet. She placed these into the boiling quinoa and covered it.

"Sorry about that. We found a slim-jim, which explains how he broke into Onstad's rental car. There were more than a dozen cases of beer from his old place of employment. We suspect he got those by illegal means. We're passing that tidbit along to their security people. We took one of his whiskey bottles. We'll compare that with the sample I took from the tree stand, to see if they match. The shocker was Munce's burner phone. He claimed he bought it off some kid, but you know how that goes."

"So Stryker did it? We were so sure Monica was behind it all."

"You never know. It wouldn't be the first time two disgruntled spouses got together to solve a problem. But I doubt they ever met each other."

"Jim and Terry will be so disappointed. They were both chomping at the bit to pay a condolence call on the Widow Munce. Jim was going to bake her a cake."

"Were they going to seduce a confession out of her? Was Jim going to put truth serum in that cake? I don't know what you expected to find out."

"You have to admit there's something strange about Monica. Can you put the silverware out? I'd like some water, too, please."

"Strange isn't murderous," Peter called from the table. "Leave the woman alone. She doesn't need any more grief right now."

"She's guilty of something. I know she's covering something up."

"Like what?" Peter asked, amused.

"I don't know, but now she's perfectly polite to me. I

can feel all this tension underneath. It's not natural. And her daughter is angry about something." Lia pulled the quinoa off the stove and removed the now-steamed packets of tilapia. She dished them up, along with the quinoa and greens.

"Yeah, I picked up on that. She's a teenager. Teenagers are always mad about something. That looks great. Much better than the sandwich I had planned."

"So, what's next? Is that it?" Lia asked.

"Not quite. We've got to tie the case up. He claims the neighbors saw him out working on his car all day, but I bet there was enough time for him to slip away. It shouldn't be too hard to break his alibi and figure out how he got down off that hill without his car. We hope to wrap it up tomorrow. Then maybe I can stop working so late. Have you decided what you want to do for your birthday?"

"No, I haven't. Really, you don't need to go to any trouble."

"Uh-uh. With this case winding down, I won't have to work this weekend unless a new corpse shows up. I want to do something fun. Your birthday is just the excuse."

"So I'm just a pretext for you?"

"In this case, yes."

"Pig."

"That's *Monsieur Couchon* to you."

10

FRIDAY, OCTOBER 18

"I see in the newspaper, they arrested William Stryker for George's murder," Jim announced. "It said he was once married to a woman who works at Dollar Hut."

"So we were totally off base?" Bailey asked.

"Looks like it," Lia said.

"Alas, my skill at ratiocination will not be put to the test," Terry said.

Lia turned to Jim. "I hope you didn't make that cake yet."

"I was going to bake it this morning. I might do it anyway."

"Do they know why he did it?" Bailey asked.

"They've got some ideas." Jim said. "But he isn't talking. According to the paper, he had George's phone and he owned the bow. That's open and shut."

"Murder by crossbow. A truly Medieval act," Terry said. "Did you know, a soldier could be trained to use a crossbow in less than a week? Whereas a longbow archer has to start practicing by the age of ten, and train continuously to keep up their skill. A good long-bowman can fire ten arrows for every single arrow a crossbowman shoots, and the range of the longbow far exceeds that of the crossbow.

"One pope banned the use of crossbows against Christians. You could only use them against Pagans and other nonbelievers. I have a vague recollection of a prof mentioning a Medieval pope who forbade the clergy from drawing the sword in battle. He said this led to an inventive bishop coming up with the flail.

"Now the flail, that's a weapon–"

"Terry? What does the flail have to do with anything?" Bailey asked.

Terry shrugged. "It's just interesting, that's all."

"Look who's pulling in. Isn't that Kate's car?" Jim nodded toward the boulevard.

KATE WALKED through the parking lot with Max on the long training lead. She was walking at heel, alert to Kate's every move. The group stared as the pair advanced to the service road, then disappeared from view as the road curved behind the rise. Kate reappeared when she reached the picnic shelter. Max was still heeling, still focused on Kate. She waved at the group in the large park before entering the small side.

"I've got to see this," Lia said. She called to Honey, Viola and Chewy and headed for the gate.

"Hey, there," Lia called from the outside of the small park. Max was dutifully following Kitty around in big circles. "Who is that you have with you, and what have you done with my dog?"

Kitty laughed. "Come on in," she yelled.

Lia entered the little park and her trio dashed forward to greet Max. Max looked up at Kitty, then raced to the end of her lead. The women walked over to the picnic table and climbed on.

"We saw Max walking with you. I can't believe it's the same dog. What did you do to her?"

"Renee explained to me that with a strong-willed or highly distractible animal, you have to find out what motivates them and offer them something they want more."

"What are you giving her? Doggie crack?"

"That's what Renee calls it." Kitty pulled an ugly brown lump out of her pocket and said, "Max come!" Max stopped sniffing Honey and raced to them. She sat, watching Kitty with an expectant look on her face. Kitty handed her the lump. Max snarfed it down and thumped her tail on the ground, hoping for more.

"What is that stuff?"

"Dehydrated liver."

"That explains it," Lia said. "Kitty, can I ask you a question?"

"Sure, go ahead."

"The police have cleared you, haven't they? Why are you still hanging around?"

Kitty sighed. "I guess I'm not sure what to do with myself. I took a leave of absence from work when I came up here to see George. If things went well between us, I was going to look into a new job and a place to live."

"You were willing to leave your friends and your job

and your life for him?"

"When you've lived without love as long as I have, it gives you a different perspective on what's important. George brought something special into my life, something I hadn't had since the night we met. I wasn't foolish enough to quit my job on his promises, but I was willing to be open to the idea that what he offered was real."

"What about his wife?"

"Naturally I didn't feel good about breaking up a marriage. George rarely talked about Monica, but I'm convinced their marriage was already broken before we met again. That thing I was missing, George was missing it, too. He broke his wedding vows with me, but I think she broke faith with him first by not being a true wife. She may have kept things together on the outside, but that internal bond was missing. I don't believe she ever thought of him as anything but someone to keep up appearances with."

"Why do you suppose he married her?" Lia asked.

"From what little I know, Monica represented a normal life to him. Very 'Ozzie and Harriet.' It took him a long time to realize it was all surface. I was married, once, to someone who slowly squeezed the life out of me. I'm now convinced he never really knew me and never cared to. It was a very empty life."

Lia sighed. "Can I tell you a secret?"

"Certainly, Dear. Sometimes it's so much easier to confide in a stranger."

"Peter wants us to get more serious, but I'm scared of exactly what you're talking about. I don't want to make that kind of mistake. How do you tell if it's going to work?"

"I'm no expert, but I did a lot of thinking after I got my divorce. I think time is your best ally in figuring that out. Too many people get married before they discover what the other person is all about. You've got to wait until the stars fall off your eyes. A good relationship strengthens over time, while a poor one shows its flaws. People either grow together or they grow apart. It's important to look to yourself as well. I had some very immature, Cinderella notions when I got married. It's important to make sure you understand your own motives."

"That's it? Just wait?"

"Just time," Kitty agreed, "and keeping your eyes open."

"Thanks." Lia paused, considering Kitty's words. "What are you going to do now?"

"I thought I'd spend today taking Max around to the other parts of the park, like you did with Honey. If Daisy is still in the woods, she might come to me. It gives me something to do, and Max enjoys the exercise."

"What about your trip?"

"I'm not due home for a few more weeks. I'd like to stay long enough to understand what really happened. I want to be more settled about everything before I go.

"I understand they arrested someone yesterday. The paper said he was once married to one of the women who worked for George, and that George helped her get her divorce. Do you know anything about it?"

"Only that," Lia said.

"He must be a very angry man."

"I HEAR BANJOS, and I'm outta here," Brent said as Peter

knocked on the door. Peter did not have time to reply before the door swung open.

Brian Dempsey was not what they were expecting. The yawning man stood five-eleven and was a touch stocky. Peter judged him to be in his mid-thirties. His hair was short, about one-half inch long, and he had a day's growth of beard. He wore sweat pants and a tee shirt. His clothes were clean. His eyes were intelligent. They held none of the bleariness of chemical pursuits, none of the animal cunning of the base criminal element Peter had been anticipating.

His expression was polite and relaxed. It occurred to Peter that he had heard no mad scramble to hide a bong or stash. He peered around Brian. What he could see of the living room was tidy.

"Brian Dempsey?"

"Yeah?"

"I'm Detective Dourson and my partner is Detective Davis. We're making inquiries about one of your neighbors, Bill Stryker. Do you know him?"

"More than I want to. Why do you ask?"

"We're looking into events that happened the morning of October seventh. Were you around then?"

"The seventh? That was a Monday, wasn't it?" He pulled a smart phone out of his pocket, clicked on a calendar icon. He yawned again, displaying well-tended teeth. "Sorry, I work nights. Monday, I don't have any classes until two. That day I had an eight o'clock dental appointment, so I got home from work around six-thirty. I had breakfast, left again around seven-thirty, came back around nine-thirty. I leave for school at one-thirty on my late days."

"Where do you go to school?"

"Cincinnati State." Another yawn. "I study electronics."

"Did you see Stryker that morning?" Brent asked.

Brian rubbed the back of his neck, frowning while he thought. "Not when I came home, not when I left for the dentist. When I came back, he was outside, working on his truck. I went in, slept until one. When I got up, I could hear him swearing from inside my living room. He was still at it when I left for class." He nodded at Bill Stryker's old F-150. "Swearing and banging on the undercarriage. That truck has interesting ancestry."

"He work on it often?" Brent asked.

"More often than not."

"Did you look outside at any time between nine-thirty and one-thirty?" Peter asked. "We're wondering if Stryker was there all morning, or if he might have left for a while."

Brian grimaced. "I never looked outside. I will say that there were a lot more parts on the ground when I left, and plenty of beer bottles. I think he was pulling the transmission."

"Were those Hudy bottles?" Brent asked.

"Don't know, but that's what he usually drinks. Is his beer important?"

"Just wondering. Does Stryker have any other transportation besides that truck?"

"Hell, half the time, he doesn't even have that."

BRIAN SAID one of his neighbors was usually home during the day and might remember seeing Stryker on the day in question. He pointed them to the woman's house, where a skinny hound was chained to the front porch. The hound failed to lift his head when they climbed to the porch, but a suspicious number of dogs set up a hullabaloo as Brent knocked on the door.

"Think she has licenses for all those dogs?" Brent asked.

"I wouldn't bet on it."

A stringy woman who looked sixty but was probably forty answered the door, accompanied by the strong odor of beer. She was vague on dates. She sometimes saw Stryker working on his truck, but she couldn't say when. In fact, she wasn't sure what day of the week it was. Brent told her it was Friday.

Peter concentrated on the road as he drove down the hill. "We've got a window of opportunity for Munce's murder. Based on the time he was supposed to meet with Onstad and when he was due in to work, it should have happened sometime between ten and one.

"Dempsey is a credible witness who puts Stryker at home immediately before and after the window," Peter continued. The postman is off for a long weekend and won't be back until Monday. No telling if he'll remember seeing Stryker or not."

"Stryker could have slipped out while Dempsey was asleep. Makes it harder, since our best scenario has him setting up in the woods before Munce arrives," Brent said. "How do you suppose he got down off this hill?"

"He had to have an accomplice. It's the only explanation. The accomplice sticks a screwdriver into Onstad's tire, then waits on Brestel where he can't be seen from the top of the hill. Stryker probably stashed the crossbow with him before he reported it stolen, just in case the responding officer asked to have a look around. His buddy drops him off with the crossbow and goes on his merry way. Stryker offs Munce and takes Munce's car. He disposes of the car, dumps it or sells it to a chop shop. Buddy picks him up, takes him home."

"It's tight," Brent mused, "but it could happen. So now we look for known associates. Why do you think he kept the phone?"

"Because crooks are stupid?" Peter suggested.

"Makes our job easier."

"Truth."

"You picked out a birthday present for Lia yet?"

"I'm working on it."

"Time is passing, Brother."

"Worry about your own woman."

"I would, but Cynth has yet to surrender to my charms. She obviously has no clue what delights are in store for her."

11

SATURDAY, OCTOBER 19

LIA ARRIVED AT THE PARK TO FIND HER FRIENDS GATHERED in the picnic shelter while their dogs lined the inside of the fence, watching. As she approached, Jim, Bailey, Jose, Terry, Kitty and a number of other regulars began to sing "Happy Birthday" to her.

Lia shook her head while she released her dogs into the park. She returned to the shelter to find Bailey and Jose lighting candles on a plain chocolate cake dusted with confectioners' sugar. The candles stood sentinel on the long side of the cake, so close together they looked like one long flame.

Jim had cut "Happy Birthday Lia" out of paper, laid the letters on top of the cake and sprinkled the sugar on top so that when he removed the letters, the sentiment stood out.

"We didn't know how old you were, so we put the whole box on," Jose said.

"Gee, thanks. You think I'll be able to blow all those out? Give me a minute while I crank up my oxygen tank."

"Don't forget to make a wish," Jim said.

Lia made a silly face while she inhaled. Making an "O" with her mouth, she blew, directing her breath at the long line of candles. Several people stepped in to extinguish the last of the flames when she faltered near the end.

"Does it count if I get help?" she asked.

"If it doesn't, it should," Jim said. He handed her a knife. "Here, you cut."

"What did you wish?" Terry asked.

"I'm not telling. But it wasn't for you to win the lottery."

"A dagger to the heart!" Terry clutched the wounded organ. "I thought we were friends."

Terry had brought a thermal carafe of coffee to go with the cake. He and Jose dispensed cups while Bailey gave out the cake. Lia took a piece of cake over to Kitty, who was passing biscuits through the fence to the assembled dogs.

"Here, I didn't want you to miss out. Jim's crazy cake goes fast."

"Thank you." She took the cake. "It was so kind of Jim to invite me. Renee wanted to come, but she had a meeting at the museum."

"I'm glad you could make it. I guess you didn't have any luck looking for Daisy yesterday?"

"No, but I'll keep trying. Have you heard from any of the rescue organizations?"

"Not so far. I hate to think of her still lost," Lia said.

"Somewhere, George is looking down and he appreciates what you're doing for her. She's such a sweet dog," Kitty said.

"Hey, Birthday Girl," Bailey called out. "Where is Detective Hottie taking you tonight? Enquiring minds want to know."

"Sorry, can't help you. He hasn't said."

"You mean he's a guy and he hasn't figured it out yet."

"Such scorn!" Lia admonished. "Bailey, you are a woman of little faith."

"I am a woman of extensive experience. I bet he still doesn't have a clue where you're going."

"He did say to wear a dress and heels. I don't know if I have any heels that don't have teeth marks."

"I didn't know you had a dress," Bailey said.

"HEY, GORGEOUS," Peter said when she answered the door. He lifted her hand and twirled her around, made a lingering inspection of her attire. "You sure do clean up well. Where have you been hiding that dress? You got any more like that?"

Lia looked down at the fuchsia silk cocktail dress decorated with gold bugle beads. "I trot this out for art openings. You don't think it's too much, do you?"

"I think it's so just right, we may have to miss our reservations." He gave her a wicked grin, pulling her close.

She shoved him back through the door. "No way we're staying in after I put lipstick on. You'll just have to suffer."

Brent's car was sitting by the curb. "Brent loaned me Celeste for the evening. He says you'll dump me for him after you ride in her leather seats."

"He does, does he?"

"We have a bet on it."

"Oh, really? What's the bet?"

"If you haven't dumped me by Monday morning, I have to buy doughnuts." He handed her into the A4.

"That doesn't seem fair. Why should you buy if you win?"

"He says the loser deserves a consolation prize."

"Oh, really?" Lia smirked. "So, where are we going?"

"We're going for a pleasant drive along Columbia Parkway. That's all I'm going to say."

"East side of town? Must be fancy."

"I'm not saying a word."

She had to admit, the A4 handled well. The sound system was superior, wrapping her in "Claire de Lune" while she sank into the buttery seats.

With most of the leaves down, Lia was able to see boat lights twinkling on the Ohio River as the Audi sped along the parkway. They drove into Columbia-Tusculum, where the parkway slowed and the road was lined with colorful Victorian houses. Peter turned right at Delta Avenue and pulled up to a valet in front of a Romanesque style brick building.

Lia burst out laughing. "You couldn't resist, could you?" she said, as she eyed the well-dressed patrons entering the restaurant.

"Can I help it if Urban Spoon says it's the best restaurant in town?"

"Uh-huh."

The Precinct was a thirty-year-old steak house occupying the former Cincinnati Police Patrol House Number 6.

"You just want to see some celebrities."

"I'm crushed. My only ulterior motive tonight is getting my hands under that dress."

Peter escorted her indoors. Lia took a seat in one of the antique barber chairs that decorated the lobby. Peter snapped a picture of her, then continued to look at his phone, punching buttons.

"What are you doing?"

"Posting this on Facebook."

"You're not."

"I am."

The hostess led them to a tiny rotunda lined with stained glass windows in a harlequin pattern.

Peter pulled out a chair for Lia. "If you'll notice, the only celebrity you can see from this table is a certain Cincinnati artist."

"Uh-huh. Keep piling it on, Kentucky Boy. At least I'm not overdressed. Where did you get that tie, anyway?" she asked, referring to his blue-on-blue Kenzo silk jacquard.

"It came with the car. Brent said I wasn't allowed to wear any of my ties here."

"You sure he's not gay?"

"Nah. He's just been reading too many Lucas Davenport mysteries. He wants to be the tough guy in the silk suit. I keep asking him if he also wants his face bashed in with a hockey stick. He seems to think John Sandford will write him into a novel without the scars. Next thing you know, he's going to show up with clocks on his socks."

"WELL," Lia said finally, eyeing the remains of her oversized filet, "at least we're going to have enough leftovers for the dogs. If I eat any more, you won't have to get me out of this dress, I'll bust out spontaneously as I'm getting into Brent's car. And no, you can't post a picture of that on Facebook."

"I'm giving up a lot here, if you expect me to pass on a chance to publicly humiliate you. I'll expect payment later. Shall we get dessert to go?"

Lia looked at her plate mournfully. "I think we'd better. I'm not going to be ready to eat again until Wednesday. Think it'll keep that long?"

They sipped coffee as the waiter took their food away to pack in one of Jeff Ruby's signature doggie bags. Peter pulled a slender pink package out of his pocket. It was an odd size, about six inches long and less than two inches wide, with an intricate silver bow. She looked at him sideways as she untied the ribbon.

"You didn't wrap this, did you?"

"I cannot tell a lie. Cynth took pity on me and did it."

Lia opened the small box and pulled out a keyring attached to an aluminum tube anodized a rich rose pink. The tube was about the size of a roll of nickels, but longer and covered in hatch marks. A small vertical line appeared on her forehead as she examined it.

"I don't want to seem ungrateful, but, what is this?"

Peter took the object from her. "This is called a kubotan. It's a self-defense weapon disguised as a key chain. Hand me your keys." Lia removed her keys from her evening bag and dropped them into his palm. Peter slid them onto the ring on the end of the tube.

He held the tube in this fist, with the keys hanging off the top, waved it back and forth. "Like this, it becomes a flail. You can use it to slash someone in the face, though that's the least effective use for it. You can also do this." He jabbed the tube up and down, like a dagger.

"You can break someone's nose or hit them in any of a number of vulnerable spots. I've got a training manual that shows you how to use this on different pressure points if someone attacks you."

He held up the tube, showing her a tiny hole in the bottom. "If you flip the safety and press the other end, it shoots pepper spray out of here. The pepper spray has a ten-foot range."

Lia smiled and shook her head, leaned over and kissed him. "Dourson, you are such a romantic. Thank you. This is an amazing present. Bailey will say that the first thing I should do with it is use it on you, but I think I know why you chose it."

"You don't want me hovering or worrying. Cynth gives classes in self-defense. I've reserved a spot for you in her next session. If I know you can take care of yourself, maybe I won't make you feel so crowded."

She leaned back and considered. Maybe this was what Jim had been talking about. He gives a little, you give a little. Thinking creatively so both of them could get what they needed: a way to be themselves and be closer at the same time.

"You're some guy, Dourson. How about we grab that doggie bag and see if we can make it home before my dress explodes?"

12

SUNDAY, OCTOBER 20

BAILEY HELD THE KUBOTAN DELICATELY BETWEEN HER thumb and forefinger as she examined it. She extended her hand so Kita could give it a sniff, then gave it a little shake and made the keys clink. "I don't know, Lia. It looks like a cross between a Medieval torture device and a heavy metal sex toy to me. He ask you to use it on him yet?"

"Ha. Ha. I happen to think it's very sweet and thoughtful. I just wish it didn't weigh so much." Lia set her coffee down on the picnic table. She stretched her arms over her head and yawned. "Sorry, late night."

Bailey gave the kubotan another shake. "Better than steak knives, I guess. Does this mean you're going steady? Are his initials engraved on this anywhere?"

Terry wandered up. "What's this? Do my eyes deceive me, or is this a twenty-first century pocket flail? A very attractive model, though you need more keys to make it effective."

"Hi, Terry," Lia said. "This is my birthday present from Peter. He says it's called a kubotan."

"Technically, a kubotan is made of hard plastic and has grooves in it, so it's lightweight and your hand fits it snugly. This is a self-defense keychain stick, a take-off of the kubotan. It was created for tactical use, primarily by female police officers.

"Its use is similar to the yawara stick and is greatly linked to 'empty handed' martial arts techniques. Of course, you'll want to deploy the mace before your antagonist ever gets close enough for you to strike them.

"But it will never replace a loaded gun," he concluded.

Lia looked at Bailey. Bailey turned white and said nothing. Leave it to Terry to forget about the last time she carried a gun, even though he had been the one to give it to her.

"No guns, Terry," she said with finality. "The wrong people will think I'm happy to see them."

"Touché," Terry said, and he wandered off to find Jackson.

LIA PULLED the kubotan out of her hip pocket and slid the key in her front door lock. The dogs milled around, tugging their leashes in opposing directions. She twisted the key and shoved the door open. The dogs preceded her as she stepped inside. She turned, shutting the door.

Strong arms wrapped around her from behind, pulling her into a bear hug, one large hand gripping the other over her solar plexus.

"Where's your kubotan?" Peter muttered threateningly into her ear.

"What is this, *The Pink Panther*? Are you going to be attacking me at random from now on?"

"Humor me," he growled.

"Okay, Cato. It's in my left hand."

"Bend your elbows and bring your hands up. Place your right hand on top of your left hand, covering the key end of the kubotan."

Lia dropped the leashes. "Check."

The dogs milled around, sniffing at the entwined couple, trying to understand why Lia wasn't getting their breakfast.

"Now, gently, because you really love me, push the butt end into the back of my exposed hand."

Lia looked down, sighted his hand and pressed the kubotan on top of the tendons in Peter's hand.

"Press in a little harder … a little harder … OW!" Peter dropped his hands.

"Okay, step away, turn around and don't flip the safety, but act like you're going to mace me."

Lia stepped away, turned, raised her arm and pointed the bottom of the kubotan at Peter's face. She applied her thumb to the button on the other end.

"Squirt," she said. "Did I pass?"

"Wouldn't hurt to get a little further away, but it'll do in a pinch." He shook out his hand.

"Did I hurt you?"

"You hear me say, 'ow'?"

"I thought that was just for effect." She took his hand. "If I kiss it, will it feel better?"

"It won't feel worse." He grinned.

She held his hand up, gave it a loud smack. "Help me unclip the dogs. So … did I pass?"

"That's one basic technique. Of course, you want to ram the kubotan into their hand about ten times harder, but you got the picture."

They released the dogs, who ran into the kitchen for breakfast. Lia doled out kibble as Peter handed her bowls.

"Are we going to do this again?" she asked.

"Probably. This and a few other moves. That'll give you a little confidence with it until we can get you into Cynth's class. The point is for you to react automatically if someone grabs you."

"And you want me to hurt you while I'm at it?"

"Only a little. Just enough for you to get a feel for the pressure points. Just as long as you don't start taking pleasure in it."

"Doing this will make you feel better?"

"Knowing you can handle yourself will make me feel a lot better."

"I think it would be more fun handling you. You have any more positions to show me, you big, bad, dangerous thug, you?" She traced a finger along his collarbone.

Peter gulped.

BAILEY SAT at Lia's kitchen table and shuffled a stack of charts. Lia and Peter sat across from her. Peter's digital recorder sat in the middle of the table. The dogs lay nearby, watching. Kitchen usually meant food.

"Are you ready for me to turn this on yet?" Peter asked.

"Go ahead," Bailey said.

"Wow," Lia said, eyeing the stack of charts. "This looks really complicated. I didn't know it was going to be so involved."

"Have either of you had your chart read before?" Bailey asked.

Peter and Lia shook their heads.

Bailey pulled Lia's chart out of the stack and turned it to face them. She briefly explained that the chart was a map of the sky and the position of the planets when a person is born.

Then she pointed out the complex arrangement of planets that made Lia an artist.

Lia's eyes began to glaze. "Wow," she said. "Interesting."

"It is interesting, because the placement that encourages you to develop your artistic talent also creates a conflict for you. Libra says you're all about partnership and cooperation, but the first house is very independent and places a priority on self and autonomy. And you're a bit of a control freak, with Pluto there."

Peter nudged Lia with his knee. She ignored him.

"Something very important is going on in your chart right now. See the little red sign outside the circle, shaped like an old TV aerial?" Bailey pointed to the incomprehensible squiggle. "That's Uranus, as it is in the sky today."

Peter raised his eyebrows, but resisted the obvious joke.

"It's passing through your house of partnership and marriage, and it will be there for about seven years. This suggests that any relationship you enter into has to allow more room than the traditional relationship, and that it is likely to have its own rules and be unusual in some way. Otherwise, it's not likely to last."

"Does that mean marriage is out?" Lia asked, deliberately avoiding Peter's eye.

"Not necessarily. It could work if it allowed for the individuality of both partners."

"Huh," Peter said. "What about me?"

"You're a Capricorn, so you tend to be conservative and believe in rules and social conventions." Bailey continued pointing out different planets. "One of the ways you can serve your purpose is to make the world a better place through a career that investigates death in the pursuit of justice."

"How about that," Peter said. "What about my anus?"

Bailey rolled her eyes.

Lia gave him a *look*.

"*Ur-an-us* is in the house of your finances for the next several years. That's also the house of your personal values, so it may just mean that you are changing your priorities. Usually, though, it means that your personal income and finances are unstable and unpredictable, and changes will be sudden. It can mean a windfall, or it could be that you lose everything."

"So I should go ahead and buy lottery tickets, but only one a week?"

"Exactly. I didn't spend much time on your individual interpretations, but there's one thing I want to point out before we go on to the comparison." Bailey held up the pair of charts. "See how all your planets are grouped tightly together? It's the same for both of you.

"That's called a bundle pattern. It signifies that you are high energy, highly focused people. It also means you are very confident in yourselves and single minded. And it is a sign that it's natural for you to believe your way is the right way. It takes special effort for you to see other people's perspectives."

"That's not me," Lia protested.

"You're a little different, because the Libra influence softens the tendency. Peter's moon is in Sagittarius. That can also dampen the effect.

"But you both have to make conscious effort to understand the other person's point of view and you have to make room for the object of the other person's focus."

"Don't you mean their obsession?" Peter asked.

"You could put it that way." Bailey put the first charts away and pulled out another that had two concentric rings, like a target.

"This is what happens when you lay Peter's chart on top of Lia's. This type of chart shows how two people relate to each other."

She pointed to a tiny 'male' symbol next to a tiny 'female' symbol. "That's Lia's Mars and Peter's Venus. Look how they're snuggled up next to each other."

"Aw," Lia said.

"This is the strongest astrological indicator of sexual attraction."

"Huh," Peter said. Lia elbowed him.

"Since it's Lia's Mars, it's likely she made the first move." Bailey looked at them blandly. Lia looked back just as blandly.

Peter held up both palms. "Don't look at me. I'll never tell."

See those little tridents next to Mars and Venus? That's the sign for Neptune. That brings in a magnetic attraction and a spiritual connection. You might even have a psychic rapport."

Lia looked at Peter. "Can you tell what I'm thinking right now?"

"Uh-huh, but not because I'm psychic."

"Peter's Sun makes a 60 degree angle from Lia's Moon. That's good for cooperation and understanding, and it's often found in successful partnerships and domestic relationships."

"Hmm," Peter said. Lia elbowed him.

"In this aspect, Peter's Sun is more active and it shows up in Lia's house of home, so he is likely to have an impact on her domestic affairs."

"Uh-huh," Peter said. He dodged Lia's elbow just in time.

"There are parental overtones to this placement, which means one of you may tend to treat the other like a child."

Peter blinked. He forgot to dodge. "Ouch," he yelped.

"Lia's Sun shows up in Peter's eighth house, which has to do with sex, rehabilitation and death. It also has to do with financial interdependence and business partnerships. So we have sexual attraction. Along with that, Lia can inspire Peter toward self-improvement and regeneration, which includes detoxing. And, at some point, you may choose to merge your finances."

"The sex part is okay, but I'm not going to drink her green smoothies, no matter what you say," Peter said.

"I find it interesting that this is also the house of death, and Lia has been involved with two of your cases, now."

Peter leaned back and folded his arms.

"See," Lia said, "it's not my fault. Blame the solar system."

LIA SHOWED BAILEY OUT, then returned to the kitchen, where Peter was tossing liver treats to the dogs. Honey was best at snatching these out of the air. Chewy always missed and snuffled around on the floor to find his. Viola refused to lower herself to such antics. Two treats lay on the floor in front of her while she gave Peter a you've-got-to-be-kidding look. Peter leaned over and handed her the treats. Viola plucked them delicately from his fingers. Lia stood in the doorway and watched him with a curious expression on her face.

He looked up. "You want to talk?"

"I don't think so. I need to process."

"You have to admit, it's interesting."

"Hmmph," Lia said. "She only said all that stuff because she knows us."

"I don't think so. She did offer to lend me her books so I could check it all out."

"Of course. You are the open-minded one."

"Be fair, Libra-Girl." Lia didn't respond. "Would you like me to leave?"

"Oh, I don't know." She sat on his lap, toyed with his hair. She didn't meet his eyes. "It's been a long weekend. I've had a really great birthday, but I guess I'm tired now. That was really intense, you know?"

He gave her a hug and put her off his lap. "It's okay. Can I leave Viola here for one more night? I'll pick her up tomorrow."

13

MONDAY, OCTOBER 21

"I HOPE YOU TWO HAD A GOOD WEEKEND," CAPTAIN ROLLER began.

Peter and Brent looked at each other. Whatever was coming, they weren't going to like it.

"Stryker's lawyer is raising hell that you never looked into his story about the kid selling him the phone. This makes a big, ugly hole in your case. While you were out carousing, Stryker met with Officer Forman and created an E-FIT of the guy he got it from. I want you to get out there and close that hole up." He shoved a copy of the computer drawing at them, then waved them out of his office.

"THIS IS NOT how I wanted to spend Monday," Brent said as they walked back into the bull pen. "Standing around a convenience store in a bad neighborhood. The locals will want to shoot us because we're interfering with their illicit business just by being there. You think anyone will tell us anything? That place is too close to Fay apartments, which is not exactly full of civic minded citizens."

"Cop? Danger? What part of that didn't you understand when you signed on? But we have a worse problem," Peter said.

"What's that?"

"You take a good look at that E-Fit?"

Brent picked up the drawing off Peter's desk. Shook his head.

"Squint your eyes a little and think back."

Brent frowned as he considered the dark hair and broody eyes, shook his head. "I give up."

"The day we interviewed Monica Munce. When we were leaving. The kid down the block with the evil eye?"

"I remember." Brent looked again. "Could be."

"Lia says he's been hanging around our widow. This could blow our case out of the water."

"Isn't that just peachy? Do we know his name?"

"No, but the funeral is tomorrow. I bet he's there. Stryker said he bought the phone around four. That fits with someone who's still in school."

"You really think there's something to this?" Brent asked. "What are the odds?"

"What are the odds of catching Ted Bundy with a traffic violation? It happens."

"You really think it could be some kid? What about school?"

"One step at a time. First we canvass the store. Tomorrow, we either see this kid at the funeral, or we find out his name and chase him down."

"BAILEY THINKS my present is a sex toy." When this didn't get a laugh out of Peter, Lia knew it had been a bad day. He slumped down on the couch. Viola jumped up beside him and whimpered for attention. He stroked her absently while he stared ahead.

Lia got him a beer and sat down on his other side. "Tell me about it," she said, combing her fingers through the hair hanging over his ears, brushing it back. It dawned on her that she was petting him, as he was petting Viola.

"We had to cut him loose. We had him and then we had to let him go."

"What happened?"

"He bought the phone off some kid. Witnesses saw it. And the postman places him at home when Munce died. Now all we've got on him is receiving stolen property, and that's iffy. Dammit! I just knew he did it. I hate being this wrong."

"So somebody saw him buy a phone. How do you know it was the same phone?"

"We don't. But we still had to release him, based on the postman's statement. The kid who sold it to him looks like that neighbor kid you said was hanging around Monica Munce."

"Really?"

"Yeah. Do you know his name?"

"Jacob. I don't know his last name, but I'm sure Bailey

has it because she had Trees research him. He's got bad grades and has been caught smoking dope."

"Big surprise. Do you remember his address? That's enough for me to run him. I hate duplicating work, but I need it on paper."

She wrote the information down and Peter stuck it in his wallet. "Are you going to the funeral tomorrow?" she asked.

"Yep. Gotta hope the doer feels compelled to say good-bye. Brent and I will be sneaking pictures of everyone and hoping for a Perry Mason moment. If no one confesses and tosses themselves on top of the coffin, we'll roust the kid and see what's what. He's young. Maybe we can scare him into telling us something worthwhile."

"You don't think he did it?"

"I'd hate to think he did it. Not exactly the same thing."

"I guess I'll see you at the funeral," Lia said.

"You barely knew this guy. Why are you going?"

"I feel connected to this. Max dumped his femur in my car. We found his remains. I'm looking for his dog. I would feel weird if I didn't go."

"I guess that makes sense." Peter nodded.

"There's this other thing."

"Oh?"

Lia took a deep breath. "I'm taking Kate."

Peter shook his head but didn't say anything.

"We'll stay in back. We're going to arrive late and leave early. There are other dog park people going, so we're going to hang with them. She just wants to say good-bye." Lia said all of this in a rush, reminding Peter of a teenager trying to talk a parent into an extended curfew.

"This could turn ugly." Peter winced inwardly. Why

did he have to sound like his Dad the day after Bailey said that stuff about parental tendencies?

"Kate's not like that."

"It's not Kate I'm worried about. Just be careful, okay? And try not to mace anyone, no matter how much they deserve it."

14

TUESDAY, OCTOBER 22

Lia drove through the iron gates of Spring Grove Cemetery and Arboretum. Kate sat beside her in the old Volvo, fussing nervously with the hem of her blouse while she stared out the window. The road dipped down under a stone arch, then opened up into four lanes fanning out into the Civil War era graveyard. Lia took the second road from the left, following a broken green line on the asphalt.

"Look." Lia pointed to a two-story obelisk keeping company with a miniature Greek Parthenon among pine and magnolia trees. They drove around the edge of a small lake, passing a pair of swans drifting by a weeping willow. "The carp in that pond are as long as your arm." Lia slowed. "Check this out. You won't see this back in Oklahoma." Ahead of them a lichen covered Gothic Revival chapel soared, complete with flying buttresses.

"Oh, my," Kitty said. "No, I don't think we have anything that old in Oklahoma."

"This is a National Historic Landmark. It's the second

largest cemetery in the country. I'm taking the scenic route so we won't arrive too early. You might as well enjoy the view."

Lia navigated narrow blacktop lanes mazing over gently rolling hills. She loved the quirky juxtaposition of monuments, from weeping angels, to a sphinx, to a dog resting on top of his master's crypt and more obelisks than ever existed in Egypt. They passed a pair of joggers stretching along the side of the road.

"I'm glad people use this for something. It's too beautiful just to keep dead bodies," Kitty said. "Do you bring your dogs here?"

"An unknown artist once called this 'a more magnificent park than any which exists for the living.' No dogs allowed, or I'd be here more often. The building on the other side of the gatehouse up front used to have a jail cell in the basement for people who drove their carriages too fast on cemetery grounds. You can still see the bars on one side of the building. They're very strict here."

Gradually the eclectic assortment of nineteenth century statuary gave way to modern gravestones, then to flat plaques embedded in the ground to create the illusion of an uninterrupted park.

"That row of cars is it," Lia told Kate. "I see Bailey's truck and Jim's Caliber. "We'll just hang in the back. It'll be fine."

"Thank you for doing this. I couldn't stand it if I didn't say good-bye to George, and I don't have the courage to come alone."

The group of mourners was smaller than it might have been. Lia suspected Monica wanted to avoid sensationalist gawkers and arranged a graveside funeral, a service which incidentally lacked chairs, as a deterrent.

Lia also suspected that dog park regulars would not have been invited except for her food deliveries. That, and the ongoing search for Daisy had likely created an obligation the very proper Mrs. Munce couldn't ignore.

People were dressed in everything from jeans to full black. Lia thought her own black broomstick skirt patterned with wild roses struck a nice balance between casual wear and formal mourning.

A clutch of women, black, white and Hispanic, stood to one side. Lia pegged them as Dollar Hut employees. One had a mass of fried blond hair with significant roots that echoed her running mascara. A young black woman wore braids spilling down her back, reminding her of Asia, a therapist she had seen the previous year. The women were mostly dressed in jeans with black tops. Some of them were probably going to work afterwards.

Lia looked over at Kate as they made their way up the slope. She was conservatively dressed in a borrowed skirt and low heels. They'd tried on a wide-brimmed black hat as a sort of disguise, but it was the wrong season and would draw attention instead of deflecting it. Kate hid behind a dark scarf and sunglasses instead.

A walnut casket was suspended over the grave, supported by a casket lowering device. This consisted of four heavy chrome rails mounted around the edges of the grave and joined at the corners by a series of gears inside a housing. The long rails could rotate and acted like spools for the casket lowering straps. With the excess rolled onto the rails, the straps formed a sling that held the casket up. When the service was over, the gears in the corner housing would be unlocked and the device would then be cranked, playing out the straps and lowering the casket into the grave at a decorous pace.

The edges of the grave were draped with green outdoor rugs that resembled Astroturf. Green rugs also covered the mound of dirt behind the casket. A spray of white roses lay atop the coffin. A photo of George grinned crookedly inside a frame of matching roses, hung on a skinny wire easel beside the dirt mound. On either side of the casket, floral tributes were mounted on more flimsy easels. A large and lurid cross of pink, spray-painted daisies stood out from the other arrangements. Lia attributed this excess of sentiment to the women from Dollar Hut.

Lia glanced nervously around the crowd, looking for Peter and Brent, hoping not to find them. A peek to the side revealed the pair observing the crowd from under a spreading oak. Peter caught her eye, lifted one eyebrow in a subtle acknowledgment. She shrugged back at him and resolved not to look in his direction during the rest of the service.

Lia and Kate stopped at the back of the group, behind Bailey and Jose. Bailey turned and whispered, "I thought you were never going to get here." She turned back toward the minister, who continued to drone on. Lia looked sideways at Kate. She suspected that behind her sunglasses, Kate was ready to bolt. She gave her arm a squeeze of encouragement and saw the woman's shoulders relax.

Lia plucked out a sentence from the reading.

"… As gold in the furnace, he proved them, and as sacrificial offerings he took them to himself …"

Lovely, cheery stuff. She found herself mesmerized by the faint drone that was the minister's voice. The service would have put her to sleep if she had not been standing up. Blinking, she focused, narrowing her eyes as she concentrated on the words.

"... He who pleased God was loved; he who lived among sinners was transported—snatched away, lest wickedness pervert his mind or deceit beguile his soul; for the witchery of paltry things obscures what is right and the whirl of desire transforms the innocent mind ..."

Did Monica pick that out? Did she guess that Kate would show up? Does she believe Kate somehow bewitched her husband and God snatched him away so he wouldn't be corrupted? A quick peek at Kate's resolute expression confirmed that the "scarlet woman" had heard every word.

Lia peered around Bailey, looking for the righteous widow. Monica Munce stood in front of the coffin, to the left of the minister. Her head was bowed and Stacy stood by her, a hand on her elbow. Lia estimated the widow's line of sight and decided that there were at least five people obscuring Kate from Monica's view. Still it would be best to leave as soon as the service was over.

THE SERVICE ENDED. Kitty watched as the crowd began to move, morphing into a line to pay their respects to the family. The space in front of Kitty cleared out. She froze, mesmerized by the rapidly widening space. She felt someone, Lia, place a hand on her arm. Monica and Stacy turned to greet other mourners and Kitty found herself staring right at Monica. Monica stared right back, her expression of shock transforming to fury.

"There she is!" Stacy squealed. "It's Dad's girlfriend! I knew she'd come!" Monica had Stacy's arm in a steely grip as Stacy struggled to pull away.

Kitty felt Stacy's pointing finger like a stab in her gut. Appalled, she turned from the goggling crowd and took off down the hill, scanning for Lia's car as she ran. She tripped over a pillow monument, falling in the grass, rolling over twice before she was able to stop herself. Knees stinging, sunglasses lost, stockings torn, and drowning in waves of mortification, she began hyperventilating. Lia caught up with her and put a hand out to help her up. Kitty waved her off, kneeling in the grass with her hand to her chest as she concentrated on breathing normally.

"Don't go! I want to talk to you!" Stacy yelled.

Kitty struggled to rise. Stacy broke away from her mother, brushing by the Dollar Hut women and stumbling into the casket lowering device. She stuck a hand out, grabbing onto the housing of the corner gear mechanism and shoving herself back upright.

As the woman with fried blond hair from Dollar Hut stumbled back out of Stacy's way, she tripped on the edge of the carpet and fell against the young black woman with long braids. Braids flying, the young woman fell against the portrait of George, knocking it over onto the pink floral cross. The women landed in a heap with roses and daisies scattered over them. George grinned in the grass several feet away.

Kitty froze as she watched the end of the casket slowly tilt down into the grave.

Oblivious, Stacy continued to run and shout, now only yards away.

As the unlocked and out-of-sync gears slipped faster, the casket picked up speed and tumbled into the grave. It echoed as it banged against the side of the vault, then crashed into the bottom with the sound of splintering wood.

Jim, Bailey and Jose ran to the graveside as the Dollar Hut women helped their two friends back up.

"Please, I really want to talk to you," Stacy panted as she drew up to Kitty and Lia on the side of the hill. Her waist-length hair was coming loose from the velvet headband that had restrained it. The headband itself was slipping forward onto her forehead. She came to a halt and took a moment to push the strip of velvet back on top of her head.

Monica erupted. Stacy turned at the sound of her mother's incomprehensible tirade and the three of them watched the chaos on top of the hill.

"Did I do that?" Stacy asked in a small voice.

Lia made a wry expression. "I think you did."

Stacy lowered her head. "I didn't mean to."

"We're not the one you should be telling that to," Kitty said gently.

Monica continued to yell incoherently as horrified mourners gathered to stare down into the open grave.

"Yeah, well I'm not going to try apologizing right now. You're George's girlfriend," she said to Kitty.

"Yes, Stacy, I was. I'm so sorry about your loss."

"I'm sorry about yours, too. How do you know my name?"

"Your stepfather showed me many pictures of you. He loved you very much. How did you recognize me?"

"I saw you, outside the store once. And the police showed us your picture." Lia winced. This hadn't occurred to her.

Monica screamed, "Get that out of there! Get it out! Get it out!"

Stacy held out her hand and Kitty took it, trapped by the need to share a moment with this girl who loved George. Stacy continued, "I could tell he cared about you. You know, he wasn't happy for a long time until you came along. I love my mother, but she was really hard on George. She tries to act like she's so nice to everyone, but she wasn't, not to him." She glanced back up the hill and rolled her eyes at her mother's hysterical outpouring.

A BURLY MAN was carefully lowering himself into the grave while a funeral home employee threw his arms in the air, objecting. Lia looked over at the oak tree. Peter and Brent remained where they were and watched impassively as the pandemonium played out. She noticed Brent holding his phone unobtrusively in his folded arms and imagined he was taking pictures.

"Try not to judge your mother," Kitty said. "Marriage can be very … difficult."

"She should have been nicer to him. I bet you're a really nice lady."

Lia saw the barrel-chested man steam down the hill, carrying a small cluster of crushed red roses, slinging them back and forth as he pumped his arms. He came up behind Stacy.

"Stacy," he ground out, making her jump as he placed a hand on her shoulder. "You need to go back to your mother. Now!"

Kitty stared at the odd bundle of roses as if it were dangerous. She edged back.

A mulish look crossed Stacy's face, then passed. "Whatever." She turned to leave and took a few steps up the hill, then turned back toward Kitty. "I'm glad I met you."

"Me, too," Kitty said, dragging up a hint of a smile.

The bull-like man glared at Kitty and shoved the mashed heart of roses into her stomach. "I'm sure you'd like these back."

Kitty clutched the roses as tears rolled down her face.

"You have some nerve, bribing the mortician into sticking your–" here he curled his lip. "–*tribute* into George's coffin. You humiliated Monica by showing your face and disrupting George's funeral. How dare you intrude on my family like this?"

"I only wanted to say good-bye to George," Kate blubbered into the roses.

"Haven't you done enough?" He demanded.

"Apparently she hasn't," Lia said, stepping forward to divert the man's attention. "You seem to think you need to add another ring to this circus. We were leaving. All you're doing is keeping us here. Stacy is the one who made a scene. Why don't you go talk to her about it?"

The man's face turned scarlet as he inflated with fury. "You leave Stacy out of this. Who are you, anyway?"

Rage is apparently a family trait. "And you are?" Lia tossed back.

"I'm Stacy's uncle. Unlike you, I belong here." He looked at Kate, opening his mouth as a prelude to more abuse.

"Problem?" Peter stood behind Monica's brother. His tone was mild, but firm. "I believe these ladies were just leaving. That's all right with you, isn't it?"

Monica's brother slitted his eyes and jutted his jaw. He turned to face Peter, who was several inches taller as well as standing higher on the slope.

"We don't need any trouble here, do we?" Peter asked. "I'm sure your family needs you right now."

Monica's brother jabbed an angry finger at Peter. "Just get them out of here." He stormed up the rise.

"My hero," Lia said, limply.

"Am I allowed to say, 'I told you so'?"

"I didn't mean for this to happen," Kitty whispered.

"Go," Peter said. "Please?"

PETER SHOOK his head as he watched Lia and Kate walk the rest of the way down the hill to the car. Monica's voice still shrilled from the hill top. He hoped Brent kept his eyes open during the chaos. It would be interesting to know what he noticed during Stacy's Rube Goldberg production.

Peter walked back up the hill against the tide of people now leaving the gravesite. Monica railed at the funeral director while his employees handed up fragments of the coffin. A seemingly chastened Stacy stood at Monica's side. Peter caught her looking sideways out of her lowered eyes. A smirk flashed across her face and vanished.

The dog park regulars were gone. Some of the Dollar Hut employees remained, probably so they wouldn't have to go back to work yet. They fussed with the garish pink cross, trying to repair the squashed and mangled blossoms.

Brent was an oasis of rationality leaning against the oak tree.

"What did I miss?" Peter asked.

"I got some lovely pictures of Monica before she regained her composure. Now that Mount Saint Monica has nearly blown herself out, she is doing an excellent job of pretending both Stacy and the offending coffin don't exist.

"Jacob," he gestured with his chin toward the young man standing apart from the family, "tried to help with the coffin but was rebuffed. He is now acting twitchy like there's something he wants to do but knows he can't. Either that, or his tie is too tight. He keeps looking over at our widow.

"Bubba seems to think he's in charge, and it's pissing off the worker bees. Bubba's wife knows that whoever's in charge, it's not her.

"The Dollar Hut crowd has been striving mightily to maintain their dignity since the coffin decided to interrupt the proceedings. I caught Shondra snickering. There were knowing looks between Monica's coworkers. I strongly suspect they find Monica's lack of control ironic for a school counselor. Amazingly, no one looked shocked by her performance.

"The widow has excellent lungs and should consider

changing careers to town-crier or pearl diver. Stacy keeps sneaking looks over here. Shame her little mishap aborted the party. We could see how long she keeps it up. Do you suppose it's my natural good looks and charm?"

"I think it's the great, big badge in your pocket," Peter said.

"I can only imagine what the mood will be at Chez Munce after this. Oh, to be a fly in the punch bowl."

They waited until, with a final look of longing, Jacob turned to go. Peter and Brent moved casually as they intercepted the boy, flanking him while looking as if they were just joining him for the trip down the slope.

"Jacob Cox?" Peter asked.

"Who wants to know?" Jacob's attempt at surliness came out petulant. Peter was certain the boy knew exactly who they were.

"Cincinnati Police," Brent obliged. "I'm Detective Davis and my partner is Detective Dourson. We understand you're a neighbor of the Munces. Family friend?"

Jacob gave a very adolescent shrug. "Mrs. Munce's my counselor at school. I do some yard-work for them. You shouldn't be talking to me without my parents."

Peter picked up here in their choreographed effort to keep Jacob off balance. "I believe your driver's license says you're eighteen. That is what it says, isn't it, Detective Davis?"

"I do believe you're right, Detective Dourson. I also believe the rulebook says we don't need your parents, young Jacob."

Jacob shrugged again. "Worth a try." He stopped by an ancient but well-kept Camry. "What do you want?"

"Your parents know you're here?" Brent asked.

"Yeah. What's the big deal?"

"We have a few questions for you. You can follow us to the station, or we can drive you there and have an officer bring you back when we're done," Peter said.

"I can't right now. I gotta get back to school."

"We'll give you a note," Brent said.

JACOB ELECTED to follow them to the station. Peter and Brent met him in the parking lot and escorted him through the tiny lobby at District Five to an interview room in the secured area in back. By mutual agreement, Peter and Brent remained silent until they entered the room, in order to unnerve Jacob.

"Have a seat," Peter said. He signaled to Brent, who left the room.

Jacob slumped into the plastic and chrome chair. Peter stood.

"What's this about?" Jacob's protest contained false notes. The nerves were real, but Peter suspected Cox had a very good idea what it was about. Still, you had to play the game.

Brent entered, carrying a large zip-lock bag and a file folder. He laid the bag on the table. It contained an inexpensive cell phone.

"Recognize this?" Peter asked.

Jacob blinked rapidly. "It's a phone." He shrugged.

"Look closer," Peter said.

"What's the big deal? It's just a phone." The wide-eyed look was now accompanied by an edge of whine.

"Not just any phone, young Jacob," Brent said.

Peter leaned across the table, hovering over Jacob. "This," he jabbed his index finger at the phone, "belonged to George Munce. Nobody knew he had this phone except one person."

"Until he died, anyway," Brent added. He pulled the E-FIT out of the file folder and placed it on the table next to the phone.

"This person," Peter's index finger now incriminated the E-FIT, "was seen selling this phone."

"So what, he looks like me. I've got nothing to do with this." The whine was now honed to a hair-splitting edge.

"Cut the crap, Cox," Brent said. "If we have to, we'll put you in a lineup and get a positive ID from our several witnesses. We just thought we'd give you a chance to come clean without the parade."

"What are we looking at, Detective Davis?"

"Let's see. On the low end, receiving stolen property. Could be theft. Then we've got impeding an investigation, interfering with a corpse and the top of the line includes your various murder charges."

"Why don't you make it easy on yourself and tell us about the phone," Peter suggested.

"Look," Jacob exploded, "I just found it, okay? I thought I could make a couple bucks. I didn't do anything to anyone!"

Peter stood up, folded his arms. "Convince us."

Jacob stared at the table. More blinking. "I was hanging out at Harvest Home Park—"

"When were you there?" Brent interrupted, keeping Jacob off balance.

"Uh –" More blinking.

"It's not a hard question, Cox," Peter said.

Brent went to a sideboard in the room, poured a glass of water out of the pitcher sitting there.

"It was after school–"

"What day was this?" Peter asked.

"Tuesday," Jacob blurted. "It was Tuesday."

"Which Tuesday?" Peter asked.

"Last week … no, wait, a couple weeks ago."

"What were you doing there?" Peter asked.

"I was just hanging, all right?"

Brent returned with a cup of water. "Here." He set it down in front of Jacob. You look like you could use a drink."

"Who were you hanging with?"

Jacob looked down, his eyes tracking his hand as he picked up the cup and took a drink. More blinks.

"Nobody. Just me."

"Anyone see you hanging with yourself?"

"I dunno. I don't remember."

"Where in the park were you?"

"On the bleachers, by the ball diamonds."

"How'd you find the phone?"

"I was just walking and it was in the grass." He took another drink, his eyes again on his hand.

"Where in the grass?"

Blink, blink, blink. "By the playground, near my car."

"So you just suddenly decided, 'no need to be a solid citizen and return it, I'll just sell it and make a few bucks'?"

"Uh, yeah. Like that."

They continued to badger Jacob while he told his story. The frequent interruptions kept him off-center and prevented him from having time to think. Eventually he finished, with an account of selling the phone to a man who fit Bill Stryker's description, at the time and date reported by Stryker.

"This is my problem, Jacob." Peter leaned over the table again. "You live four houses down from Munce, but you just so happen to find his phone in a place he is not known to frequent, the day he goes missing. Instead of attempting to return the phone to your neighbor, you wipe the memory and sell it. When Munce goes missing, you don't consider it important enough to tell anyone. And when it turns out your neighbor is not missing, but ripped to shreds by a pack of coyotes, you're too busy covering your sorry ass to let anyone know about it."

Jacob jumped up and shouted, "How was I supposed to know it was his phone? It's a prepaid!" He blinked furiously as he sat back down and folded his arms mutinously across his chest.

Brent's Atlanta accent tended to come out during interrogations. It was now so thick, Peter could smell magnolias. "Depending on when, exactly, you 'found' that phone," Brent drawled, "it either rang your ear off or else it had an exceptional number of new voice and text messages on it. Are you telling us you just ignored that?"

"I want a lawyer."

Peter waved Brent off. He turned to Jacob. "We're done with you. For now."

They escorted the red faced adolescent back to the lobby. Brent scrawled a quick note on the back of a business card and handed it to Jacob. "For school," he said. "They can call me if they need verification."

"Screw you, Asshole," Jacob said, tossing the card on the ground.

Cynth walked into the building just in time to catch Jacob's furious exit.

"My, my. Making friends?"

"I'm having better luck with him than I am with you," Brent said. "Why won't you go out with me?"

"Um, because you're getting lucky with teen-age boys? I wonder if I should report you."

The desk sergeant snickered. Cynth flashed her ID at the card reader on the door, letting herself into the back. Brent spun to catch the door before it closed again. She was already down the hall, her long braid swinging behind her.

Peter shook his head, tsking as he picked up the rejected business card. He put an arm around Brent's shoulder. "Real men don't beg."

"That must not have been a real man who was leaving plants at Lia's studio door last year."

"That was not begging. That was wooing."

"Uh-huh. 'Brent, she's not taking my calls,'" Brent mocked in falsetto. "'Oh, Brent, what am I going to do?'" He started choking theatrically as Peter's friendly arm slipped around his neck. Gamely, he rasped, "You were whipped from the word go."

Peter dropped his arm as the door swung open again. Brent straightened up as Captain Roller walked through, on his way to lunch with one of the lieutenants. He called over his shoulder, "My office. First thing tomorrow. I expect progress."

"Where are we going?" Brent asked. "Dinner is across

the street." Brent pointed to the small Chinese restaurant across Ludlow Avenue.

"Our food won't be ready for another ten minutes. I want to take a quick look in here."

Peter turned the corner, stopping at a tiny storefront on Telford Avenue.

"Oh, no," Brent said. "Not again."

"It'll only take a minute."

"We're looking for a murderer. Have you forgotten? Tomorrow morning? Roller? Progress?"

"Dust it off, Cupcake, you'll survive." A tinny bell jangled as he pushed open the door to the jewelry store, Brent on his heels. The interior was dim, the walls lined with glass-fronted, barrister bookcases set on top of matching oak cabinets. Each shelf was dedicated to a single semiprecious stone, containing loose stones, rings, necklaces, earrings and bracelets in a wide variety of ethnic and artistic settings.

"This is more like it," Peter said.

"I'm so happy for you. Let's go"

"Do I bitch when you waste time flirting with Cynth down in IT?"

"Yes, you do."

"That's lovely, isn't it?" a smoky voice said.

Peter looked up from the coral and turquoise Native American cuff he was examining to see a familiar face surrounded by spikes of copper and lime green. "Desiree, isn't it? You're a ways from the Comet. New job?" Peter could feel Brent salivating next to him. He unobtrusively stepped on Brent's foot and applied a gentle pressure. Brent cleared his throat and stepped sideways.

"You've got a good memory, Detective. Second job. I

decided to get serious about life after Luthor died. I'm learning how to make jewelry while I bartend. What case are you on today?"

"No case, looking for a ring for my girlfriend."

"You've come to the right place. What do you want this ring to say?"

"Excuse me?"

"A ring is significant, but you're not looking at engagement rings, so you must want to say something different. There's a whole language around stones."

"Huh."

"For example, diamonds are a symbol of innocence and constancy. So horribly patriarchal and boring. When is her birthday?"

"She just had it. October"

"Birthstones are a good place to start. For October, you have your choice of moonstone, tourmaline, coral and opal. Coral is believed to prevent ill fortune and offer protection from skin disease."

Peter shuddered. "Not a message I want to send."

"Then there's moonstone. Legend says, if you give your lover a moonstone necklace when the moon is full, you will always have passion. Moonstones can also reunite lovers who have quarreled."

"There you go, Brother, just what you need," Brent said.

"We don't fight. We discuss. There's a difference." Peter turned back to Desiree. "Tell me about the other stones."

"Tourmalines are healing stones. They heal emotional wounds. Pink tourmaline opens your ability to surrender to love." Desiree gave him a winsome smile with this.

"Giving tourmaline might be considered manipulative or even insulting, don't you think?"

She blinked. "You might be right. I never thought if it that way." She led them over to the last case. "Opals enhance creativity. They are the stone of love, but only to faithful lovers. They're supposed to bring misfortune to an unfaithful lover. Otherwise, the Romans considered it a stone of hope and good luck."

"There you go," Brent said. "Insurance. Guaranteed karma if it doesn't work out."

Peter said, "I like how opals have so many colors in them. She enjoys a lot of color." He started to mention that Lia was a painter, but considering Desiree's history with Lia's former boyfriend, didn't want her making connections.

"Most opals are made into cabochons. These are rounded, with a flat back instead of faceted. We also have natural stones in the matrix." She gestured to a bracelet featuring an oddly shaped opal with bits of rock attached, wrapped in an amorphous setting.

"Huh," Peter said. He straightened up. "Thank you, Desiree. I may be back." He turned to Brent. "Time to go, Grasshopper." They exited the shop.

"How many more jewelry stores are you going to drag me into, Brother?"

"None."

"Seriously? You've given up? Hallelujah."

"Nope, I made up my mind."

"But you didn't buy anything. What exactly did you decide?" Brent asked, suspicious.

"I'd tell you, but you know the drill. I'd have to kill you. Cynth would be so disappointed."

THE DOGS CROWDED around Brent as he hauled the sacks of Chinese food through Lia's front door. "Now I know why Peter volunteered to carry both laptops." He and the dogs made a sort of train heading into the kitchen, with Viola whimpering, Chewy bouncing and Honey taking advantage of her superior size to keep the lead. "No, Chewy, down. No jumping. Honey, that's Italian leather you're drooling on. Lia! Call off your dogs!"

Lia snorted, breaking off her hello kiss from Peter. "Sure thing, Brent. Shall I pull out the pepper spray?"

"I don't care what you do, as long as you– Honey, that's my crotch!"

"Sounds like one of your better dates," Peter called out. "You sure you want help? We'd hate to spoil the mood." Peter wrapped his forearm around Lia's neck. "Quick," he whispered in Lia's ear. "Where's your kubotan?"

"You're getting even with me for today, aren't you? Brent, I need a hand out here," Lia called. "Cato's at it again."

Peter tightened his grip. "Things could have gone smoother, but Brent wouldn't have been nearly so entertained. I'm suspecting Kate didn't tell you about her coffin insert."

Brent walked out of the kitchen. Alone. "The food," he announced, "is on top of the fridge with your *pets* gathered around it like pagan worshippers. If you want dinner, you may retrieve it. You people must live like savages. Please don't conduct foreplay in front of me, it offends my sensibilities."

"Hand me my kubotan, it's on the little table by the door."

"You sure you don't want me to mace him for you?" Brent asked as he passed it to her.

"Thanks for offering, but you'd probably hit me with the overspray. Okay Mighty Sensei, your devotee awaits."

Peter tightened his arm. "Notice how you can't breathe?"

Lia gave a strangled nod.

"Turn your face into the crook of my elbow." Lia complied. "Better?"

Lia took a deep breath. "Much."

"You know where my funny-bone is?" Peter asked.

"I didn't know you had a funny-bone, Dourson," Brent said.

"Ha, ha. Press the kubotan into my funny-bone. It should be easy, since you're looking right at it. Gently now, this is just for demonstration purposes."

"Food is getting cold, Bossman," Brent said.

Lia positioned the kubotan in her hands the way he'd shown her and shoved it into the outside of his elbow.

"Ow!" Peter dropped his arm. "I said, 'gently,' not 'dent me.' When did you turn into a sadist?"

"I'm hungry. Sorry about the dogs, Brent. They've never had the opportunity to see if you're a soft touch. I'll put them out back for now." Lia turned to Peter. "I'll dish out the food if you'll distract the hairy horde. Brent, you can set up the laptops on the coffee table. Darling, I had no idea you were talking about surveillance videos when you asked if we could have Brent over for movie night."

Peter was still shaking out his arm. "I saw a few art films in college. This should be right up your alley."

"I got a grade for watching them. What are you going to give me for watching these?"

He leaned over, nipped her earlobe. "I'll think of something," he whispered.

"HAVE I MENTIONED," Brent said as he sat on the couch with his chopsticks and a bowl of moo shoo pork, "how very amusing that little drama was that you staged with Stacy?" He still eyed the dogs, even though they had given up. They were now lying on their beds on the other side of the room, pretending there wasn't food around.

"What exactly was Monica screaming about?" Lia asked. "I was too busy getting Kate out of there to find out."

"Good thing," Peter said, "or she would have been screaming about you. Mostly it was about shoddy caskets that pop open and shatter and how dare they humiliate her by tossing her husband's bones around like that. She let everyone know she was suing the funeral home for sneaking in the coffin insert. She also demanded that we arrest Kate for trespassing."

"Trespassing?" Lia asked.

"Trespassing," Brent confirmed, "and a number of other things. It was quite the debacle. The pictures are priceless. I would post them on Facebook, but she'd know where they came from and Roller would not be amused."

Brent swiped at his pants leg, then lifted a pair of blond hairs with two fingers, holding them away as if they were contagious. "I presume these are Honey's. You know, I was going to offer to steal you away from Peter, but the dog pack is a nonstarter. I can't accept dog hair on my clothes. You give up the dogs, then we can talk."

"Um, thanks for the offer?" Lia said.

"Smooth, Romeo," Peter said between bites of his egg roll. "I don't know why women aren't falling all over you."

"Where are these movies you promised me?" Lia asked.

Peter pulled a trio of thumb drives out of his pocket and plugged them into the computers. He opened video files featuring a grid of smaller screens with a different birds-eye view of the store on each one. He increased the speed so the people on the screens were jerky dolls scampering about, Keystone Kops style.

"What are we looking for?" Lia asked.

"Anything that involves George and another person. Anything that looks hinky. People we recognize. The trick is not to fall asleep while we're doing this."

"Can you tell me what happened with Jacob?" Lia asked.

"Are you sharing vital case information with a civilian?" Brent asked.

"It's all right, Brent. I took a blood oath," Lia said.

"I figure she's less inclined to get into trouble if she knows what's going on, since this is so close to home. Do you want to do the honors?"

"I see. You want me to participate in this breech of ethics so I can't rat you out."

"Something like that," Peter agreed.

"Oh, ye of little faith. Oh well, in for a penny." They kept their eyes on the tiny screens while Brent recapped the interrogation. "The kid told the truth about selling the phone, but it's obvious he was lying about where he got it and who was with him at the time."

"How could you tell?" Lia asked.

"The kid was blinking more than Hugh Grant. Excessive blinking frequently accompanies perjury and prevarication. So I did this neat little trick that Peter taught me. I got him a glass of water. When he was talking about finding the phone, he had to look at his hand to pick up the glass. When he talked about selling the phone, he didn't."

"Weird," Lia said. She noticed two clerks yakking on screen, ignoring a customer. She wondered if George saw these infractions, and what he did about them. "How does that indicate lying?"

"Nervous people lose the ability to complete small tasks they normally do without thinking. They can still do them, but they have to concentrate. It's called unconscious competence versus conscious competence."

"Are there conscious and unconscious incompetence?" Lia asked.

"Indeed there are." Brent pointed with his chop sticks. "You can be bad at something and not realize it, like most people when they're singing in the shower. Or you can be bad at something and realize it, like knowing better than to grab the controls on an airplane."

"Then there was the bonus."

"Which was?" Lia asked.

"We got his fingerprints. They unfortunately did not match the prints on the murder weapon.

"Hold everything." Brent leaned over and hit the spacebar on one of the computers, pausing the screen. "There's Onstad, in the housewares department with Munce."

"Does she have a candlestick with her? The rope?" Lia asked. "Maybe the lead pipe?"

Peter rolled his eyes and shook his head while he paused the other computers. "Back it up a bit so we can watch the whole thing."

Brent obliged, making a note of the time stamp at the beginning of the sequence then starting the video again. Kate was back in linens, lingering over some towels when George walked up. George took a quick look around before he approached Kate.

"Aw, they're holding hands," Lia cooed.

The pair talked while pretending to confer over curtains. George took another quick look around, then took Kate's face in his hands and kissed her thoroughly.

"Reality TV at its finest," Brent said. "The man has moves,"

"Isn't this better than 'The Bachelor'?" Peter asked.

"Only if she slaps him," Lia said. "Or maybe if the women clerks gang up on her in the parking lot."

"Vicious," Brent said.

"That's my girl," Peter said, giving Lia a squeeze.

Dinner was finished. The remains were in the fridge and the dishes in the sink. Lia was drowsing with her head on Peter's lap. She found the videos did not lose anything when viewed sideways.

"Huh," Peter said. "That's interesting." He pressed the space bar and paused the video.

"What is it?" Brent asked

"Stacy, in the store," Peter said. "Talking to Carleen. I didn't realize they knew each other. Let's keep an eye on her, see what she's up to in Dad's store."

Lia sat up. They all leaned forward, peering at the

screen. Peter gave a running commentary. "There she is, heading toward the back of the store. ... Now she's looking around ... spots something or someone. ... She's out of this camera ... into the next ... hurries toward the door to the back. ... Now she's in that little hallway. Probably going to the restroom. ... Nope, into Dad's office, and out of camera range."

"Fascinating," Brent said. "Wonder what she wants in there."

"Door is opening again, here comes our girl ... Whoa!" Peter said.

"Bingo," Brent said.

"Huh?" Lia said. "What just happened?"

15

WEDNESDAY, OCTOBER 23

"I don't know why you need Stacy again," Monica complained as she and her daughter entered the interview room. "Or why we needed to come all the way out here. I don't appreciate having to take time off from work. I had to cancel appointments. You're not the only ones with an important job."

"Mottthhheeeerrr," Stacy whined.

"Hush," Monica snapped.

"Please be seated," Brent said. "Can I get you some water?"

"Water? How long are you planning to keep us here?" Monica demanded.

Stacy rolled her eyes to the ceiling and huffed an aggrieved sigh.

"That depends on Stacy, Mrs. Munce," Peter said.

"What has Stacy done? I insist that you tell me!"

"Mrs. Munce, we are conducting a formal interview," Peter explained. "We will be asking the questions. You are here to advocate, should Stacy's rights be in question. You may, of course, terminate this interview at your discretion. However, I think you'll want to hear what we have to say.

"You are not here to answer questions at this time. It would be helpful if you would remain silent. We need to find out what Stacy knows, not what you want her to say."

Monica glared at Peter. "Stacy, sit up straight. You know better than to slouch like that."

Stacy ignored her mother and stared at her hands, her long hair curtaining her face. "What do you want to know?" she mumbled.

"Stacy," Brent began, "we were reviewing security tapes taken at your stepfather's store the night before he disappeared."

"So?"

"How well do you know Carleen Thomas?" Peter asked.

Stacy shook her head and continued staring at the table. "Just a little. From the store."

"Stacy! What did I tell you about associating with the trash in that place?"

"They're just people. There's nothing wrong with being *nice*, Mother. Aren't you always telling me to be *nice* to people?"

Brent set two glasses of water in front of Stacy and Monica while giving Monica a warning look.

"Stacy, what did you and Carleen talk about that night?" he asked.

Stacy took a sip, while eyeing Brent. "Nothing. I just said hello and said I was going to use the restroom in back."

"Did you?" Peter asked.

"Did I what?"

"Use the restroom."

Stacy locked eyes with Peter for three very long seconds. She dropped them back to the table. "No."

"Tell us about that. What did you do instead, Stacy?" Brent asked.

"Why are you bothering to ask? You already know, don't you!" Stacy accused. "Why don't you tell her!" She jerked her head at her mother, whipping her hair around. She shoved it back behind her shoulder, angry.

"All right," Peter said, "why did you take your stepfather's second phone, Stacy?"

"What?" Monica screeched. "Stacy, you didn't!"

"I didn't mean for anyone to get hurt," Stacy pleaded.

"What do you mean, Stacy? What are you talking about?" her mother demanded.

"Mrs. Munce, please let us ask the questions," Brent said. "Why did you take the phone, Stacy?"

"I just wanted to scare her off. I didn't want George to leave."

"Are you talking about Kate Onstad, Stacy?" Peter asked.

"Yeah, her."

"What made you decide to scare her off?" Peter asked.

"George kept saying on those Kindle notes that he wanted to be with her forever. I knew he was going to leave us. So I thought I could pretend to be him and break them up."

"How did you try to break them up, Stacy?" Brent asked.

"I already hacked his Kindle account. I knew he used

either my name or DaisyBug for his password, so it was easy. Anyway, he usually left his Kindle at home. I think they were passing Kindle notes when he was hanging around the house, like kids sneaking notes in class. He probably figured it was safer than chatting online.

"I stole his phone. I knew they were going to meet that Monday, so I …" Here she stumbled. "I punctured Kate's tire that morning."

Monica shot up straight and drew breath to speak. Brent gave her a quelling look. She settled back in her chair.

"Didn't you have a student council meeting that morning?" Peter asked.

"I didn't go," she said quickly.

"I suspect," Brent said with an extra coating of Tupelo honey, "that if we check the attendance roster at that meeting, you were there. I also suspect you made sure people knew you were there, because you knew somebody was letting the air out of Monica's tire. Who did you ask to help you, Stacy?"

"I just wanted everything to go back to normal," Stacy mumbled.

Peter gentled his voice. "Who helped you, Stacy?"

Her head bowed in misery, Stacy said, "Jacob did."

At this point Monica launched into a screaming rant. "I told you NEVER to go near that boy! How could you do this to me! Do you see what he did? He killed George!" The rest of Monica's rant was lost as her voice shrilled beyond coherence. Peter and Brent stood back, waiting for her to wind down.

Stacy shouted back at her mother, her voice escalating. "He did not! He did not! He did not!"

"Should I pull out my Taser?" Brent asked Peter, leaning close so Peter could hear him over the cacophony.

"Give them a minute."

Monica stopped to glug down some water.

"Mrs. Munce?" Brent asked. "May we step outside for a moment? You'll be able to see Stacy the whole time, I promise."

They went out of the interview room. Peter could see Monica watching Stacy through the tiny window in the door. Brent would handle her.

"Detective Dourson?" Stacy asked timidly.

He looked over at her, lifted his eyebrows.

"What's he saying to her?"

"Just getting her to calm down so we can continue our interview."

"I wish she wasn't here. You see how she is. It'll be worse when we get home."

"Do you want us to call Children's Services?" Peter asked.

"No, she won't hit me. She just yells, and it'll last for hours. Normally, she wouldn't lose it in front of you. She'd be all polite and concerned. I think this has really flipped her wig. Tonight it's going to be all 'this is going to ruin me' and 'I didn't give you all the things I never had to see you throw yourself away on that white trash.'"

"I'm sorry about that. We really have no choice. You're only sixteen."

"Yeah. Two more years of this shit. You see why I didn't want George to go? He was my only defense."

"You're doing really well. You're telling us the truth, and that's important. What made you decide to be honest?"

"You're thinking things about Jacob that aren't true. He called me yesterday and told me. He didn't tell you everything because he wanted to protect me. He was going to let himself get charged for something he didn't do. I can't let him do that."

Monica returned to the room, followed by Brent.

"What did you say while I was gone, Stacy? You really should not have been talking while I wasn't here." Peter noted that Monica's voice was octaves lower and a hundred decibels softer. He thought he detected slight hesitations that suggested she was struggling with her control.

"I told him I was being honest because if I'm not, everyone will think Jacob did something he didn't do."

Monica stiffened.

"Remember our bargain," Brent said softly. He remained close to Monica.

"Please, Stacy," Peter said, "tell us what happened, in your own words. We won't interrupt. Do I have everyone's permission to turn on a recorder? Mrs. Munce?"

Monica jerked a nod. Peter set up his recorder and Stacy began talking.

"Jacob and I started seeing each other last spring. I met him when I was tutoring students for the SATs. I took them early and did really well, so they asked me to help." She turned to her mother. "I knew you didn't approve of him, so I asked George what to do."

Monica drew in a sharp breath and her nostrils flared. Brent gave her a repressive look before she could interrupt. Monica clenched her lips together until they were barely visible. She crossed her arms and glared back.

"George suggested that Jacob start doing some yard

work at our house as a way for you to get to know him better, and maybe you'd realize that he's better than you think. George said he was a punk when he was Jacob's age and it was love that made him realize he didn't want to live that way. He understood.

"I stumbled on the Kindle thing, like I told you. I was telling the truth when I said I didn't realize it was George leaving the messages. I just thought it was really cool that two old people that hadn't seen each other since high school finally got together again and were so hot for each other. When he asked her to come to Cincinnati, the things he said made me realize it was George. Then he started talking about finding a way to be with her.

"I knew that meant leaving us, so I freaked. At first I thought, hey, most internet relationships don't survive the face to face. It's not real, you know? But she came, and the messages kept getting hotter.

"I thought I could mess things up and make her think he was breaking up with her, and she'd leave. He was asking her to stop by the store, so I started driving by, hoping to catch her.

"I saw her and saw what car she was driving, and I knew where she was staying because that was on the Kindle. I knew about the other phone because he told her on the Kindle when he was going to call her, and when she could call him, and the number he gave her wasn't his regular cell number. They always arranged their calls when George was working, so I figured out he was keeping the other phone at the store.

"I picked a day when I knew they were going to meet, and the night before, I stopped by the store and stole George's phone so he couldn't talk to Kate. I knew he'd just figure one of the customers snuck into his office and took it. I forgot about the surveillance video being back there. If he hadn't died, I would have been so busted."

"What happened after that, Stacy?" Peter urged.

"The next morning, Jacob went to Kate's motel and stuck a screwdriver in her sidewall. I wanted to make sure she couldn't meet George. She started calling and sending texts, and I ignored them. Then I sent her a text that said not to call anymore, ever. And I went on George's Kindle and left her a message, pretending to be him. I said I was really sorry, but I couldn't be with her anymore, and please don't make things any harder than they were already by contacting me, meaning him."

"That's all we did. Then Dad didn't come home, so I freaked and gave the phone to Jacob and asked him to get rid of it. I didn't know he was going to sell it. He ran into Mr. Stryker and since he sort of knew him, Jacob figured he wouldn't ever tell anyone where he got the phone. That's all that happened!"

"Stacy," Peter asked, "how did Jacob know Bill Stryker?"

"Um, not sure, exactly. Dad showed me a picture of Mr. Stryker and a picture of his truck months ago, because I was coming around the store and Carleen was having problems with him. Jacob and I were driving past the store, and I spotted him sitting in that old truck, staring at the store. I pointed him out to Jacob, and Jacob said he knew him, and he was a jerk."

"Did you tell your dad about seeing Stryker?" Peter asked.

"Yeah, but since he was sitting outside the limits of the restraining order, there wasn't anything anyone could do."

"Stacy," Brent said, "why are you so certain that's all Jacob did? If he knew Bill Stryker, he probably knew about the crossbow. We already know he knew about Kate Onstad's car."

"He wouldn't do that! If he did, why would he sell Dad's phone to the guy who owned the crossbow?"

"Because," Brent said, "sometimes people just don't think."

"But why would he kill George? He liked George!"

"We don't know, Stacy," Peter said. "That doesn't mean he didn't do it."

A VISIT to each school office determined that while Stacy had been in class all day on October 7, Jacob had been missing and had an unexcused absence. The secretary also informed Peter and Brent that Jacob was currently absent.

"Damn kid said he wanted a lawyer before we could ask how he knew Stryker," Peter said. "Looks like we get to call him back in."

"When we find him, you mean," Brent said. "We lose him and Roller will be all over our asses."

The school secretary had been kind enough to give them work numbers for Mr. and Mrs. Cox. Calls to Jacob's apathetic parents revealed that they had no idea where their son went when he was truant, and that they had given up on finding out. Mr. Cox, especially, treated the call from the police as an inevitability he had been expecting for a long time. Peter put out a BOLO for Jacob's car.

"Looks like we're headed back up to Balmoral," Peter said.

"Just when I thought this day couldn't get any more interesting," Brent said.

Stryker was not home. Dempsey was, and he identified Jacob as someone he'd seen around Stryker's place a number of times several months earlier. "Not recently though," he said. He had no idea what the kid had been doing with Stryker. Peter left his card in Stryker's door with a note to call him, which he was sure Stryker was going to ignore.

"It's curious," Brent said as they drove back down the hill. "Stryker knows Jacob and he gives us Jacob's face, but not his name. Why do you suppose that is?"

"I figure Stryker was totally pissed that he wound up with that phone. He's pissed enough at Jacob to give us his face, but he still has a thing about not being a rat, so he doesn't tell us who he is. Or he wants to be truthful enough that witnesses will verify his story and get him off the hook. Maybe he didn't really want us to find Jacob. Maybe Jacob knows things he doesn't want Jacob sharing. Maybe all of the above."

"Whatever it is that young Jacob might know, it must implicate him as well, because he sure didn't volunteer it during our interview," Brent said.

"Criminals."

"You said it. You think the Widow Munce could clue us in on the Cox boy?"

"I'm sure she'd love to," Peter said, "but she won't without Jacob's signed release of information. So let's track down the parents again and find out from them what Jacob Cox has been up to that has him visiting the school counselor."

"HOLD ON A MINUTE, ASIA." Lia pulled her cell phone out of her pocket, checked the screen. She was sitting in the therapist's office, a warm and stylish room featuring tapestried armchairs and soft throw pillows. Restful slate blue walls complemented richly hued artworks, including a small yellow, gold and green painting of Saint John's wort. Lia had traded it to her in lieu of a portion of her fees.

"Did it ring? I didn't hear anything," Asia said.

"No, I just wanted to make sure I hadn't butt-dialed Peter before I said anything. I've got to figure out how to stop doing that.

"The other day he told me I accidentally called him while he and Brent were waiting to talk to his captain. I was singing to the dogs and they were chiming in. Before he could switch his phone off, Brent reached over and put it on speaker. Roller's secretary found it very amusing. She thought I sounded like the love child of Kate Bush and Tom Waits."

Asia laughed. "That's a compliment, isn't it?"

"I hope so. Depends on how she feels about Tom Waits."

"We haven't talked in months," Asia said. "What brought you in to see me today? Are your symptoms coming back?" Asia referred to Lia's bout with acute stress disorder the previous year.

"Not that. It's Peter."

"What about Peter?"

"We've talked about my relationship with Peter before, my trust issues, and I'm making progress. Now Peter is talking about moving in together again, and I'm not sure I want to take that step. But I don't want to endanger our relationship. I'm comfortable the way things are. I've been talking to my friends about this and it occurred to me I should discuss it with a pro."

"I see. As I recall, your biggest issue is loss of autonomy."

"That, and the financial issues. And I know it's selfish, but I like having my place exactly the way I want it."

"How much time are you and Peter spending with each other?"

"I see him at least twice a week. He usually stays over."

"How do you feel when he's gone? Do you miss him?"

"Not when I'm working. Sometimes at night I miss him. Cuddling with Honey and Chewy isn't quite the same."

"Are there any other reasons for you to set limits on your relationship with him?"

"I haven't talked about this with anyone before, but I like knowing when I'm going to see him and when I'm not going to see him. It frees me up to go about my life.

"When I was living with Tom, everything had to include him. If he wasn't there, I wound up waiting for him and wondering when he was going to get home. And if I wanted to do something and he didn't want to, then I never got to do it. I had less room in my head for making art.

"I know part of it was him being a jerk, but part of it was me getting wrapped up in the relationship and not setting limits. I'm not sure if I can set those boundaries if I get that close to Peter. What we have right now is so good. I don't want to screw it up."

"I see," Asia responded. "I've thought about this a lot, what it means to be single and to be married, looked at it from the outside and the inside. It's a huge issue for many people.

"No person is ever really single, not a healthy person, anyway. We all need others to survive: physically, emotionally and spiritually. As a longtime, single person, you've built up a community of support. Your dog park friends provide you with human contact, even during those periods when you are totally immersed in your work and think you're shutting the world out.

"A mistake many couples make is to believe that their partner is all they need. When they do that, they start closing themselves off to other relationships. They may even take on a 'you and me against the world' mentality. Then they begin to expect things from each other that the other person just doesn't have the capacity to give. No one person can be all things to another human being.

"I think, on some level, you're aware of this, above and beyond your intimacy issues. It's critical that you build a definition of intimacy that has a place for community. Your community, Peter's community, and the community you share.

"Does Peter have friends of his own?"

"He's got Brent," Lia said. "He likes Jim and Jose at the park, but they've never done anything together away from the park. They've got a softball team at the station and he plays."

"What does he do on his days off?"

"If we're not doing something together, he mostly watches sports on TV."

"Normally I would be concerned about him spending all his personal time vegging out. However, Peter has a very demanding job and he's interacting with people much of the time. It's quite possible that he needs time to himself to regenerate.

"Whereas you spend your working hours alone and need stimulation and social engagement when you're not working. It's a fundamental difference. In many couples, it would be a major source of conflict. In your case, your needs may be complimentary. Peter might need private space as much as you need your autonomy."

"It's not just that. He's also very protective. I find it a bit stifling."

"Protective, how?"

"He's concerned that something will happen to me again. He gave me a kubotan for my birthday." Lia fished her keys out of her pocket and handed them to Asia. "It's got pepper spray, too."

Asia examined the rose-colored tube. "I've seen these before. This is designed for police duty. How do you feel about having it?"

"I'm thinking it's his way of protecting me when he's not there, so he doesn't worry about me so much. He also signed me up for self-defense classes."

"That may be so, but how do you feel about it?"

"Kinda warm and fuzzy, in an odd way."

"Has Peter ever attempted to limit who your friends were or your contact with them?"

"There was last year. He didn't want me being around anyone alone."

"Are you referring to the 'Bucky' situation?"

"Yes, back then."

"How do you feel about that in retrospect?"

"I didn't like it at the time." She shrugged. "Turns out he was right to be concerned. If I had listened to him, I might not have a bullet hole in my leg."

"Does he still try to restrict your friendships?"

"No, why?"

"Sometimes controlling behavior is misinterpreted as 'protective' and it winds up isolating a woman from her other relationships. It's one of the first signs of an abuser."

"Oh, no, nothing like that. He wants me to keep the screen door locked if I have the front door open, park near streetlights at night, stuff like that.

"He's unhappy about me associating with this woman, Kate, but that's because she's connected with a murder he's investigating. She's a person of interest. Someone stashed evidence in her car. He says he doesn't want me near someone who has drawn the attention of a murderer."

"How do you feel about that?"

"He has a point. I like Kate, and I can't help running into her since she's staying with my best customer. But I'm willing to take precautions."

"Does Peter get angry when he knows you're seeing her?"

"He'll sigh, but he lets it go."

"Sounds like you think his concern is reasonable. Is that correct?"

"Pretty much."

"Does he ever suggest that you don't need to work so much and that he would like to take care of you?"

"No, huh-uh."

"How would you feel about it if he did?"

"I wouldn't like it. My art isn't just about money, it's my life. Anyone who loves me should understand that. Why do you ask?"

"I haven't talked to you in a long time, so I don't know how things have been going with Peter. This is another one of those red-flags for an abusive partner. Sometimes the offer is perfectly generous, but other times it's a way for a man to make a woman totally dependent on him, so he can gain control."

"No, it's nothing like that."

"Okay. I just had to make sure."

"You're scaring me a bit. Peter is not abusive or controlling. He's just old-fashioned and he's a cop."

"I don't want to alarm you. Most likely, an abuser would have started showing his true self by now, and he would not have given you a weapon that you could turn against him, not unless he was very sure of his control over you.

"I think you'll be fine," Asia concluded.

"Boy, that sure makes my issues with Peter sound petty."

"Your issues are not petty at all. You have an absolute right to pursue the kind of life that is going to make you happiest. It's so much better for you to be asking questions at this point instead of jumping into a commitment and finding out the terms later."

16

THURSDAY, OCTOBER 24

TERRY POINT AN AUTHORITATIVE FINGER IN THE AIR. "As Samuel Johnson said, 'Marriage is the triumph of imagination over intelligence. A second marriage is the triumph of hope over experience.'"

Lia leaned over and whispered to Bailey, "Wasn't that Oscar Wilde?"

"Don't tell Terry he's quoting Oscar Wilde," Bailey whispered back. "He'll have to wash his mouth out."

"When I lived in Alaska," Terry continued, "I had a bumper sticker that said, 'In Juneau, you don't lose your woman, you lose your turn.' Relationships there are extremely inbred."

Bailey leaned over to Lia. "The way I heard it, in Alaska the women say, 'The odds are good, but the goods are odd.'"

Lia stifled a snort.

"What's that you said, Bailey?" Jose asked. "I couldn't hear it."

"Never mind," Bailey said.

"When anyone bugs me about how many times I've been married," Terry soldiered on, "I say, 'You fall off a horse, you can either sit on the porch sniveling, or hitch up your pants, go out to the corral, and saddle something else.'"

"But four times?" Bailey asked.

"What can I say? I like women," Terry declared.

"Apparently, they don't like you," Jim observed.

"I'm glad you said that. I wasn't about to," Bailey said.

"Hey, my average relationship lasts longer than most TV series. Or NFL careers, for that matter."

"I don't want to be a TV series. Did you learn anything from your four marriages?" Lia asked.

"Sure. I can now repeat my mistakes perfectly, every time." Terry ended the topic by turning to Jose and launching into his thoughts about the registration of ammo and the latest commentary by Rush Limbaugh.

"Looks like the sensitivity portion of today's programming is over," Bailey said.

"Speaking of sensitive, I can't believe you didn't warn me ahead of time about Sunday," Lia said.

"Warn you about what?" Bailey asked.

Lia turned to Jim. "I let her do her astrology thing with Peter and me and she pops out all this stuff about financial interdependence and domestic partnership. Some birthday present."

"You wanted me to lie?" Bailey asked. "I thought you wanted to know if it made sense to go to the next level."

"I don't know what I wanted," Lia grumbled. "It was just a shock, hearing that."

"Astrology is powerful stuff," Bailey said. "Besides, I

said all that stuff about Uranus meaning you had to have a nontraditional relationship. Doesn't that make up for it?"

Lia's phone beeped. She pulled it out of her pocket, checked the display.

"Hey, Jerome. What's up?"

"I meant to call you yesterday, but I got busy and forgot until this morning."

"No problem. What's going on?"

"I saw a German Shepherd when I was out making deliveries. She looked like the dog in your poster."

"You saw Daisy?" The voices around her hushed.

"I think so. I'm sorry I wasn't able to stop and check her out, I was running late."

"That's okay, tell me everything you remember. Where was it?"

"It was on Knowlton, where Fergus ends. This skinny dark-haired woman was walking her. They were headed toward Hamilton Avenue.

"I was thinking, most people walk their dogs around the same time every day, and they usually have a route they stick to. If you hung out at the right time, you might see her."

"When was it?" Lia asked.

"It was right around eleven."

"That's great Jerome. Thanks for calling me."

Lia stuck the phone back in her pocket. "Okay, who's up for surveillance?"

BAILEY AND JOSE had to work all day and couldn't help. Lia pulled the first shift, 10:30 a.m. to 12:30 p.m., Terry was on next from 12:30 p.m. to 2:30 p.m. Jim drew the late shift. He met Terry a few blocks down from the end of Fergus.

"No luck," Terry said. "I had to fend off an amorous Chihuahua and I met a couple of pit bull mixes, but no German Shepherds to speak of."

Jim sat in his Caliber, working on his third crossword of the afternoon. Fleece sat at his side, occasionally pawing his arm for attention. He figured Daisy's current owner had been headed to Hoffner Park when she was spotted. That was where he'd take a dog if he lived in the neighborhood. He was positioned so they would have to pass by him, whichever direction they had come from.

He was puzzling over the clue, "Image on Irish euro coins," when he spotted two children with a large dog crossing Fergus on the north side of the street. He quietly got out of his car and took Fleece up the sidewalk so he would intersect with them.

As the children approached, he could see them more clearly. The eldest was a girl around eleven or twelve with dark, stringy hair and jeans that were too short. She wore her tennis shoes without socks. Her brother was about five or six, with a round face and an intense look about him. The dog did indeed look like the picture of Daisy in his pocket.

When they got within range, Daisy started straining toward Jim and Fleece. Jim walked closer so the dogs could sniff each other. "Friendly dog you have," he said. "What's her name?"

"Xena," the girl said. "Mom says she's like the warrior princess on TV."

"She does look like a warrior princess. You must be really strong to walk her all by yourselves."

The girl shrugged. The boy, who was petting Fleece, looked up and grinned. "Yeah," he said.

Jim stroked 'Xena's' head. "Sure is friendly. How long have you had her?"

"Since she was a pup," the boy piped up. "That's what Mom says to say, since she was a pup."

The girl gave her brother a quelling look. "We gotta go, Mister. We're not supposed to talk to strangers." She moved to go past him.

"You going to the park?"

"Yeah!" the boy said. "The park! The park! The park!" He hopped up and down for emphasis. His sister rolled her eyes.

He moved aside. Daisy craned her neck as she walked by, watching Jim with intelligent eyes. He wondered if she remembered him.

He walked Fleece down the block, then turned around and headed toward Hamilton Avenue, keeping the children in sight while they crossed at the light and turned South. He arrived at the corner in time to see the children cutting into the park.

Jim went back to his car, then circled the block. As he drove, he examined the array of modest Victorian era, clapboard shotguns. He passed a vacant lot and noted an overgrown greenbelt running behind all the houses.

The renaissance that was spreading through Northside was just starting to take root on Knowlton. A few houses were fully refurbished. A couple had scaffolding on front, a precursor to coming improvements. Some were slipping into ruin in the clash of income levels that was characteristic of the area.

He wondered which of the pastel colored houses was theirs. Not one of the rehabs. He noted the ones with peeling exteriors, listing porches and dull colors, zeroing in on one painted an unfortunate shade of Pepto Bismol pink with a cyclone fence in front and a rusty bike chained to the porch. The original porch columns with their gingerbread trim were long gone, replaced sometime in the Seventies with scrolled aluminum supports. Broken concrete steps led to the porch.

The children appeared, not walking so briskly now. He imagined they were tired. Perhaps they didn't want to go home. He checked the time. It was now four forty-five.

Jim experienced a small satisfaction when they stopped at the Pepto-pink house and opened the gate. He considered his options. He wasn't prepared to create a fuss about the dog in front of the children. He now knew where Daisy lived. She wasn't going anywhere. He'd advise Lia, and the group could decide what to do the next morning.

17

FRIDAY, OCTOBER 25

"WE KNOW DAISY HAS A HOME, AND SHE HAS KIDS TO PLAY with. Monica doesn't seem that interested. Are we even sure she wants the dog back?" Bailey asked.

"She has a home," Jim said, "and there are kids, but we don't know if it's a good home. In that neighborhood, people are likely to let their dogs run the streets and dump them when they get inconvenient. Daisy eats a lot of food and the family living in that house isn't doing too well. Best case is they love her and feed her but don't give her proper medical care. If she gets sick, they put her down. If the Munces don't want her, we can find her a better home than this one."

"We need a positive ID," Terry said. "I venture to guess that our scarlet woman knows Daisy better than anyone outside the family, and Daisy knows her as well."

"She's not a scarlet woman, just a sad case. How would you like it if the love of your life was torn apart by coyotes?" Bailey asked. "Lia, do you know if Kate's coming today?"

"I'm pretty sure she is. If she's not here soon, I'll give her a call."

"You should go during the day, while the kids are in school. Better for them," Jim said.

"Less drama for us that way, too," Lia said. "If Kitty says she'll do it, I'll go with her since I know her best."

THEY DROVE Lia's old Volvo for two reasons. First, she was used to having dogs in the back seat. Second, Lia was afraid Kate's new Altima might give this family visions of a reward they didn't deserve, considering Daisy had been wearing a collar with tags. If Daisy somehow lost her collar, they still never posted a free 'found ad' for her.

It was shortly after 11:00 a.m. when Lia pulled up in front of the neglected house.

"Oh, my," Kate said, "this feels a bit creepy, don't you think?"

"It's just poverty," Lia said. "Poverty isn't evil. There could be many reasons why the house is the way it is. Could be they just moved in and haven't had a chance to fix it up yet. Maybe someone is sick and can't work. At least we know they like animals. They can't be all bad."

They climbed the broken steps. The bell was out of order, so Lia rapped sharply on the door. Inside, a dog responded by barking. The sound was deep and powerful.

"That does sound like Daisy," Kate said.

After a few minutes, the door cracked. Daisy shoved her nose through the door and whimpered excitedly. Kate knelt down to greet her. Daisy continued to fight with the door until she wiggled through. She was all over Kate, licking her face and wagging her tail. Kate gave up and sat on the porch and hugged the dog.

"Xena! Down! Bad!"

Lia looked down to see a short, bony woman with dark hair that had been fried in a way she normally associated with over-bleaching. She looked middle age, but she also looked haggard, like she had lived hard and was possibly younger. Deep lines were carved around her mouth and her eyes had dark circles under them. The woman pushed past Lia and grabbed Daisy's collar, dragging her back into the house. She bent over to hang onto the straining dog. Daisy rasped as she panted, fighting to get back to Kate. The woman looked up from this position. "I'm so sorry." There was a touch of hills in her voice. "She isn't very well behaved. What can I do for you?" Her smile was forced, as if she knew she should be friendly but would just rather not.

"My name is Lia, and this is Kate. We're here about your dog," Lia said. "We believe this is the same dog that went missing at Mount Airy Forest a little over two weeks ago. She pulled a folded flyer out of her pocket and showed it to the woman.

The woman barely looked at the picture. "I don't know what you're talking about. We've had Xena all her life." Her eyes went flat. Her chin lifted in defiance, belying Daisy's frantic attempts to reunite with her friend. She yanked Daisy back inside and attempted to shut the door. Lia stuck her foot inside the jamb, wincing as the door banged into it.

"I don't want this to get ugly," she called through the

cracked door, "but I'm certain this is Daisy. I can prove it at the SPCA. She's been microchipped," Lia bluffed, hoping it was true. "If we have to, we'll file a complaint with the police. I'd hate to have to do that, because you found Daisy and took her in, and we're grateful for that. But it's time —"

"Is there a problem?" Lia twisted around to see a well-muscled man behind her on the porch. "Honey," he called to the woman, "why don't we all go inside and discuss this like adults?"

The woman relinquished her hold on the door. Lia pulled her foot out and shook it.

"That's better," he said. "You ladies come in and we'll figure this out."

Relieved, Lia followed him into the painfully neat but shabby living room. Kate followed.

"Have a seat," the man said, closing the door and flipping his hand at a nubby brown sofa.

Lia and Kate sat. The woman released Daisy, who scampered back to Kate. Kate began scratching her ears and cooing. Daisy lolled her tongue and closed her eyes, wallowing in canine bliss.

"I'm going to tie Xena out back while we discuss this." He grabbed Daisy's collar. Daisy stiffened her legs, digging in. Her nails scraped across the wood floor as he dragged her out of the room. Lia could hear the back door open and his muttered commands to the dog. The door shut, and Daisy began immediately hurling herself against it. The rhythmic thuds were punctuated with howls.

The women waited silently for the man to come back, observing each other. Lia surveyed the living room. A large, boxy TV sat on top of a composite board media center. Apart from the sofa, there were three dinette chairs with torn vinyl upholstery mended with duct tape. An upside down milk crate served as a side table between two of the chairs.

There was something red hanging on the back of the woman's chair that drew Lia's attention. She'd seen that particular shade of stop-sign red before. She felt a vague sense of unease. Something about the red thing. It was a smock, like clerks wear in some stores. It slammed into her brain: this woman worked for Dollar Hut.

"Look," she said, standing up, "Why don't we talk about this some other day. Kate and I are running late."

"Sit back down." Pivoting at this command, Lia discovered a gun pointed at her chest. Speechless, she watched as the man turned to the woman. "Carleen, I told you this would never work, but you had to keep the damn dog, didn't you? 'The kids love her,' you said." His face twisted as he said this.

"Billy, I'm sorry—"

"First you whine until I get another phone because I can't talk to you from my number, somebody might see it on your records. Look what good that did! Nearly got me going down for murder. Now it's the damn dog. They know you got the dog, Carleen. They're going to think it's awfully funny that you had George's dog all this time. When are you going to listen, you stupid bitch?"

Carleen cowed.

"Carleen?" Kate said. "George's assistant manager Carleen?"

"You know her and you didn't say anything?" Lia asked, incredulous.

"George told me about her. I never saw her up close.

And she had blond hair."

"How's your grand plan now?" Billy sneered at Carleen. "All this trouble over your pansy-assed boss." He turned to the women on the sofa. "Do you know what this bitch did? She gets jealous because the boss she thinks is someday going to wake up and run away with her is now fooling around with some fat broad from out of town. She thinks if she gets rid of the competition, meaning you—" He pointed the gun at Kate and snorted. "–she'll get to have him all to herself."

"This is all your fault, Billy!" Carleen wailed. "If you hadn't told me how you'd seen them fooling around in the woods from that stupid tree house of yours, this never would have happened. But you had to call me up, laughing about it. You couldn't keep it to yourself, could you? You had to tell me all about it."

Billy snorted. "So what does she do? She breaks into my house and steals my crossbow and decides she's going to fire a few bolts at you—" He waved the gun at Kate again. "–to scare you off, like you were in the line of fire of some deer hunter. Only the day she goes out there, you're not there.

"So when her pansy-assed boss sees something up in the trees and decides to find out what it is, she goes spastic and pulls the trigger by mistake. Wouldn't you know, the bolt rips right through his neck and he bleeds out before she gets down from the tree.

"What I wouldn't give to see that. A couple times shooting at targets in the back yard, and she thinks she's the big hunter! "I shoot years. I never had such a perfect kill shot and she aces it by accident. There go all her fancy plans."

"Then she drags that dog back with her and calls me. 'Oh, Billy,'" he mimicked "'I really screwed up, Billy. I want you back, but I need your help. Please, Billy, you gotta help me.'"

"So *I* take care of the body, *I* get rid of the car, *I* dump my own six-hundred-dollar crossbow, and what do *I* get? 'We can't be seen together Billy, not yet Billy, you have to call me on a different phone Billy.'" Billy continued his vicious falsetto. "All that and she has to keep the stupid dog.

"Carleen, did I ever tell you what a kick it was, watching those 'yotes rip into your boss? I had the best seat in the house, up in that old blind. I sat up there and thought about all the trouble he caused while they pulled him apart. I wanted to take pictures for you, but that wouldn't be smart.

"We're doing this my way, now, Carleen. Get the electrical cords out of my truck, the long ones." He tossed her his keys.

Fearful, Carleen scampered out the door. Lia kept her eyes downcast, submissive.

Keys. I have my keys. I'm not helpless. Thank you, Peter, for being such a good boyfriend. She stretched her shoulders, moved her hands casually down beside her hips.

"Hands back where I can see them." Billy walked up to her, swinging the gun in her face.

Lia tracked the gun as it swung inches from her, carefully returning her hands to her lap. She looked at Kate sideways. Kate pleaded with eyes shining white all around, terror coming off her in waves.

Lia remembered that feeling. She'd had a gun to her head and she'd been shot once. It no longer petrified her.

She was able to think, and that was the important thing. She had to pay attention, look for an opportunity. Right now there was nothing she could do. *Best to continue acting compliant.*

Carleen returned with a pair of orange, heavy-duty electrical cords. Each coil looked to be twenty or more feet long. Lia had one of these in her studio for running her power tools.

"Hands in front of you, and get in the chairs," Billy said. The two women obeyed. He walked over and put the muzzle of the gun against Kate's head. Lia's stomach clenched as she imagined how Kate must feel at that moment.

"This is how it's going to go," Billy announced. "I keep this gun right here while Carleen ties you up." He poked the side of Kate's head with the barrel for emphasis. "The minute either of you tries anything, it goes off. Understand? Carleen, tie the skinny one's hands to the back of that chair. Then tie her ankles to the legs. Make it tight."

Unable to do anything else, Lia allowed Carleen to pull her hands behind her. She thought about the kubotan in her hip pocket. *So close!* Yet what good was it against a gun?

Carleen fussed over the slippery cord and the knots, irritating Billy, who yelled at her. Finally she was finished with Lia and went over to Kate. Lia hid her relief when Billy moved away from Kate to let Carleen tie her up. She had a feeling that he'd stick that gun right back into Kate's head if he knew how much anxiety it caused her.

Billy walked over and pressed the muzzle into Lia's temple. She froze up, her mind blanking out. Slowly, one breath at a time, she regained control of her thoughts, using an exercise she learned in therapy. *Thank you, Asia. I can handle this.*

When Carleen was finished, she turned to Billy with an apprehensive look.

Billy pulled the third chair in front of his prisoners, reversed and straddled it. He draped one arm across the back of the chair and scratched his head with the muzzle of the gun.

"This is fucked up … Gotta do this right. First thing, the dog has to go. I'm taking it down to the pound. They'll get their damn dog back and nobody will have any reason to come looking for us. You're going to watch these two. Keep the gun on them." He handed the weapon to Carleen. "Where's the collar that mutt came with?"

"It's in the junk drawer in the kitchen, Billy."

Lia could hear him rooting around then banging the drawer shut. He walked back in. "Give me my keys. I'll be back in half an hour, tops. Think you can keep them under control that long?"

"Yes, Billy."

"You'd better, if you know what's good for you."

Billy slammed the back door on the way out. The three women waited. Lia heard the starter of a truck crank, grind, crank again, then catch. The truck pulled out and the tension in the room slipped several notches.

"Carleen," Lia broke the silence. "You've got to untie us!"

"I don't have to do any such thing. I let you go, he'll kill me."

"It was an accident when you killed George. That's manslaughter. You won't serve five years. You know he's not going to release us. That makes you an accessory to murder. You could get life for that. This is way out of control, you've got to see that."

Carleen turned flat, mud-brown eyes on Lia. "All I have to see is what will happen if you're not here when he gets back. You hear what he said about George? He'll do that to me if you're gone, only he won't bother to kill me first."

"You can tell him something," Lia improvised. "Tell him someone came after us and forced their way in. You can leave with us. You don't have to stay here with him."

"And what am I going to do about my kids, huh? You think it's easy, raising two kids with no one to help? George used to give me money sometimes, but now he's dead. Billy's all I've got. 'Sides, he ain't gonna forget I asked him to take care of George's body for me. You think anything you say is gonna make a difference?"

While Carleen ranted, Lia twisted her left hand, stretching, attempting to reach two fingers into her pocket. *So close!* She brushed against the tips of her keys. She slid a key between her index and middle finger and carefully began to work it upward.

"What are you doing? Why are you twisting around like that?" Carleen walked over behind Lia, grabbed the keys and yanked them out of Lia's pocket. She shook them in Lia's face. "What did you think you were going to do with this, use the keys to cut the cord?" She snorted and dropped the kubotan on the milk crate, then sat down backwards on the third chair, holding the gun steady on the chair back.

Lia glanced over at Kate. There was an intent expression on Kate's face, a subtle shift to her shoulders. *Is Kate untying herself?* She scrambled for some way to distract

Carleen, give Kate time. How much longer would Billy take? The SPCA was barely a mile away.

"What are you and Billy going to do after we go missing? People know where we are. It's not going to work, Carleen."

"Billy will think of something. They haven't found the car and they won't find you, either. They won't be able to prove anything."

Lia shifted in her seat. "You keep telling yourself that." *Just keep talking.*

"Why are you squirming like that?" Carleen stood up from her chair and walked back over to Lia, checking her knots.

"You try being tied up in one of these chairs." She shifted again. And she prayed.

Hands freed, Kate launched herself at Carleen's back. Carleen shrieked and the two women fell over. Kate's ankles were still tied to the chair and it banged against Kate's legs then twisted and slipped over to the side, dragging her legs with it. Carleen flipped over, flailing her free arm as she kept the gun out of Kate's reach. Kate grunted as Carleen shoved a hand in her face, pushing her away. Kate dug her short fingernails into Carleen's arm. Kate had longer arms, but she was still hampered by the chair and Carleen had wiry strength from her years lifting boxes of stock at the store.

Frantic, Lia looked for a way to help. She could work at her bonds, but she didn't have time to undo them. She had to act fast. If Carleen rolled close enough, maybe she could lean back and drop a chair leg onto Carleen. That would hurt.

Carleen held the gun back over her head with one

hand, and pulled Kate's hair with the other, trying to get Kate to let go of her wrist. Lia rocked her chair to the side and dumped herself on top of Carleen's exposed hip. Carleen lost her grip and the gun skittered across the floor. Kate clawed for it, dragging the chair.

Her hand fell on a black workman's boot.

Billy bent down, picked up the gun. "Looking for this?" He pointed the gun down at Kate's face, out of reach of her hands. "The only reason I don't shoot you right now is I don't want blood all over the house. Get up Carleen."

Lia thumped down on the floor sideways as Carleen worked her way out from under her. The small woman stood up painfully. Her face was bleeding where Kate scratched it. She rubbed the hip Lia fell on and looked fearfully at Billy.

"I leave you for ten minutes and you can't even control a couple of tied-up women with a gun in your hand. I oughta smack you good, Carleen."

"Sorry Billy. I didn't realize—"

"Shut up, Carleen! I gotta think … Tie her back up," he said, nodding at Kate. "Get her loose from that chair and tie her hands behind her back. We're going for a walk … You, girlie." He jerked his head at Lia. "We're going to untie you. You make one wrong move and your friend is dead, blood or no blood."

"Where are we going, Billy? Somebody will see us."

"We're going out the back way, through the woods. Nobody will see us this time of day. I left my tire iron out back. We can use that on them. I don't want to use the gun if I don't have to. Get the duct tape. Can't have them screaming. We'll either dump them in the woods or break into the back of that foreclosure on Chambers."

Carleen finished tying Kate's hands and went for the tape. She came back with the tape and a pair of scissors, cut a strip of tape off, then applied it to Kate's trembling mouth.

"Okay, now pull the electrical cord down from her hands and tie it around one ankle," Billy instructed.

Carleen complied.

"Leave about a foot and tie it around the other ankle … run the rest of the cord up through her hands and give it to me … get the other one. Put the tape over her mouth first. Billy turned toward Lia to supervise. He had unconsciously dropped the nose of the gun while he was directing Carleen. It was no longer pointing at Kate, but down, toward the floor.

Carleen knelt down, wrestling with a strip of duct tape. Lia felt Carleen's hot breath on her face as she laid one end of the sticky tape on Lia's cheek and stretched it across Lia's mouth. While Carleen was blocking her from Billy's view, Lia slipped one loose hand behind her, grabbed the kubotan off the milk crate.

Lia flipped the safety off the kubotan and swung it over Carleen's shoulder, pointing the bottom end at Billy.

Sorry, Kate.

She depressed keyring swivel, releasing a cloud of pepper spray across the room.

Billy and Kate screamed while Lia rammed the end of the kubotan into Carleen's temple. Billy dropped the gun and fell, clutching his eyes. Carleen yanked Lia's hair, drawing tears. Lia struck Carleen again with the kubotan, hitting a pressure-point in her shoulder.

Kitty rolled on the floor, sightless, groping for the gun through a haze of pain. She felt the barrel between her tied hands and snatched it toward her, fumbling, scrabbling to get a firing grip on the weapon while Billy howled. She pointed blindly in the direction of his screams and pulled the trigger. The gun roared in her ear and the recoil send her arms flying up over her head. She ignored the ringing in her ears as she lowered the weapon and fired again.

Stunned, Lia and Carleen stopped their grappling to see the red stain spreading on Billy's shirt. Carleen pulled away from Lia and ran to him. She pawed through the pooling blood on his clothing, looking for the wound in his side as more blood streamed over her fingers. Kate fired again, this time hitting the sofa. Lia freed her other hand and began dragging herself and the chair across the floor to help Kate.

The front door blew open as a trio of officers poured in with guns drawn, Peter and Brent two steps behind them. The officers quickly assessed the circumstances. Brent relieved Kate of the gun while the others surrounded Carleen and Billy. An ambulance siren sounded in the distance.

Peter stood over Lia, taking in the strip of duct tape dangling from her face and the tangle of her legs, the chair and electrical cord. He stooped down to untie her. "You okay, Babe?"

"Babe," she muttered, "is a pig."

18

SATURDAY, OCTOBER 26

Peter sat on the picnic table next to Lia, holding her hand. They were surrounded by the usual morning crowd, plus Kate, Max and Daisy.

"… I was sitting at my desk, reviewing reports when I get this butt dial from Lia. I'm about to hang up when I decide to listen in for a while and maybe make a loud, rude noise at an inopportune moment. Only instead of hearing her gossip with Bailey, I hear all hell breaking loose. Then I hear Stryker's voice. When I heard Carleen's voice, I knew where you must be. We had all available units meet down the block with their sirens off. We were in the process of surrounding the house and figuring the best plan of action to avoid a hostage situation when we heard Stryker screaming. All bets were off then, but before we could break in, the gun went off."

"So I maced Kate for nothing?"

"It's quite all right, Dear," Kate said, patting Lia's free hand. "You didn't know."

"Not nothing," Peter said. "You gave us the opening to rush in and grab Stryker and Thomas before Carleen got her wits about her and grabbed the gun from Kate. Things could have gotten a lot worse. There's a reason hostage situations usually last for hours.

"Carleen became hysterical and began talking before we could get her properly Mirandized and into the station. She seems to think she's a victim in this. Never mind it was her prints on the crossbow.

"Stryker clammed up and demanded a lawyer. Thanks to your statements, we've got him on accessory after the fact and interfering with a corpse. I heard him planning over the phone, so we've got them both on conspiracy to commit murder.

"What was up with Carleen's hair? Why did she dye it brown?" Kate asked. "I might have recognized her if it wasn't for that."

"Apparently Stryker is a Fundamentalist at heart. Carleen only became a blonde after her divorce because Stryker would never let her bleach her hair. Wouldn't let her wear nail polish or make up, either. When he agreed to come back, he insisted she dye it brown and get rid of the cosmetics so she wouldn't look like a whore anymore."

"Unbelievable," Lia said. "I can't understand why she turned to him."

"He was the one person she knew who wouldn't balk at helping her out. I'm sure there's more to it than that. Domestic violence is complicated."

"I'd like to know," Jim said, "how Daisy wound up with you, Kate."

Kate smiled. "Lia arranged it."

"Stacy called me," Lia said. "She got my number off one

of our posters. When the SPCA called Monica to tell her they had Daisy, she told them Daisy's owner was deceased, and could they please find the dog a good home. Stacy overheard, and she didn't want Daisy going to strangers. She asked me to step in. Kate offered to take her."

"Poor Stacy," Kate said. "I think she got the worst end of the deal."

"She's tougher than you think. She holds her own with Monica, and she'll be 18 before long," Peter said. "That will give her leverage, if she chooses to use it."

"How so?" Lia asked.

"As crazy as Monica is, I don't think she wants to be left alone. Once Stacy's an adult, she can leave home. She's smart enough to get a scholarship for college, so Monica can't hold her education over her head. If Monica wants Stacy to stick around, she'll have to treat her better. I have a feeling Stacy will be okay."

"What about Jacob?" Jose asked.

"He offered to pay restitution to Avis for the tire and he's doing community service. Rumor has it he's going to be picking up poop here at the park.

"He also heard a couple of his classmates talking about the bottle bombs in his chem lab, so he did his civic duty and turned them in. And, Heaven help us, he asked me what it took to become a cop."

"Maybe that will keep him out of trouble," Lia said.

"Kate," Bailey asked, "what are you going to do now?"

"Daisy and I," she hugged the dog, "are going back to Oklahoma."

"What about Max?" Jim asked.

"Peter had a suggestion–" Lia said.

Peter looked toward the corral. "And here she comes." He waved his arm overhead. "Hey, Chris!"

A tall, stocky woman with a skinny dog drew near. As she got closer, Lia could see the broad face, dark hair and hooked nose of Native American ancestry.

"What a handsome Shepherd," Bailey said as the dogs approached the newcomer and began sniffing her hindquarters.

"That's Boo. She's a Belgian Malinois," Chris said. "They're cousins of German Shepherds, bred for scent work."

"Oh!" Lia said, "You're the one who came out to the crime scene the day we found the bones."

"That was us." She stroked Boo's head. "Boo did all the work. I just interpreted. I understand one of these dogs found the remains first."

"That's Max," Lia said, pointing to the dog now engaged in a mock-battle with Boo.

"I've been looking for a second dog to train. Peter suggested Max had an aptitude for scent work. I'd like to run her through a couple tests, if that's okay."

Kate and Max followed Chris and Boo to the small dog park. The rest of the group moved up front to the fence so they could watch.

"I need three volunteers," Chris said.

Lia, Jim and Bailey left their dogs with Peter and went over. Chris signaled Boo to lay down. She then had Kate hold Max's lead while she pulled a plastic jar out of her pocket and removed a liver treat. She showed the treat to Max, but kept it out of reach. She took the treat over to the trio of volunteers and asked them to hold their hands out. She placed the treat in one palm, out of sight from

Max. The trio was instructed to close their hands into fists and walk to the other end of the small park. There they were to spread out, then hold their fists up, two feet apart.

When everyone was in position, Chris unclipped Max. Max bounded across the park to Jim and jumped up by his left hand. Jim grinned, told Max to sit and gave her the treat.

"So far, so good," Chris said.

Next, she had Kate take Max around the picnic shelter to the niche in back that was used to hose off dogs. Chris took another liver treat and put it inside a Kong ball. She then tossed the ball into the middle of the park.

Kate released Max on Chris's command. Max began searching, nosing around in the grass. It took her five minutes to find the ball. She was busy digging the treat out when Chris retrieved the ball, giving the delicacy to her.

After that, she removed a rag from a plastic bag and allowed Max to sniff it. She took it to the far side of the park, then had Kate release Max to see if she would retrieve it. Chris did this several times with different rags. Max retrieved rags that held scents of decomposition and live humans. She was disinterested in the rags scented with chemicals associated with narcotics, bombs and arson.

"She's got a good nose and she's a high energy dog. She's definitely got potential," Chris said.

"Did Peter tell you she's an escape artist?" Lia asked. "How will you ever manage her?"

"It's likely she's bored and wants something to do. If I give her a job that involves taking her to the woods, she may get enough stimulation that she doesn't need to run off. She's highly food motivated, so that's the tool I'll use to train her. Presuming the rescue is willing to let me adopt her."

"What if she doesn't work out as a scent dog?" Lia asked.

"Many dogs who start training don't wind up qualifying. I still need a friend for Boo, and they seem to get along."

"I'm sure they'll be delighted for you to have her, since you have a strategy to work with her."

"I'll call them today," Chris said. "Let's go, Boo." Boo fell into position at Chris's heel.

"That's what I call a happy ending," Bailey declared as they watched Chris exit the park.

EPILOGUE

SUNDAY, NOVEMBER 10

LIA AND PETER SAT ON THE BACK STOOP, ENJOYING THE brief spell of Indian summer. The dogs milled around in the fading light, checking their scent sites for signs of intruders, refreshing their spots, and looking for stray sides of beef.

Lia breathed in deeply, tilting her head back. "I don't know why I think I'm going to miss this. Chances are it'll be 70 in January."

"True." Peter tipped his beer, then set it aside on the steps. He took Lia's hand in his, bounced their joined hands on his thigh, then brought it up to his lips and kissed her knuckles. He looked off into the darkness. The sky was indigo, fading into black with one bright star above the horizon. *Venus,* he corrected. Not a star.

"Do you remember the first night you grilled dinner for me? We slow-danced here in the yard while night fell.

I looked up and saw the first star and I made a wish." He took another swig from his beer. "Do you want to know what I wished for?"

"I don't know. Do I?"

"I wanted to get in your pants."

Lia sputtered, "I'm glad I wasn't a forgone conclusion."

"You never are. It's one of the things I love about you."

"Oh, really?"

"I got you something." He pulled a hinged velvet box out of the pocket of his windbreaker and held it out.

Lia eyed the little box, the box that was sized just right for a ring, as if it were fanged and venomous.

"Aren't you going to open it?" Peter asked, eyes wide and innocence.

"And ruin the suspense?" Lia stalled.

"Chicken," he accused amiably.

"Uh-huh."

"Excuse me, that should be *ma poulette*, as long as I'm calling you a barnyard animal." He popped open the box with his thumb. A small lump flashed color as light from the kitchen hit it. "I thought you might like this." He slipped his finger through the end of a long silver chain and lifted. He drew the chain slowly out of the box until the small rock swung free, dangling between them.

"You." She poked him in the chest. "You did that on purpose, making me think you were going to propose. That was a dirty trick."

"I have to get my kicks where I can." He grinned and chucked her chin.

She stuck her tongue out at him, then reached over and took the gem in her hand, turning it slowly so the color winked. It was an opal, oval shaped, about a half inch in diameter. The stone was surrounded by a thin layer of matrix. It nestled in an arrangement of inter-woven silver strands.

"It's beautiful. It looks like an egg in a nest."

"It's about us."

"Is it now?" She tilted her head, gave him a coy look.

"I wanted to give you something special, something to remind you how I feel about you. I was 12 when I found that opal. I went on a rock hounding trip out to Nevada with my Boy Scout troop. The scoutmaster's brother was a rock guy, and he showed me how to polish the top of it. Opals are fragile, so we left the rest of it alone. He said we might destroy the stone if we cut it, so we kept it in the matrix with this window on top so you can see how beau-tiful it is inside."

"You kept this since you were a child, and you're giving it to me?"

"Yep. I thought about a ring, but rings seem to be about commitment, and I don't want this to be about that. And a ring isn't practical for you since you work with your hands."

"So, what is it about, Barnyard Whisperer?" The air between them seemed to tingle while she waited for Peter to gather his thoughts.

"You gave me a piece of yourself when you left me that painting a year ago. I wanted you to have a piece of me.

"This is like a talisman. People wear talismans around their neck, don't they? So you can keep a part of me near your heart. And the opal is precious and beautiful, like this thing we have between us. Our relationship is a living thing, like an egg. We have to protect it and nurture it. It's full of wonderful possibilities. It's still an egg, so we don't know what it's going to be yet."

She leaned into him and kissed him. "I love it. You have unplumbed depths, Kentucky Boy." She handed him the charm and turned her back. "Put it on me?"

Peter undid the clasp and draped the necklace around her. He cinched it, then rubbed her back.

"There's more."

"More?"

"When I talked to Alma that time, she said in a good relationship, partners are each other's heroes. I want you to know that you're my hero."

"Really?"

"You look for the good in people and you remind me to look for it, too. I spend all my time protecting people from the harm others do, and many of the people I deal with couldn't care less about anything besides themselves.

"Then there's you, spending all your time making the world a more beautiful place. When I'm with you, I remember there's another side of life. I love what I do, and it's important. Being with you gives it more meaning. You remind me of what I'm protecting."

She leaned her head on his shoulder, wrapped her arms around him and gave him a squeeze. "You're my hero, Kentucky Boy."

Peter grimaced. "I can't be much of one. I never seem to show up in time to rescue you."

"You show up. That's what matters."

MAX'S SONG

She's the Max
She's the big kahuna
She's the Max
She likes to eat canned tuna
She doesn't use a spoon-a

She's the Max
Her name should be Houdini
She's the Max
She thinks that I'm a meanie
She always tries to flee me

She's the Max
And she brings back treasure
She's the Max
It's her one big pleasure
Admonishments don't faze her

Simba, model for the cover of *Maximum Security*, is the winner of my Cover Dog Photo Contest. His dad, Jerome Wilson, owns Northside Grange, just like in the book.

Brian Dempsey is an old friend who agreed to appear in this novel (Congratulations to Brian and Tammy on their recent marriage.)

Named places in *Maximum Security* are real. Dollar Hut is the one exception, though you have probably been in a store like it. Individual homes are a combination of several houses. They are true to the neighborhood, but do not exist as described. There is a very private copse of evergreens in French Park, though I have never had occasion to put it to the same use as Peter and Lia.

The quote Terry cites regarding marriage has been attributed to both Samuel Johnson and Oscar Wilde. I leave it to you to decide who the true author is.

The synastry reading Bailey does for Peter and Lia is based on real charts. For anyone who is interested, Lia

Anderson was "born" 6:30 a.m., October 18, 1982 in Cincinnati, OH. Peter was "born" 9:10 a.m., January 3, 1981, Mammoth Cave, KY.

Grave disasters, such as the one which occurred in this book, do happen. Google it, if you don't believe me.

In *Maximum Security*, Carleen is a victim of domestic violence, and Asia questions Lia out of concern that Peter's protective behavior may in fact be a prelude to abuse. What may not be obvious is that George is a victim of Monica's verbal and emotional abuse.

Domestic violence is a complex issue taking many forms. Many of the initial behaviors may seem harmless or even flattering. One thing that is consistent with domestic violence is escalating boundary violations: the abuse always gets worse.

If you need information or help, please contact The National Domestic Violence Hotline at www.thehotline.org or 1800-799-7233

ACKNOWLEDGMENTS

A book does not appear in a vacuum. Behind every author is a group of people who make it possible for the author to share their vision with the world. The dog park regulars who inspired my series have embraced the books and become my street team.

John Cunningham is my lead salesman. Desiree Willis is a beta reader and my aspiring PR director. Angie Hall is my most brutal beta. She and her husband, Paul Kramer, have always been there when I needed support, no matter what or when. She-who-refuses-to-be-named turns her gimlet eye to my MS, providing that last proof-read/edit before publishing. Ski donated a Kindle Fire to the cause, changing my life with functionality apps. Marti Dourson wrote an article about me. Tom Sansalone is my rock.

Other supporters include Sarah Schellenger, my neighborhood librarian; and writer Stephen Scott, my biggest booster.

I am blessed in my friends.

ABOUT THE AUTHOR

Carol Ann "C. A." Newsome is an author and painter who lives in Cincinnati. She spends most mornings at the Mount Airy Dog Park with a zombie swamp monster named Gypsy Foo La Beenz.

Carol loves to hear from readers.
Contact her at
gypsy@canewsome.com

Would you like to stay in touch?
Sign up for Carol's newsletter at
CANewsome.com

facebook.com/AShotInTheBark